# DARK AWAKENINGS

Volume 2 in the *Little Girl Lost* Trilogy

by
## Cindy Hanna

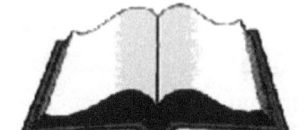

**CCB Publishing**
**British Columbia, Canada**

Dark Awakenings: Volume 2 in the Little Girl Lost Trilogy

Copyright ©2010 by Cindy Hanna
ISBN-13   978-1-926585-85-7
First Edition


Library and Archives Canada Cataloguing in Publication

Hanna, Cindy, 1965-
Dark Awakenings / written by Cindy Hanna.
(Little girl lost trilogy ; v. 2)
ISBN 978-1-926585-85-7
Also available in electronic format.
I. Title. II. Series: Hanna, Cindy, 1965- . Little girl lost trilogy ; v. 2.
PS3608.A558D37 2010   813'.6   C2010-903649-2


Cover photo: Nadya Leuven – Photographer, Belgium

Publisher:   CCB Publishing
             British Columbia, Canada
             www.ccbpublishing.com

*I dedicate this novel to my husband—the love of my life. I cannot, nor would I want to, imagine an existence without you. Mere words cannot express how grateful I am that you support and encourage the actualization of my dreams. Your calm, steady, consistent demeanor helps me maintain a true course in all my endeavors. From the bottom of my heart, I thank you for your love, understanding and, above all, patience.*

# CHAPTER ONE

## Perhaps I'm Weird....

I guess I'm weird. But then normal isn't exactly my style. I mean, what's normal about being a hooker and stripper who has premonition dreams? Despite my exotic side, I'm one of those people who enjoys going to the market. You know, aimlessly strolling up and down the aisles, no list. Just fake it as I go.

Like to eat healthy. Zoom through the canned food aisle like a commuter hitting a break in traffic. Boxed food items don't hold my attention. But the meat section, complete with choice cuts, that's one place I'll linger.

I'm a carnivore and damn proud of it. There's nothing as satisfying as sinking your teeth into a good porterhouse steak seared to perfection. How when your knife cuts into it, the juices gush from its perfectly pink center. The taste so heavenly, it melts in your mouth.

And the produce section, piled high with arranged stacks of fruits and vegetables kept fresh by automatic misters—oops, there they go again. Tiny beads of water seductively dripping off the contours of the produce. Some droplets get caught in the dimples and leafy bits, while others caress every curve. The fruits and vegetables look as appealing as a swimsuit model's six-pack.

Tucked within these colorful displays of produce are the bins of nuts and dried fruits. The sight of them makes me laugh. Not heartily, but a reserved, embarrassed sound that rises from somewhere buried deep within. The nuts and dried fruits remind me of when I got arrested for shoplifting them as a teen. Remembering is good. Used to hide from it. Caused all sorts of problems. Now I embrace my memories, even the hard ones.

1

As I pass the display of onions, their flaky skins catch my eye. Can't stop thinking about them. Smelly vegetables whose centers—their heart and soul—are well concealed by layers. Man, now I'm craving onion rings.

I've learned that we have two choices. We can bumble our way through life with blinders on, unaware of what and how various events affect us, or we can embrace that knowledge and learn from it. For the majority of my life, I did the former. Not out of choice, but out of necessity.

Didn't come from a Norman Rockwell childhood—quite the opposite. Mine was full of abuse and drugs. Spent my life hating my Self. What had happened to me. What I had allowed others to do to me. How I'd willingly set myself up to be used and then tossed aside like an old rag.

A year and a half ago, I began absorbing what life presented me and allowed these new feelings to flow through me, awakening my Self and self-awareness. At first, this proved challenging, for I'd become a pro at concealing my feelings. I'd also mastered the art of masking the unpleasant events that affected me. Taking those first few steps to waltz through my emotions, whatever they were, revealed that I had two left feet.

I stumbled my way through. At times, flailing so much against my Self that I wondered if I might be going mad. I wasn't. I was experiencing my own feelings for the first time. This proved exhausting and frustrating—at first. But then I saw a small crack in the shell. The tiniest glimmer of hope. I began to see my own transformation through the eyes of those around me and became fascinated in others' reactions to my positive change and growth. From it, I drew strength and gained a bottomless appetite for more self-improvement.

And so, I began to peel back my own layers, the protective shell in which I'd encased myself to block the daily hurt, abuse and hatred that had been directed toward me. I dug into that flaky skin with a new enthusiasm for life. Some layers peeled away with ease. Like yanking off a band-aid. If I did it fast and furious, it only stung for a short while. Others revealed the screaming demons that dwelled just below the surface. Those I bucked against the most. The ones that made me want to curl up into a tight ball and pretend that I'd never taken the lid off my Pandora's box.

Truth be told, I did run from some buried memories. The ones that proved all-consuming. I peeked at them from around protective corners, taking in minute doses until I'd built up enough immunity to not be destroyed by them. Each time I discarded another layer, I gained strength.

Can't believe how much I've grown. How much I've changed. My looks. The way I talk. How I think. Everything is different—better. I look back at the mess my life was a year and a half ago and can't believe that was me. I'm not that person anymore. I've learned how to deal with life's difficulties. How to set goals. How to reach out to others for help and to assist them.

I'm still working on it—my Self. Don't know if I'll ever get to my core. Every time I strip back another layer, I grow and evolve and gain more awareness to my Self. Guess it's like remodeling a house. My ma cautions to never finish that job, for when you do, you'll find yourself with a "For Sale" sign on the front lawn. This may be the same. Perhaps the day I find my core will be my last, for where else will I need to journey?

"Excuse me. Excuse me, ma'am."

Ma'am? They can't be referring to me. Looking around, I'm discouraged to discover that, indeed, I'm the one being addressed. When did I become a ma'am? Never mind.

A frazzled-looking mother around my age—early thirties—pushes a shopping cart, occupied by an adorable little fair-skinned toddler doing his damndest to change his ethnicity by finger-painting the smeared chocolate part of an Oreo across his entire face.

"I'm sorry?"

"The onions—a red one. Could you?"

"Oh, sure." I select a medium-sized one and hand it to her. She never glances at it but tosses it into the belly of the cart along with her other "survival" needs: chips, boxed main courses, cookies and frozen microwavable meals. Shoppers like her come to the store hungry, only to discover later that they have purchased none of what they need, but plenty of useless stuff. Poor woman, she'll be back.

I grab an onion for myself and a few staple fruits—bananas, pears and some grapes—before heading over to the meat department. Once there, I gaze, almost in a trance, at the delicious cuts of raw meat beckoning me. Mmmm…meat. Wasn't I just ragging on that woman for shopping while hungry? Hypocrite.

I select a couple of New York strip and T-bone steaks. Add them to my hand-held basket. Geez, it's heavy. Gotta think about working out my arms. I walk to the only register and stand at the back of the line. God, I hate that! Why do they bother building ten check stands when they rarely use more than three? Maddening.

I reach for a trash magazine. You know. The ones where the details of celebrities' lives are splashed across the front pages for the world to dissect. As if they have no skeletons in their own closets. But then, celebrities *do* choose to put themselves in the public eye. If they didn't want attention, guess they should've stayed in the private sector instead of pursuing a life in front of the camera. I know. Been there, front and center. Well, okay, maybe it's a bit of a stretch to compare a stripper to a celebrity, but hey, we both put ourselves out there.

A second before my hand lands on the magazine, I freeze. My attention is captured by the man standing several customers ahead of me. Even from behind, he's sexy. I'm drawn to the musculature of his back as it pulls against his T-shirt. I swear. Some people could literally wear a burlap bag and make it look good. I hate them!

This man is one of those—good eye candy. I lean a little to the side to get a better view. Just as I suspected, he's got a tight ass framed by his jeans. Nice! My eyes travel down his legs. Mmmm… long and muscular. Continuing my scan, I take in the traces of salt and pepper in his hair, and his bronzed skin, not burnt and tough like a day worker's but a natural Mediterranean color.

The man finishes his transaction and, gathering his bags, proceeds to the exit. Damn! The woman in front of me is blocking my view. Move your fat head, bitch! I need to see his profile. Too late, he's already out the door. Thanks! There goes what would have been tonight's fantasy….

As I move forward in line, I'm bitter toward the woman in front of me. Don't even know her, and yet I hate her! How dare she rob me of my eye candy!

I place my basket on the conveyer belt and watch it inch toward the checker. Still a couple of people to go before it's my turn. Oh, shit! Forgot the ice cream. I turn to the customer behind me, a man in his late seventies, and cringe at the thought of asking. But the desire for a frozen treat outweighs my hesitance. "Excuse me." The man doesn't respond. I try again—louder. "Excuse me."

The man cranes his head toward me. "Yes?"

"Would you mind if I grab a container of ice cream?"

His face lights up. "Oh, no. Go right ahead."

"Thanks! Be right back."

Standing in front of the display case, door open and letting out the cold, I can't decide which flavor. Hate people like me. Get in line before they're done shopping. Step out to grab "one more thing" and end up holding up the whole line.

Ah, hell! I'll just get them both. Wait! Then I'll have to work out more. Damn, I'm getting old. Not like when I was stripping and could dance off the calories. Fuck it—I snatch both containers and proceed to the checkout where the checker has just begun scanning my items. I shoot an apologetic look to the elderly man behind me as I slip ahead of him to finish my transaction.

A few minutes later as I near my car, groceries in hand, my heart skips a beat, recognizing the muscular back and flashes of bronzed skin. As I get closer, I can see the delicious ringlets of dark hair that play with his collar.

I slow my pace. What am I gonna do? Can't let him get away. I'm almost upon him when he closes his trunk. Thinking quickly, I allow one of my bags to slip from my hand. As the contents spill to the ground, he turns. Perfect! I bend down to gather my scattered items and say, "Ah! I'm such a klutz."

"Here, let me help," the man says, chasing after my onion. "Aha! Got it," he says, capturing it. He returns and places it in my hand, allowing his to linger a moment longer than necessary.

I look up. Our eyes lock. An electric surge pulses between us. "Thank you," I manage.

He smiles, flashing a brilliant set of white teeth with the tiniest of gaps between them. He's one of those. The lucky ones. The kind with naturally straight teeth. I think back to my childhood, plagued with headgears, neck gears and braces complete with metal wires rashing the insides of my mouth, and I hate him.

As he pulls his hand away from mine, he says, "Glad to help. We can't have rogue onions rolling amok in the parking lot."

I stand there frozen. Say something, stupid! I used to be so smooth with the johns. But this guy's blue eyes hypnotize me. The most brilliant light blue I've ever seen. Out of place against his skin tone and almost black hair, they cast a spell on me. The man cocks his head to the side and scrutinizes me. Probably to determine if the idiot standing before him is worthy of further conversation. My knees feel weak. My heart is beating double-time, and still I say nothing. What the hell's the matter with me?!

The man half chuckles, "Hmmm…." and then says, "Well, I've got to go. Perhaps we'll meet again…."

My powers of speech return, and I manage to squeak out, "That'd be nice." Offering my hand, I add, "I'm Sally."

Clasping mine, he says, "Hello, Sally. I'm Carlos."

"Nice to meet you, Carlos."

# CHAPTER TWO

## An Evening Stroll

Princess, my yellow Lab, greets me at the door, tail wagging, when I get home. You'd think I'd been gone a week, not just an hour. Love her greetings. They make me feel special. Loved. Can't imagine being without her. She's been there through everything. Always cheerful. Always accepting. Find myself talking to her a lot. It's comforting. I swear she understands me. She tilts her head at all the right moments and barks her reply when asked a question.

"Hey, girl!" I shuffle down the hallway to the kitchen where I deposit my bags on the counter, dog at my side. "Been waiting?"

She barks.

"Good girl." I rummage through the groceries and find what she's waiting for, a treat. Tearing open the bag, I hand her one. No circus tricks for my gal. Never saw the point in making a dog do tricks for a treat. You either appreciate and reward your pet, or not.

I put away the groceries and set a New York steak on a broiling pan. While I preheat the oven, I gather fixings for a salad: mixed lettuce, glazed walnuts, crumbled Gorgonzola cheese, pomegranate seeds and raspberry vinaigrette dressing.

While my steak cooks, I make the salad and set Princess' food out for her. When my steak is done, I serve myself. My knife glides through the fibers of the meat as if it were softened butter. Placing the juicy morsel in my mouth, I lean back and close my eyes. Mmmm, that's good!

After eating, Princess sits by my side waiting for me to finish washing the dishes. "I know, girl." Drying my hands, I reach for her leash and clip it to her collar. She nearly pulls me out the door.

You'd think the dog would get bored with this routine. Or at least not act as though it's her first time on a walk. We take one every evening and hike local trails and mountains when time allows. Used to go more during the week. Not so much any more. I enjoy her enthusiasm. It's contagious and makes me smile.

Being happy is good. Spent *way* too much time unhappy. For a while there, my life was nothing more than one long tragedy after another. Never had enough time to come up for air before the next thing would hit. Of course, getting addicted to crack didn't help. Only added to my troubles. Handing control of my life over to a chemical…. What was I thinking? Oh, yeah, I wasn't. At the time I was young, naive, hurting and wanted to stop my emotional pain. Using was one of the stupidest things I ever did.

A block into our walk, as always, Princess relaxes and settles into an even stride. She anticipates my moves and reads me so well. We wind our way through the maze of our neighborhood's tree-lined streets.

Every now and again we come across a car parked at the curb. Most are pulled into driveways or tucked away in garages. Wait. What was that? I slow my pace. Look around. Though it's dark, the streetlights allow me to scan the area. I don't see anything. But I *feel* it. I'm being watched. I look down at Princess. She appears relaxed. I shake off the feeling of unease and resume my pace.

# CHAPTER THREE

## Safe? Right....

Seeing Sally slow her pace, he ducks behind a tall hedge. He smiles when he sees her turn.

*Love your nervousness, cunt.*

He watches her scan the area, then look down at the mutt who seems to reassure her. He remains concealed as she continues on. He waits, then resumes following her.

Hidden across the street from her house, he waits. Looks down at his watch.

*Any time now.*

His homework had been thorough. He knew Sally went on an evening walk about this time each day. He'd have preferred her to be alone. But he knew her mutt was no *real* threat to him. Least, hadn't been so far. And he'd done this a few times—stalked Sally, but always at a greater distance.

But tonight's different. He wants her to *feel* him. Wants to scare her. He likes that—scaring people. Makes him feel more powerful. More in control. And he craves control above all else.

Whatever he wants, he gets. And what he wants now is to rattle Sally's cage. Make her uncertain. Question her safety.

*Safe? Right.... Bitch ain't safe. Not with me around.*

# CHAPTER FOUR

## This Old House

Princess and I round a corner, and our house comes into view. It's a grand two-story Craftsman from the turn of the century. As I climb the steps to the wrap-around front porch, the oversized rocking chairs catch my eye. James had insisted upon them. Said they made it feel like home. 'Course, he was right. How many nights did we spend on this very porch, watching for shooting stars? Or Sunday mornings spent sharing the paper over a steaming mug of coffee for me, hot tea for him?

I remove Princess' leash and sit in one of the rockers, rhythmically tilting back and forth. Can almost feel James rocking beside me…. Perfectly synchronized. Never did that with anyone else…just James. But that's done now. Part of the past.

Princess lies down beside me. For a few minutes, she balances her head between her front paws. Then, without warning, lets out a big sigh. You know the kind. The one that says, "Okay, guess we're gonna be here for a while. Might as well get comfortable." She exhales, then flops over onto her side, grunting.

I rock a while longer, and she begins to fall asleep. In the process, she snortles. Similar to the sound a horse makes. Love it when she makes that noise. That's when I know she's settling in for a long snooze. I rock for longer than intended. Don't feel rushed. The stresses of life no longer weigh heavy on my shoulders. The feeling is liberating.

I watch Princess' rear legs run in her sleep. Bet she's chasing a fat squirrel with a bushy tail. She loves pursuing critters up trees. Honestly, you'd think she'd tire of never catching one. She doesn't.

She tackles each hunt with the expectation that this is the one—the time she'll catch the little bugger. Gotta give her points for not giving up even in her dreams.

I gaze at the stars and spot a shooting one near the horizon. "One, two, three," I count aloud, then close my eyes and make a silent wish. My younger brother Eric and I used to play this game when we were kids. I open my eyes and get up. Princess wakes and rises with me.

The cold makes me shiver, and we go inside. As I pass through the living room, I look at the decorations and furniture. I smile at the two black-and-white photos hanging on the wall above the sofa. James had picked them up while in Europe before we were together. The images captured in them—one of a lichen-covered stacked wall in the country, the other of buildings lining the waterways of Amsterdam—are peaceful.

My eyes travel downward to the new sofa. It was sad to let the old one go. If I close my eyes, I can picture it and how it still smelled of James' cologne. But change is good, they say.

I notice the awkward chunky coffee table and smile. Another of James' pre-us possessions. Couldn't bear to part with it. Something about its simplicity. I tilt my head and appreciate the refinishing. Angel and I did a good job. The table looks fresher, almost new.

And then there's James' dark distressed leather armchair. He loved that chair. Would sit in it for hours reading a book before a crackling fire. Used to enjoy hearing the leather creak as he shifted his weight.

I pull my eyes away from the chair and head upstairs. As I climb the steps, my hand glides along the solid railing. Everything in this house is sturdy and made from dark woods. I like it that way. Gives it character.

At the top of the stairs, I see one of Princess' tennis balls lying up ahead. I grin and race her to it. Arriving a moment before she does, I place my foot over it. She drops down on her front legs, rear in the air, tail wagging like a puppy, and attempts to grab it from under my foot. I mess with her for a bit. When she turns away, I give the ball a gentle kick down the hall. She pounces after it, takes it in her mouth and shakes it as if it's a raw steak.

Princess sees me approaching, turns and heads into my bedroom. Sometimes this room is hard to enter. Even though it's been almost a year and a half....

Ah, James...the pain of losing him still stings. To think of what we had and lost.... In the blink of an eye, it was gone. So senseless. It's getting better, though. Most days are easier than before. Some are worse—much worse. But that's okay. It's part of the healing process. It's horrible to lose one's spouse. Especially when I needed him most, but I'm getting better. Peeling back the layers of my onion is helping.

I pass through the bedroom into the bath to the ball and claw cast-iron tub. Such a cool tub. Don't make them like this anymore. It was James' idea to install the suspended oval curtain rod so he could shower. Me, I love to sink into a tub full of scalding water overflowing with mounds of glistening bubbles. Makes me feel pampered.

I reach through the shower curtain. Gotta take that thing down. Never use it. I set the plug and turn on the water. Sitting on the tub's edge, I watch the swirling liquid through the rising steam. I pour some bubbles from an expensive body shop—a gift from my mother—into the stream of water. At first, I'd protested the lavish gift, but she'd insisted. I smile as the room fills with the calming scent of lavender. The mounds of silky bubbles look like fluffy clouds.

I close the bathroom door to trap the steam. Although old houses are nice, they sure can get drafty. Guess people didn't mind the cold as much back then. I shed my clothes and let them fall in a heap on the floor. I chuckle softly. James hated this habit of mine. Although I would always scoop them up and put them in the hamper when I was done, it drove him mad that I could stand to let my shed clothing lay in a crumpled heap while I bathed. He was just the opposite. As each article of clothing came off, it was folded and stacked in a neat pile. Never understood this extra step. I mean, the clothes are dirty and going in the hamper. What difference does it make if they're folded or not?

I leave my clothes on the floor and, turning off the water, slip into the inviting tub. The moment I do, the warm soothing water washes away the day, and I close my eyes, lost in the luxury of my bath. What is it about a hot soak?  How does it instantly relax, heal and cleanse?

I lay my head against the high back of the tub.  Perfect height.  Not like those modern tubs whose lip bites into the back of your neck.  This tub hugs and supports my shoulders and neck and allows me to relax to the point that I almost drift off to sleep.

I soak until the water is cool and the chilled air seeps in.  I turn on the faucet to add more hot water, only to discover that I've used it all.  Damn!  Gotta get a bigger water heater.  Reluctantly, I pull myself from the tub and reach for my bath towel.  I pat myself dry then wrap my hair.

By this time, the steam has begun to dissipate, and I can start to make out my likeness in the mirror.  I don't turn away.  As the mirror unfogs, my image takes form.  I see how my auburn hair shines in the light.  It used to be longer, but I cut it to just below my shoulders.  I admire the curvature of my hips and cinched-in waist and smile at my full breasts.  A woman's body.  I lean in to survey the slight mask of freckles splashed across my nose and cheeks.  Guess they're always gonna be there.  Funny.  I thought…I don't know…that I'd outgrow them? *Can* you outgrow freckles?  Guess not, at least not in my case.

I hear the muffled ringing of the phone in the other room.  Throwing on my robe, I venture to the bedroom and pick it up.  "Hello?"

A familiar, "Hey there, Sally girl," greets me.

"Angel!"  I flop on the bed and tell her about meeting Carlos.  She asks an endless barrage of questions, and I tell her what a fool I'd made of myself with my muteness.  I remove the towel and absentmindedly run my fingers through my hair, combing out the tangles.  My hair's more than halfway dry by the time I hang up, and I can't stop thinking about Carlos.

I throw on a pair of sensible flannel pajamas, not the lacy lingerie I used to favor, and climb into bed.  I reach for my spiral-bound journal.  Never got out of the habit of journaling in a simple notebook.  Guess it reminds me of the original one James handed me, as my doctor, when I was an inpatient at the drug treatment facility.  God!  It's only been four years?  Seems like a lifetime ago.  So much has happened, and yet….

I open my journal and begin writing.

*I'm so torn. There's James' memory. All that we shared. His presence is everywhere in this house. And I like that. Comforts me. But.... Then there's Carlos. Why's he having this effect on me? Not like I was looking to find someone. Haven't felt this way about another man since.... Don't know what to do. What would James have wanted? Never had a chance to talk about it. Thought we'd grow old together. Have plenty of time to work those things out. Life didn't play out that way. Has it been long enough? What's the right amount of time? Would I know? Yeah. Guess I do. Think that's why Carlos is having this effect on me. Maybe it's time for me to move on. Allow another part of the healing process to occur. Doesn't mean I have to forget James or what we shared. Think that's what James would've wanted—me to go on living. Not be alone. Find happiness. Is that with Carlos? Who knows. Perhaps I'll take baby steps. Have a dream or two about Carlos. If that works out, then....*

I sigh. Cap my pen. Close my journal. Turn out the lights. Looking at the clock, I realize it's still early. Perhaps there's time for a dream or two about Carlos....

# CHAPTER FIVE

## New Beginnings

I awake the next morning, glowing. Thoughts of Carlos still linger. Mmmm, such delicious fantasies. I roll over and view the clock. Still time. I roll back and resume my Carlos fantasy.

I wasn't clumsy or awkward with words. Oh, no. I seduced him with my sultry voice, luring him into my world. Wrapped my leg around his upper thigh and pulled him close. Clawed my nails up and down his back, much to his delight. Stood on my tiptoes, nuzzled my lips against his neck to nibble and kiss just below his jaw line. Tasted the saltiness of his neck. I felt his body respond and trembled with the urgency of my own needs. And our passion had continued. Lost in each other, we forgot time, space and our own identities. The only thing that mattered was merging as one…. And in my fantasy, we had.

With the greatest effort, I extract myself from my Carlos fantasy. I pull myself out of bed, let Princess out and then take a bath. I smile as I wash myself, imagining that the hands that bathe me are not my own, but those of Carlos caressing each and every curve of my body…. I finish washing, towel dry and throw on a pair of jeans, boots and a sleeveless blouse.

I get the Sunday paper from the front walkway, then pour myself a cup of coffee and fetch a yogurt from the fridge. Settling in at the kitchen table, I skip the sections announcing world events and turn to the ad section. There I find it—my call-out. It reads:

**Ladies, tired of not being able to face what's reflected back at you in the mirror? Interested in taking control of your life and changing it for the**

**better?  If so, I've got the solution—pole-dancing classes.  During my six-week course, you'll shed some unwanted pounds, become comfortable with and accept yourself and have a brighter outlook on life.  If this appeals to you, please contact Sally Whitmore at 555-4344.**

Smiling, I lean back and take a sip of my coffee.  I hear the front door open and with it, Angel's voice.  "Hey, girl.  Where are you?"

"In the kitchen."  I look up and admire my friend as she enters the room.  I swear she hasn't aged a day since we met.  Petite, five-foot nothing, 100 pounds tops, the only change is her new shoulder-length bob of jet-black hair that shines and swishes from side to side.

It finally happened.  We grew up.  Out of nowhere.  One day we were being our crazy selves, flying by the seat of our pants, the next we assumed normal respectable lives.

Seeing Angel, a thousand memories of shared experiences flood my mind.  Hanging with our group of druggie friends in high school.  Having sex with all the boys in that group.  Running away from home and beginning a life of prostitution that led to my getting pregnant.  Angel by my side as I delivered that child on one of the same grungy beds where I'd laid hundreds of johns.  Fleeing our pimp to become strippers.  Angel helping me through overcoming my addiction to crack.  Her shoring me up when my second son, born premature, lost his battle to live.  Holding me together when my husband died in a car accident.

I smile as Angel passes by me and heads straight for the coffeepot.  Grabbing a mug from the holder on the counter, she pours herself a cup—black—and holds the pot out.  "More?"

"Sure."

She freshens my cup, then returns the carafe to the warmer.  Angel leans over the newspaper.  "So, is it there yet?"

I tap my finger on my ad.  She reads, then looks up.  "So, you ready?"

"Think so."

"First class tomorrow?"

"Yes."

"How many students?"

"Five."

"Nervous?"

"A little. This is so strange, yet feels so right. More and more housewives are finding pole dancing is an excellent form of exercise. Builds self-confidence and self-esteem. Breaks them free of their shells and taps into what lies beneath."

"Nice commercial." Angel smiles and looks up with her caramel-colored eyes. "What do you have to lose?"

"It's not what *I* stand to lose, but *them*."

"The women?"

Nodding, I say, "I wanna make their lives better."

"Like yours?"

"The ones who need it the most are the ones who think the least of themselves. The ones who've been broken by their life choices and society. I can relate. After everything that's happened—losing my son, James dying, falling apart and then getting better—I wanna help other women find their strength so they can heal." I pause to swirl my coffee before taking a sip. Unable to meet my friend's eyes, I mumble into my mug, "What if this is a stupid idea?"

"It's not like you had this crazy thought and jumped right into it. You took your time. Really thought it through.... Give it a chance."

Can always count on Angel. She's been my best friend for fifteen years. Can't believe all the stuff we've been through. How she's always supported me. Heaven knows I've tested the limits of our friendship. Can't recall the number of times she covered for me and helped put the broken parts of my Self back together. All those times I disappeared and kept her worrying while I was off on three-day crack binges. Why'd she stay? Never would have made it through half the stuff I did, if it hadn't been for her.

Changing the subject, I ask, "Wanna see the room?"

"Sure!"

We top off our mugs. I add cream and sugar to mine and then head for the stairs. As we cross the living room, Angel points at the coffee table. "Did a good job."

"Sure did."

We climb the dark staircase. I grin as the eighth step creaks under my weight. One of the many quirks I love about my house. We round a corner at the top. Stretched before us is a wide hallway. To the left is my room. Farther down is a closed door. Arriving in front of it, I rest my hand on the knob. "Promise to give me your honest opinion?"

"I will."

I swing the door open, revealing a flood of light filtering in through two walls of wrap-around windows. In the center of the large room is a raised stage with a single gleaming brass pole. Five additional poles surround it on a lower level. Rays of sunlight streaming through the tree branches reflect off the poles and create a dappling effect on the light tan walls and floor. As Angel enters, I hear her gasp. "Wow!" she says while rotating slowly. "You and your mom did a great job!"

I beam.

"It's nicer than any studio I've ever seen! They're gonna love it!"

"What about the mirrors? Too much?"

Angel surveys the floor-to-ceiling mirrors on the two windowless walls. "No. They make it bright."

"And, if someone is uncomfortable with them, I can always draw these closed," I say, pointing to curtains.

Angel's eyes wander to the newly built-in service counter where the closet used to be and says, "Remember when we packed away James Charles, Jr.'s stuff?"

"How could I forget?"

"Never told you how much I admired your strength. How you dove right in. Got the job done."

I look at Angel. "That wasn't strength. I couldn't bear the visual reminder that my baby was gone."

"You're healing."

"Time helps."

Angel walks to the center of the room, and runs a hand up and down one of the gleaming brass poles. Turning to me, her face displays a devilish grin. "Wow! This brings back memories…. Remember how nervous we were when we auditioned for Luigi at the strip club?"

"Yeah. What was up with that? After tricking, you'd think taking our clothes off would've been easy, but...." I look at the wall clock. "Wanna get going?"

We arrive in Hollywood, park the car and stroll Sunset Boulevard. Walking along the strip takes me back. I was such a naive eighteen-year-old. Desperate to escape the pain of my brother's death, I was lured by the drugs my pimp offered and what I mistook as the exciting life of a prostitute. Thought it'd be fun to get paid for having sex. It wasn't. Thought I'd feel better about myself. I didn't. Thought I could stop any time. Impossible with a pimp like Ax.

Seems like yesterday that Angel and I, on rare occasions, used to come here to get slutty outfits to better lure johns. Yup, Hollywood was the place back then.

Based on the window displays, it looks like it still is. Every imaginable sleazy getup is represented here. And the shoes! This is the place to get every variation of jaw-dropping come-fuck-me heels. Bold colors, animal prints and clear acrylic. Such extreme heels that it defies reason that women can walk in them. And the boots.... Where do I begin? There are short, thigh-high, patent leather, ballerina and crotch-height ones.

Today's shopping spree involves finding a specific item—stripper shoes. Can't pole dance without the right heels. And, although I've instructed my new students on the exact pair to get, I have procrastinated buying them myself. So here I am. Shopping at the last minute.

Navigating several blocks from where we parked, Angel and I enjoy looking in the windows along the way. I point to a mannequin. "Look at her hair." Pastel pink and cropped to a fashionable bob. "Remember when I wanted my hair that color?"

Angel laughs. "Yeah. Just *one* of your many crazy ideas."

"Hey!"

Angel lists them. "The whole pink hair thing, the almost-getting-tattooed phase before they were in fashion—especially for women—and let's not forget the how-short-can-I-wear-my-skirt-without-getting-arrested period." Angel pauses.

I shrug. "You know I had damn good-looking legs!" We pass by a nail salon and stop. "Wanna get our nails done?"

Angel looks at her watch. "Is there time?"

Entering the salon, we stand before the limitless display of nail enamels ranging from subtle to neon. Picking up a particularly offensive shade, I hold it up to Angel. "There was a time I would have gone straight for this one." I replace the bottle. "Thank goodness I acquired some taste."

We laugh, and then both select shades of dark red and take a seat. An hour and a half later, with our toenails and fingernails gleaming, we continue toward the shoe shop, only a block away. Entering, we mock the majority of the foot-torturing accessories displayed. On the back wall, I find what I'm seeking—a pair of clear acrylic five-inch heels with clear straps, rhinestones across the toes, and a one-inch platform. I smile. They're worthy of melting any stripper's heart. A short time later, shoes in hand, we leave the store and head to Angel's car.

That evening, bubbling with anxiety, I make a run to the market to pick up a few things. As I round the corner to head down the last aisle, the one closest to the produce, I'm surprised to spot him—Carlos. Although he is turned away from me, I recognize his back and tease of dark curls accenting his tanned skin just above the collar.

My heart skips a beat. My tongue grows thick in my mouth, and I swear I've forgotten how to speak once again. Ignoring the betrayal of my body, I head toward the stack of cantaloupes, right beside him. The closer I get, the clammier my palms become, and I have to readjust my grip on the hand basket lest it slip from my hands. How should I initiate contact this time? Already done the dropping-of-groceries ploy. Probably should go with a new approach this time. I don't know. Perhaps I'll try the less dramatic, yet still effective, "hello."

I take my time approaching. Like a lioness closing in on its prey. No need to hurry. I watch him. Scrutinize his movements. Relish every delicious step that brings me closer to him. Twenty feet.

Fifteen. Ten. Wait! From behind one of the display tables, a boy of about four speeds his way toward the man—my man. He's clutching a small bunch of bananas. "Daddy! Daddy! Are these good?"

I freeze.

His back still turned to me, Carlos reaches down and lovingly scoops up the boy, bananas and all. The child shoves the fruit so close to his father's face that Carlos is forced to lean back to focus, and then he says, "They're perfect. Good job."

Before Carlos has a chance to turn, I abruptly change course and head toward the farthest checkout. All the while, my mind is rapid-firing questions. A son? He didn't mention a son. But then we didn't really have much of a conversation. Married?! Is Carlos married? If so, where's the boy's mother? This could change everything, making Carlos off limits. Shit!

# CHAPTER SIX

## Unease

I purchase my items, barely hearing the checker when she tells the amount. Gathering my bags, I head to my car. My mind swirls and protests against what I saw—Carlos with…a son. I quicken my pace. Want outta here. To create distance between what is threatening to foil my fantasies about him and me.

Halfway to my car, the hairs on the back of my neck begin to prickle. Thinking Carlos may have spotted me and is coming out, I don't turn but walk faster. Anxious to make it to my car. Don't want to see him. Not now. Can't. Gotta think this through first.

Each step I take convinces me I'm being watched. Followed. Expect to hear Carlos call my name any minute. I approach my car. Fumble with the keys. Get in. Backing out of my space, I look around, thinking I'll spot him. I don't. What? But why did I feel watched? Followed? If not Carlos, then who? Jesus! I really gotta get a grip.

Princess greets me at home and shadows me as I put away the few things I purchased. I click off the downstairs lights and head upstairs, anxious to work things out in my journal. Sitting on my bed, I write:

> What's going on with Carlos? A son? Never occurred to me. But married? What if she was there? Watching? Okay, that puts a different spin on things. Slow down. Don't get carried away. Maybe he's

*divorced. Didn't seem like the cheating kind. What am I saying? I don't even know him. Besides, what's the "cheating kind" look like? And then there's the whole felt-like-I-was-being-followed thing. But when I looked...nothing. Maybe I'm just stressed about my first class tomorrow. Mind's working overtime. That's gotta be it. I hope.*

I close my journal. Reach down to pet Princess. Turn off the light and go to sleep. But mine's a restless one, filled with bizarre dreams.

\* \* \* \* \*

Walking my neighborhood. Darkness surrounds. Eyes. Cruel ones. My house. Winding streets. Rogue onions rolling amok in the parking lot. First one. Then a truckload. I'm buried alive by them. Choke and gag on their peeling skins—what's revealed. More eyes— watching. Warning flags. Past. Present. Future. Shared laughter. Healing. Darkness. Time/space shopping continuum. Day indiscriminately meshing into the veil of darkness. Race of a lifetime.

\* \* \* \* \*

I awake as always from my premonition dreams, bolting upright, covered in sweat. What the hell? Thought they were gone. Haven't had one in...forever. Why the hell won't they leave me alone? Or at least give me something I can work with. Hate how the images they present are so jumbled. Can't make heads or tails of them. Only after, then I know what they were trying to foretell.

I feel the start of a headache. Always get one after my visions. Wish they'd come when I'm awake. But no, they always invade my sleep.  Maybe if I were awake during them, I could make sense of them.

Though I know it's useless, I try to fit the fragmented pieces of my premonition dream puzzle into place.  My headache worsens, and the images from my dream fade into uncertainty before I can connect them.  Fuck!

I lie down and stare at the ceiling for a long time before exhaustion and sleep overtake me.

# CHAPTER SEVEN

## The Waiting Game

He slides down in his car seat, watching the car pull up in front of Sally's. Narrows his eyes, recognizing the driver.

*Fuckin' cunt—Angel!*

Sally gets out of the passenger seat, grabs a bag, waves and heads inside as Angel drives off.

*How dare she be happy.*

He curls the side of his mouth into an evil sneer.

*That'll change. Always does when I make my point. And I've been* so *good at that.*

He leans his head back and settles in. Doesn't mind waiting. It's part of the game. And he likes games. Is good at them. Waiting. Calculating. Figuring out his best advantage.

A while later, he hears a car backing down her driveway.

*So, where we going?*

He follows her from a safe distance, one not to raise her suspicion—at least, not yet. They drive a bit, and he recognizes the path she's taking.

*The market, huh?*

Sally pulls in the lot well ahead of him. He passes that entry, opting to circle around the corner and pull in another. She's already walking into the store when he enters the lot. He parks a few aisles over from her car. Turning off his engine, he resumes the waiting game.

Bags in hand, Sally exits the store. He notices the way she looks flustered.

*Hmmm, and I haven't even started my fun...yet.*

He sees her quicken her pace halfway to her car.

*Excellent!*

Doesn't look around though, until she's in her car and pulling out. He lets out a pleased sigh as she leaves the parking lot.

"Until next time, bitch!" he says aloud, starting his engine and driving the other way.

# CHAPTER EIGHT

## Pre-class Jitters

Huh? What is that? The circuits in my groggy brain attempt to connect. The clock. My stupid alarm clock. Who the hell invented them? He should be shot, brought back to life and then shot again! Without opening my eyes, I reach over and slam my hand against it. The annoying machine skitters across the nightstand and crashes against the wall. With a satisfied grin, I listen as it pathetically beeps out its last wakeup call. It manages only a half dozen or so before it falls forever silent. Excellent!

Perhaps I should keep track of how many of these contraptions I've destroyed over the years. Images of alarm clocks, their intricate wires and circuit boards spilling from their shattered cases come to mind. I can't help but smile at the pretty picture it paints.

Eyes still closed, I begin my getting out of bed routine. Some might call it stalling. I prefer to think of it as making sure that I'm fully prepared to face whatever the day might throw at me. My regimen begins with a leisurely cat-like stretch. Still lying in bed, I reach my arms overhead and interlace my fingers. Facing the palms of my hands outward, I push them away from my head, grunting. Several joints crack in the process. Geez, when did that start? Used to be able to stretch and work out without anything aching or popping. Now I creak in the morning. Great! I'm sure a walker isn't far behind. I slowly allow the stretch to work its way down the entire length of my body, wiggling this way and that as more joints crack into position. Finally the stretch reaches my feet, and my toes curl.

I throw the covers back, attempting to convince myself that I will soon get up. I open my eyes and try to focus. Who am I kidding? I slam my eyes shut and roll over, covering up in the process. My body melts against the mattress once more.

Feel like I didn't sleep at all last night. And based on the snarled sheets, it's clear I tossed and turned—a lot. Can't stop thinking about it. The class. Is this a good idea? A stupid one? One that'll help? Or hurt? No wonder I'm so tired.

My need to pee becomes incessant. I try to ignore it. No use. Reluctantly, I open my eyes and peek over the edge of the bed. Princess, determined to eke out every possible moment of rest, is still asleep. Good girl. Stepping over her, I pad my way to the restroom, rubbing the sleep from my eyes and combing my fingers through my hair.

I sit on the toilet and rest my face in my hands while thoughts plague my mind. Today's the day! No turning back. Am I gonna be able to provide what I want for these women? Or am I just setting us all up for failure?

Getting up, I flush and go to wash my hands and face, and brush my teeth. As I reach for a towel, Princess comes in and sits beside me. "Wanna go out?"

She springs to attention and wags her tail, several barks escaping. I grab my robe from behind the bathroom door. Slipping in an arm, I smile at its plush softness. Not like those skimpy lingerie robes I used to wear.

Here's the thing. A robe is a robe. Right? By definition it's supposed to cover you up and offer warmth. Well, the ultra sheer, damn-you-look-hot "robes" I used to wear offer none of the above. They're just for show. Pretty packaging for what lies underneath.

I nuzzle my chin against the plush shoulder of my robe. Now *this* is what a robe should be. Sensible. Warm. And revealing just enough to entice onlookers without the wearer freezing to death in the process. What they say is true. Age really is accompanied by wisdom.

I head downstairs with Princess bounding down the stairs ahead of me. When she gets to the bottom, she turns and barks at me to hurry. "I'm coming, girl." I let her out, then pour myself a cup of coffee. By the time I've fetched a yogurt from the fridge and added cream and sugar to my mug, Princess is at the door.

I open it, and she bounds in. Acting as if she hasn't seen me in weeks, she circles, barks and rubs against my legs. I have to steady myself against her weight so she won't knock me over. She calms down, giving me the opportunity to prepare a bowl of food for her.

We eat our breakfast in silence. Well, not exactly in silence. Princess is an enthusiastic eater who smacks, licks and pushes her dish from one end of the kitchen to the other before she's done eating. I find myself staring at her as she licks every square inch of her bowl, making it spin like a noisy top against the tile floor.

Done, she looks up as if asking for more. "No more," I say. "We girls gotta watch our figures." She lies down and begins grooming herself. Meanwhile, I finish my yogurt, pour myself another cup of coffee and head upstairs with Princess hot on my heels. Who needs a shadow when they've got a dog like mine?

Heading toward my closet, I shoot a quick glance at the clock. Two hours before class begins. This is really happening. My stomach fills with spasmodic butterflies, and I begin to lose my focus. Shaking off the nervous feeling, I set about choosing what I'll wear.

First I pull out a pair of jeans and a camisole top. Standing before the full-length mirror set in the corner, I hold the items against me. Ach! These won't work. I toss them on the bed and try again. Every outfit seems wrong. Before long, my bed is covered with a mountain of rejected clothing. I look at the clock again. Geez! Half an hour gone. How did *that* happen?

I go to the closet, near desperation. Aha! I know. Why didn't I think of this earlier? I put on an outfit and stand before the mirror, admiring my selection. My feet are strapped into my new come-fuck-me stripper heels. And the mini-skirt I've chosen accentuates my trim legs. The camisole I first chose and then rejected complements the outfit. Nodding my approval, I hear the phone ring and answer it.

"Hello?"

"Hey, girl," comes Angel's voice. "Wanted to wish you good luck today."

"Thanks."

"How you doing?"

"Better now. Had a wardrobe dilemma but figured it out."

"You ready?"

I draw in a deep breath and exhale. "As ready as I'm gonna be."

"You'll do great."

"Thanks. Hey, don't mean to cut you off, but that whole wardrobe thing has me running late. Call you after class?"

"Sure. Break a leg."

I hang up, then finish getting ready. It's amazing how easily I slip back into wearing five-inch heels. Seems like just yesterday I was stripping in them. Putting the finishing touches on my makeup, I look at the clock. Only fifteen minutes till show time.

I head to the studio, flip on the lights, open a few windows and make sure the music is cued up. Next, I set a pot of coffee to brewing and check the mini-fridge to make sure there are enough waters and creamer. I pull several mugs out of the overhead cupboard and set them on the counter, double-checking the basket of sweeteners. With each new act and ticking of the wall clock, my heart beats faster. It's almost time. I step up on the main stage and run my fingers up and down the pole. Maybe just one or two moves.... It'll help calm me.

Just as I'm getting into position, the doorbell rings. Oh, God! This is it! They're here. Take a deep breath. You know. Breathe in, now out, and in again. Steady....

I take a final look around the room, then head down to answer the door. For the moment, I forget how to breathe. How stupid is that? I've been doing it since I was a baby. It's supposed to be involuntary. And *now* I forget how to breathe. What the hell? I close my eyes and try to calm myself before opening the door.

The bell chimes a second time. I reach for the handle and pull the door open. Standing before me is a pleasant though nervous-looking woman dressed in a black leotard and matching top, with a bag slung over her shoulder. "Hi, my name is Carol. Is this where the pole-dancing class is?"

I muster my most reassuring smile. "Sure is. My name's Sally. Come in, please." I step aside to grant the woman passage and note her meticulous appearance as she enters. Not a hair is out of place, and her outfit is flawless.

She turns to face me. "I hope it's all right that I'm a few minutes

31

early. Always am. Bothers some of my friends. Makes them uncomfortable. My being early isn't making you uneasy, is it?" She doesn't wait for an answer before continuing with her rapid monologue. "What was I thinking? Of course it'll make you uncomfortable. Here, let me wait out in the car until the others arrive." She suddenly looks grave. "There *are* others. Right?"

I'm so stunned by her incessant speech that it takes me a second to process that she's paused so I can answer. "No. I mean, yes, there are others. No need for you to wait in the car. I'm sure the others will be here any minute. Why don't I take you up and show you the studio?"

"Are you sure? Only if it's no bother."

"Come on. We can have a cup of coffee while we wait." Hold on! What the hell am I saying? A cup of coffee. Surely, this woman's already consumed fifteen espressos. "Or perhaps you'd prefer water?" I add.

"Coffee sounds good."

Great. Of course it does. I'm gonna be the only pole-dancing instructor to kill off her first student with a cup of coffee. I mean, how much more stimulation can this woman's heart take without checking out? I try another tactic. "Actually, I'm not sure if the coffee's done brewing yet. Sure you wouldn't prefer some water?"

"Well, if the coffee's not done...."

As we enter the room, the sharp acidic aroma of freshly brewed coffee greets us, and I see the woman's eyes twinkle with delight as she spies the full pot. Damn! I hear the doorbell ring downstairs. I look at Carol and motion toward the carafe. "Feel free to help yourself. There's creamer in the fridge." Not giving her a chance to respond, I head downstairs.

As I swing the door wide, a perfectly chiseled, five-foot-nine, alabaster-skinned, redheaded woman on the other side retracts her hand, poised to press the doorbell a second time. "Thought maybe I had the wrong address when you didn't answer right away," she says.

Great. I've got overly jumpy Carol caffeinating herself upstairs and Miss Judgmental standing before me. "Are you here for the pole-dancing class?" I ask.

"Yep."

"Then you're in the right place. Come in. My name's Sally. And you are…?"

"Trish."

"Pretty name. Is that short for Patricia?"

"No. Just Trish," she says while noisily smacking her gum.

Wow! This is going great. Can hardly wait to meet the others. "Why don't you come in?" I say. "I'll take you up to the studio. One of the other students has already arrived."

As we ascend the stairs, I'm concerned about how wired Carol might be. We arrive in the studio moments later where, ironically, I find a much calmer Carol. Hmmm…she must be hyperactive. I've heard caffeine calms hyperactive people.

I introduce the two. Trish sizes her up, sniffs and comments, "My, aren't you the eager beaver."

Standing slightly off to her side, I read Trish. She uses her tough girl act to cover for her insecurities. Know her type well. Used to be just like her…. I show Trish to the service counter where she helps herself to a bottled water, while I pour myself a cup of coffee. The three of us talk for a few minutes before the doorbell rings again.

I leave Trish and Carol to themselves and head down to greet my next student. Arriving at the door, I'm surprised to see who I presume are the remaining three of my students.

Pam's in front of the other two and introduces herself. She's pretty in a Midwest kind of way—not cover girl material. I sense a mystique hidden just below her surface, clamoring to make its way free. Her aura is alluring. To her left, a compact stout woman with dull mousy brown hair and lifeless eyes tells me her name is Molly. To Pam's right is Alicia. When she offers to shake my hand, I can't help but notice her nicotine-stained fingertips and the hard edge to her features. It's evident from the heaviness on her face that hers has not been an easy life.

I welcome them and lead the way up to the studio where I introduce everyone. Trish is instantly put on guard by Pam's height, just under her own, and her easy buoyant disposition. Of course, I'm sure Pam's tanned complexion and sassy curls that frame her soft features don't help. I'm going to have to watch those two. Oil and water....

Molly seems to be almost in physical pain when asked a question and literally shrinks back from the others. Alicia and Trish seem to hit it off for no apparent reason. I sense a common thread, not all that dissimilar to my own past.

By this time, Carol is on her second cup and Trish has almost finished her water. Pam helps herself to a mug of coffee. Alicia takes a water. And Molly refrains from treating herself to anything.

I allow them to finish their beverages and mingle for a few minutes. All the while, thoughts tumble their way through my mind. Man! What have I gotten myself into? I mean, look at them. Each is a train wreck of despair and a hard life. Who am I to think that I can make a difference? With every fiber of my psyche protesting and telling me to abort, I begin my first pole-dancing class.

# CHAPTER NINE

## Class Has Begun

Looking at my merry bunch of misfits, I realize that I'll have to draw upon my people skills if I'm to succeed, and I say, "I thought we'd begin by introducing ourselves." I can't help but notice the apprehensive looks that mask my students' faces, suggesting that they hide their feelings. "Some of you appear a little skeptical." A little? More like jumping out of their skins. "How about if I begin? My name's Sally Whitmore. I'm thirty-two. My life used to be really messed up. I was a prostitute, crack addict and a stripper." I grab hold of the pole beside me and circle it. "Spent a lot of years hating myself, having no self-confidence and loathing what I allowed others to do to me. And then I hit rock bottom." I pause to notice how the women are entranced and have relaxed as if hearing my story has allowed each of them to connect with me. "I imagine that each of you has your own tale to tell. Like mine, some might not be so pretty."

Trish spits out, "Yeah? My heart breaks for you."

Inwardly, I recoil from her verbal attack but hide my reaction, knowing that it'll only embolden her. I let go of the pole and look at Trish. I emit no anger or judgment. Instead, when I speak, it's with compassion and understanding. "The thing that turned my life around was when I began to like my Self. The day I could finally look at my reflection in the mirror without turning away was the day I knew I was on the right track. That's what I want to give each of you. The opportunity to lose a few pounds, build your self-confidence and self-esteem and learn to accept who you are."

"Wow!" Trish says. "You act all uppity for someone who was such a mess."

"Why would you say that?"

Trish sniffs. "All educated…put together. Like you're better than us."

"My experience brought me to my knees," I say as I begin pacing before my students, making eye contact with each. "It taught me to look to myself for the strength I needed to gain a better life. I'm humbled by each of you showing up here and giving me the chance to—"

"To what? Turn us into little…yous? Ha! Thank you, no. Like myself just the way I am."

I note Trish's tough-girl in-control appearance punctuated by her hair pulled back into a stern ponytail. She's perfectly chiseled. Wouldn't doubt that she's sporting an eight-pack under her cropped T-shirt. And I can see the defined musculature of her thighs through her leggings. Her fresh minimalistic makeup tells me she likes to keep things simple. I bet her life is anything but. I realize that now is the time for me to take control. If I push too hard, Trish will spin on her heels and bolt. I can see it in her eyes. I approach her and say, "Then why did you respond to my ad?"

"Thought it might be fun."

"That's it?" I say, raising an eyebrow.

Her bluff called, Trish says, "Mostly…."

I smile at her. "All I'm asking is that we each give the other a chance." Without taking my eyes from her, I continue, "I've told you a bit about myself. What's your story?"

"Ex-stripper. Like you."

"How long?"

"Five years."

I see an opening. "Tough work, isn't it?"

In between noisily smacking her gum, Trish answers, "You can say that."

Good, we're forming a connection. She's realizing that I'm not the enemy. Maybe there's hope for her…. "Would you like to demon-strate a move or two for us?" I say.

Trish sizes me up, probably in an attempt to see if I'm mocking her. Deciding I'm not, she says, "All right," as she heads to the pole

I've been circling.

She rests her back against it and leans her head back as if connecting with it brings her comfort. Slowly, she rocks her head from side to side and then spins herself so that she's facing the pole. Reaching high above her, she grabs hold and, hand-over-hand, inches her way up, her feet wrapped around it beneath her. Once up a distance, she lets go with her feet and pushes her body out perpendicular to the pole.

It's then that I see her true strength. Her muscles don't shake or strain. In fact, she seems perfectly at ease. Our eyes lock. She holds the pose a minute longer and then releases herself, returning to the floor with grace.

Alicia says, "That was amazing!"

I turn my gaze from Trish to Alicia. "Why don't you tell us a bit about yourself?"

"Well, I'm not sure I can ever do *that*," she says, pointing at the pole. "But I'm looking to do something that will make me feel better about myself."

There's an awkward long pause where I don't know if she's going to continue or not. I wait. We all do. Alicia stands there, voiceless. I take in her faded looks. Bet she used to be real pretty. But now she appears...used up. I recognize that look. Her black eye shadow, eyeliner and dark-toned glossy lipstick complement her black drastic short haircut. Her black clothing adds to her macabre look but with a hint of sexuality. Well, maybe more than a hint. Her low-cut sexy dress is short enough to reveal the tops of her gartered stockings. I'd bet anything that she's wearing a black g-string to match. Surprised she's not wearing lingerie as her clothing. Where did that come from? That was just catty. I shake my head and say, "Anything else you want to share with us?"

"Not really."

All righty then. Isn't she the little talker? I look at Carol. If ever we needed some enthusiasm, now's the time. "What brings you here?"

"Well, aren't we all looking to improve upon ourselves?"

"What are you hoping to gain?" I ask.

Carol tilts her head, lost in thought, before answering, "I guess I want to learn how to have fun. You know. Let my hair down." A nervous laugh escapes her. "I'm always so in control. Everything in its place. Everything perfect. Spend a lot of time attending to those things. But no one ever seems to notice. Feel like I'm missing life…like it's passing me by. I'm tired of fussing over insignificant things like making sure the house could pass a white-glove inspection. I flit from one meaningless task to another. By the end of each day I wonder where the time's gone, and what I have gained." She stops and views our stunned faces. "Oh, was that too much to share all at once?"

"I find your enthusiasm refreshing," I reply. "Too many never get up the courage to reveal themselves to others."

I turn my attention to Molly, who looks as if she's been the victim of a pink explosion. Her T-shirt and short skirt are complementing shades of pink. Her nails, both finger and toes, are painted Barbie pink. She looks like a girly-girl. Hell, even her make-up is done in subtle shades of pink. Well, all except her false lashes that are jet black and so thick they resemble two caterpillars crawling across her lids. Her vibrant attention-drawing pink selections contradict her wallflower behavior. She's barely spoken three words since arriving. What's her story?

"So, Molly, what brings you here?" I ask.

"I signed up."

Was that sarcastic? Hmmm…. "Actually, I was wondering if you could tell us a bit about yourself."

"No."

"No, you can't tell us, or no, you don't want to?"

"Don't want to."

Wow! This is going great! How the hell am I ever going to get her to dance on a pole? She won't utter more than a few words. Can't tell if she's messing with me or if she's the most uptight person on the planet. Realizing our exchange has ended, I turn my attention toward Pam. Her vibrant personality draws me in.

Her lips, body and hair shimmer with glitter as if Tinkerbell herself has sprinkled pixy dust on her. I sense a bit of boldness to her. Her curls bounce enticingly with every move of her head. As if her glittered self isn't enough, her clothing is just as gleaming. Her top sparkles while her skirt shimmers like the wet skin of a seal. Wonder what this put-together-looking woman could want from my class. Curiosity gets the better of me, and I ask, "Why did you sign up?"

Her eyes twinkle and her posture assumes a more self-assured pose. "Like the rest of you, I'm looking to improve myself. You'd never know it, but I have huge anxieties when having to talk with people. Not one on one. I thrive on that. Large groups, that's when I fall apart. It presents a problem with my job."

"How so?" I ask.

Pam looks down, rubbing her hands together in a nervous gesture. "One of my responsibilities, as an inspirational speaker, is to give presentations to large bodies of successful executives. I choke every time before I take the stage. Get so worked up that I feel like I'm going to either pass out or throw up. Tried everything: classes, tutorials and self-help books on how to calm yourself. None work. It's always the same. I end up in the ladies room, following a presentation, praying to the porcelain god."

"That's awful!" Alicia says.

Pam smiles at Alicia. "I'm hoping this class can get me over that. I'll try anything. Besides, it sounds fun. I'm an easy-going person who *loves* to have a good time!"

Pam stops to look at Molly. "I think you and I have a lot in common."

Molly looks at her but says nothing.

"From your clothing, you look like an interesting person just waiting to discover herself."

Molly surprises everyone when she responds, "How does that make us similar?"

Pam beams. "Because I, too, am that excited interesting person— most of the time."

The slightest hint of a smile pulls at the edges of Molly's mouth.

I can't help but be encouraged by the bonds that have already begun to form amongst my students. My students. Wow! That sounds strange. Who would have thought I would be leading a class?

One to help women feel better about themselves. Looking at the clock, I realize that class is half over and decide it's time to shake things up a bit. "Okay, ladies, let's get familiar with the pole...."

# CHAPTER TEN

## Flaunt It!

Several of the students look intrigued. One looks indifferent and Molly, as expected, looks downright terrified. "Now?" she asks. "We're going to start dancing *now*?"

I offer her a reassuring smile. "No better time...."

"Ah, geez," she mumbles under her breath.

Rather than get frustrated, I decide to soothe her. "It'll be okay. First, let's go over a few basics." I survey each of my students' outfits. Each took into consideration my wardrobe guidelines. "Let's have each of you take off your shoes."

"Why?" questions Trish.

"So you'll be able to move easily without having to think about staying steady on your feet." I note her heels. They match my own— the ones I suggested each woman get.

"I'd prefer keeping mine on," Trish counters. "Make me feel sexier when I work the pole."

Yeah, and probably superior. "That's fine," I tell Trish. As I speak, the remaining women remove their heels. Heading to the stage, I pass the bookshelf and start the music. Slinky rhythm-and-blues resonates from the speakers. I caress the pole. Mmmm.... Love its cold feeling. Always have. When I used to strip at Luigi's Gentleman's Club, some of the girls used to complain about the poles. Not me.

I grip the pole above my head with one hand. The other, I place on my thrust-out hip. "It's important to connect with your audience when you dance." Seductively, I circle the pole, locking eyes with each woman. I sense unease from a few of them. They wanna look away but are curious about what I might do next. I could string this along.... Make them squirm.... Done it before, at the club. But I won't. Not this time. Instead, I allow my moves to become one with the music, and continue with the lesson.

"Maintain eye contact," I say. "Use your eyes to tease. Seduce. Draw the audience into *your* world. You're in control. Make them *feel* that from the way you look at them."

Still holding onto the pole, I run my free hand across one of my breasts, and then travel the contours of my curves, mesmerizing the women with my movements. I can tell from the looks on their faces that I have them. They're hooked, fascinated and a little appalled. Yes! Right where I want them. I close my eyes and roll my head in a seductive circle. As it returns to the center, I open my eyes—slowly, as if coming out of an amazing dream.

Hooking my knee around the pole, I spin around it. "The trick is in finding moves that accentuate the best attributes of your body," I say. "I happen to like my legs." Turning, I lean my back against the pole, welcome its coldness through my top and reach above my head to grab it with both hands, while thrusting out my chest. With purpose, I hike up my left leg and, pointing my toe, extend it, as I slide down the length of the pole. Throughout my demonstration, I don't think a single woman has blinked. Excellent! Got them. Even Molly's looking more relaxed.

Grinning, I stand up and look at my expectant students. "Before we get started, there're a few things I need to mention. Guess they're my rules. First and foremost, you need to be in the right frame of mind to be an effective pole dancer."

"What does that mean?" Carol asks.

"That you check your modesty, inhibitions and worldly baggage at the door. Here, we're all the same—beautiful, sexy, uninhibited."

"Not me," Molly mumbles.

"Don't say that. *Here,* if you'll allow me, I'll make you feel beautiful. Size and shape are not viewed the same in this class as in the rest of the world. Here you'll learn to embrace your appearance and who you are."

Molly makes shy eye contact and asks, "How?"

I can't help but smirk. "Practice makes sexy."

"What?"

"In this class, we'll spend a lot of time practicing in front of mirrors as we learn contemporary moves and explore new seductive ways to carry ourselves. We will scrutinize ourselves to determine who we are. Pole dancing is an art form of self-expression. Having the mirrors present allows each of you to view what is being expressed from within. The more time you spend practicing in front of them, the more confident you'll become, allowing you to seamlessly flow from one move to another. By doing so, you'll experience a sense of accomplishment and through that, your self-confidence will evolve."

"But each of us is so different," Carol says. "Some are more outgoing than others. How can we all benefit?"

"Glad you asked. We'll take things slow in the beginning. Experiment with music, for example. Some will be inspired by heavy rock, while others may prefer slower, more soulful music. What you wear and how your day has gone will also affect how you dance."

"You said we were supposed to check our baggage at the door," Trish says.

"I did. And you should. But despite our best efforts, some of it will seep into the studio. I'll show you how to use those feelings to enhance your pole dancing. For example, if you're more emotional one day, express that in the way you move—slower, more controlled. If you're frustrated, then you'll probably prefer a stronger song that you can match beat for angry beat."

"How long does each dance last?" Pam asks.

"The length of one song—about three minutes. Long enough, but not so long as to exhaust you. During that time, you'll string together a collection of anywhere from five to ten moves."

"You mentioned that you have a list of rules," Pam says. "Are there any more?"

"Just one—the most important. Whatever you've got, flaunt it in a way that's fun, sexy and empowering."

Several of the women smile at the concept, seeming to be excited. I like that. Their questions are good, demonstrating that they are eager to delve into the unknown. The new. The unlikely. The more I'm around them, the more I like this group of broken women. They're full of potential. Lumps of clay, ready to be molded…. And by helping them find themselves, I'll make myself stronger. That's what I need—to heal them.

Guess it's time to get this party started. "Each of you needs to stand next to a pole." The women fan out around the room, each connecting with the pole that calls to her. Standing on the stage next to my own shiny pole, I take them through a series of warm-up stretches, watching each out of the corner of my eye, to see if any have difficulty with flexibility or if any get winded. To my surprise, all are rather limber and well conditioned. Good. Like that. Nothing worse than a bunch of women pulling muscles right and left because they're out of shape. We're off to a good start.

"We'll begin with several basic moves. Nothing too complex, but when coupled with others, watch out! I want you to think of the pole as your own personal tall, gleaming, slender dance partner. Be as naughty as you dare with it. Fill your mind with seductive erotic thoughts and let them guide you as you familiarize yourself with the pole." Another slinky rhythm-and-blues piece begins playing. Perfect get-to-know-your-pole-better music. Glad I decided to stick with these tracks for today's class. "Whenever you approach the pole, don't be shy about it. Take control. Be decisive in your moves. This first time, you might wanna mimic what I do."

Wrapping my left arm high on the pole, I extend my left leg, place my other hand on my raised right hip and thrust my chest out. Everything about this position cries out confidence. I see a look of apprehension on Molly's and Carol's faces. Can almost hear the thoughts pass through their minds. Ignoring them, I dance around my stationary partner, hugging it to me. Loving it. Stroking it. All the while, I maintain eye contact with the students as I gently sway my hips from side to side. Feeling the music, I arch my back, push my chest out farther and let my seductiveness flow free as I strut my way around the pole. "Okay, now each of you try."

Trish jumps at the opportunity without hesitating. Had a feeling she would. Head thrown back, eyes closed, she gets lost in the music as she spins and shakes to the beat. Her moves are advanced and improvised. Again, not unexpected. I sense she's a showoff. A stand-alone. The longer I'm around her, the more I begin to understand *why* she's here. She's so engrossed with her routine that I doubt she would hear if any of us cried, "fire." She's a natural in her element.

Carol begins, spasmodically seducing her pole, or possibly threatening to hurt it. Her moves are stiff and intense—not in a good way. "That's very good, Carol," I lie. "But you might want to tone it down just a tad. Don't want to wear your pole out on the very first move." A couple of the other women chuckle. Eager to please and get it right, Carol slows her moves as she learns to "lead" the pole where she wants it to go.

Then there's Alicia. Her cropped black hair sways as she flaunts her sexiness to the max. Well, damn! You go, girl! For someone who looks so used up, so expired, you sure resurrect when working a pole. There's a glint of sheer unadulterated mischief in her eyes. I sense a little temptress in her. What's her *whole* story?

Molly hasn't moved. Not one step. She's looking at the pole as if it's the enemy—rather complex, better left undiscovered. What am I gonna do with her? How am I supposed to make any progress, if she can't even *look* at the pole without getting threatened? How am I gonna get her to *touch* it? I sense there's another, more adventuresome Molly. Hiding below the surface. Or maybe further down. She's there, yearning to be born. I know it. It's okay, Molly, I'll figure out how to help you.

Pam is stationed on the pole to Molly's right and is getting to know it with great enthusiasm. Noticing Molly's frozen stance, she offers, "Try this," as she circles her pole, shaking and shimmying her hips. Molly looks over and then approaches her own pole with determination. With a stiffness resembling that of the Tin Man left out in the rain, she robotically encircles her pole.

God! That's not seductive. It's more like preparing for the kill. Damn, I've got a lot of work to do with her. But…at least she's interacting with the pole. That's an improvement. She walks around her pole once and looks at Pam, who gives her an encouraging smile. For the second time, I see something that, in the loosest of terms, might just be considered the beginnings of a smile. Cool!

"That was great." I say. "You all did a wonderful job. Now let's up the ante a little." The minute the words leave my mouth, I regret them, for Molly's evolving almost-smile morphs into a fallen frown. Oh, well, maybe this move will be less of a challenge for her. Yeah, right, and the temperature is falling in Hell.

"This one doesn't require much movement," I say. "But its visual impression packs a wallop." Standing with the pole directly in front of me, I place both hands on it just above my head. I hold that pose for a few beats before dropping my left hand to my hip. Still holding onto the pole, I gyrate my hips, envisioning them as a slow-moving top, spinning on an erotic axis. Wow! My mind comes up with the strangest images. Didn't have sexy tops like that when I was a kid. As expected, Trish's already fully engaged in advanced hip gyration before I instruct the class to try. Damn! She's got moves. Fluid and flawless. Wonder if she gyrates in her sleep like that? Or at any other time....

Pam's left her own pole and is standing behind Molly. With her hands on Molly's hips, she walks her through the motions. Molly's movements are stiff and unyielding. Instead of swinging her hips to and fro in one fluid motion, she progresses through a series of jerky convulsions. Might be better if she signed up for a tribal war dance class.

I relieve Pam so she can return to her own pole. There, her enthusiastic energy shines through her moves. I give Molly a few pointers on how to loosen up. She incorporates several, and her movements become somewhat less of a train wreck in appearance.

Carol, too, has managed to slow herself down a bit and is letting the beat of the music guide her nether regions from side to side, as is Alicia. At least the majority of my students are showing promise. The jury's still out on Molly. Honestly, the woman has three left feet and a stick up her rear at least a mile long. Okay, that was mean—true, but mean.

I leave Molly with her pole and return to my own. "Since that last move had you wiggling," I say, "I'm going to introduce another that promises to shake things up." The women watch as I position myself with my back a few inches from the pole. Reaching behind me, I grab it with both hands just above shoulder height. I bend my legs a little and thrust my chest in and out in rapid succession.

Was that a small gasp I heard from Molly? Really, her reactions are becoming a bit of a bore. What's her story? She signed up for this. And it was clearly advertised as an interactive pole-dancing class. Shaking off her prudish reaction, I taunt my audience a bit more. Making eye contact with each, I pose and pout as I transfer my hands from the pole and tease my hair with slow and purposeful motions. I run my fingers through its silky softness as if I've never felt anything so divine. In the subtlest way, I slide my hands down, landing each upon a breast, where they stroke and grope as I continue to sashay my hips from side to sexy side.

There's a knowing grin on Trish's face. She flaunts her own style with the pole. Using every bit of her five-inch stilettos to her advantage, she pushes her chest out and ruffles her hair as if her very existence depends on it. And perhaps it does. I'm sensing that about her. Her need to one-up.

Molly, having gone rigid, is attempting her own rendition. It doesn't come close. Instead, she resembles a fish writhing out of water, gasping its last breath of air. But I must admit, I'm impressed that she took it upon herself to attempt this one without any additional promptings from Pam or me. Maybe there's hope....

Carol soon masters this move, allowing her ample chest to take center stage and lead her through. She even takes it a step farther by cupping each of her breasts and sighs as she pushes them together. Well, who knew?

Alicia mimics Carol's moves, and then improvises some of her own. After shaking her own chest, she playfully glides the middle finger of one hand along her outer thigh upward while holding onto and circling the pole. She caresses her hips, the lengths of her sides and then her breasts, tracing little circles around each nipple. I don't miss her suggestive moves. The others do, absorbed in their own dances. Not me. I catch her slight intake of air and the manner in which she rolls her head back, lost in pleasure. Sensed there was naughtiness in her. I'll bet we have a *lot* in common.... For someone so tight-lipped about why she's here, she's certainly expressive with the pole.

Pam, attempting her own interpretation of the moves, pauses every now and again to circle her pole, holding on with first one and then the other hand, eyeing it as if it's a piece of raw meat and she a hungry lioness. Her spirit is contagious. I see several of the other women looking at her as she tousles her hair and uses her chest to entice.

Pam's got a great nurturing personality that shines through in her moves. Funny how pole dancing does that. It takes what's buried within you—your essence—and brings it to the surface. Already I'm detecting things about each woman that they thought they could keep concealed from me. They don't know. Can't see it. Their self-expressive dance—their comfort level, or awkwardness, reveals parts of themselves they thought were hidden. They'll learn. We all will.

Since we're on a roll, with several of the ladies already inventing some of their own creative moves, think I'll make this last step a deal breaker. It'll be the one that shows me what each of my students is all about. What they're willing to reveal. What they intend to keep hidden. And how much work I have to do with each.

I position myself with my back against the pole, grabbing it with one hand near the small of my back. With my legs stationary, I playfully twist my upper body to look at my students from over my shoulder. I use my most sultry voice and say, "Okay, ladies, let's bring it home with this last move." I rotate, look over my other shoulder and, winking, add, "Really make it count."

Turning slowly, I face the pole and, as if greeting it, bow deeply at the waist. I grab the pole with one hand down by my knees, and rest my other hand on my rear, which is turned up high in the air. Continuing downward, I slide my hand effortlessly from my rear down the length of my straight leg, tracing each defined muscle. When my hand reaches my ankle, I reverse the movement of my fingers and, reaching farther behind me, trace up and down the back of my legs as if feeling along the exposed seam of a pair of stockings. Deciding it's time to finish, I begin rising—slow and graceful, letting my hand explore my thighs, breasts and finally the side of my face.

I notice that Trish and Pam are already duplicating my moves, while throwing in a few of their own for good measure. Alicia's enjoying the seductiveness of these moves and, if possible, is making them even more so. Carol's struggling to maintain perfect form and have fun while doing so. And Molly...she's actually embracing this move. Strange. I would have thought it would have thrown her. Perhaps she's softening. Becoming less inhibited. Feeling more comfortable. Good for her.

I smile at the women, tell them they've done a great job and lead them through a series of cool-down exercises. In closing, I say, "Be sure to practice what we covered today in front of a mirror, if possible. And if you're feeling bold, you may want to try some of the moves in your heels so you can get used to them."

I dismiss my students and, as each puts her shoes back on, say that I look forward to the following week when I'll really heat things up. Most look intrigued. Trish looks indifferent and Molly, as expected, looks frightened. Hope she'll be back. There's so much potential with her....

# CHAPTER ELEVEN

## Feeling Sexy

No sooner does the door close behind my last student than I rush to the phone. Excitement nearly chokes me as I wait for Angel to pick up.

"Hello?"

"Just finished my first class!"

"Tell me everything!"

"They're the most hopeless gathering of misfits imaginable."

I fill Angel in on each student's oddities. How their personalities either clashed or meshed. "Once we began dancing, their true personalities came out. You know, all the things they thought they could keep concealed."

Later at the mall, Angel and I enjoy touring through our favorite shops, picking up items here and there. Some we need. Others are impulse buys. Nice to be able to do this. Thinking back to our time spent hooking, I ask, "Remember how Ax owned us?"

"How could I forget?" Angel says, visibly shivering. "He treated us like animals. Took our money. Freedom. Youth. Your son."

I nearly spit out, "Bastard! Glad that part of our lives is past."

We stroll the mall for a bit and then stop for a treat—one of those huge cinnamon buns, drizzled with a sugary glaze and mounds of candy-coated pecans. Mmmm.... The minute we get in line, my mouth begins watering. Just a few more people....

Peeking around the person in front of us, I see some deliciously enticing samples, bite-sized pieces with a convenient toothpick sticking out of their centers. I sigh and strengthen my resolve. I can wait. It's almost our turn. Damn! The man, three customers ahead, must be ordering for an army!  He's a large man.  No, large doesn't do him justice.  He's *huge*.  He orders several of *everything* on the menu.  I'm not gonna make it.  "Be right back," I say.

Angel's face erupts into a knowing smile.  "Was wondering how long you'd last," she calls after me.

Arriving at the platter of samples, I look back and say, "Very funny.  You want one or not?"

"Well, since you're there…."

"That's what I thought," I say, selecting two of the largest pieces.  Popping one into my mouth, I grab another for good measure and head back.

Angel eats hers and asks, "Hey, how come you get two?" while chewing.

"Finder's fee," I respond, sliding my second piece off its toothpick and grinning.

Finally it's our turn.  We order a cinnamon bun to share—always do—with a couple containers of milk.  Not a word is spoken as each of us cuts slice after slice from the fluffy bun.  We scoop up as much excess glaze and nuts as possible before placing the morsels in our mouths, letting them melt on our tongues as we savor their sinful sugary goodness.  We wash down bites with sips of ice-cold milk.  Not as good as it would be if it were in actual glasses.

Why is it that milk always takes on the flavor of the container it's in?  You'd think they'd package it in glass bottles.  But, no.  Probably costs too much.  Eats into the manufacturers' profit.  Great, so they make us suffer.  My only consolation is that they, too, have to drink container-flavored milk.

As Angel and I scrape the last few crumbs and drizzles of glaze off our plate, we regain the ability to communicate.  Before, we were too engrossed in our feeding frenzy to bother with small talk.  Angel swallows the remainder of her milk before asking, "Anyplace else you want to go?"

"Hmmm—" I begin, not bothering to finish my own thought.

Angel chuckles.  "I know that look.  Spill."

"What?"  I try my best to look baffled by her comment.  Failing miserably, I add, "I was hoping we could swing by the lingerie store before we leave."

"Really? The lingerie store. Any special occasion?" she says, heading in that direction.

"Not really. Just looking."

"Girl, I know you better than that. The only time you go to the lingerie store is 'cause there's a guy on your mind. Who is he?"

I'm embarrassed to find myself blushing. Me? Blushing? What's up with that? And with Angel? We've been friends so long that she can practically read my thoughts. Why am I suddenly self-conscious? In an attempt to salvage my dignity, I say, "I don't know. It's silly, really. Don't even know him. But I can't stop thinking about him."

"Carlos?"

"Yeah. How weird is that?" I ask, as we enter the store.

"Not strange at all, based on the way you described his looks," she says, laughing. "Not to mention the way you're blushing. Girl, if I'd bumped into someone as gorgeous as you make him sound, I'd be obsessing over him, too."

We rummage through the items on the nearest rack. "That's the problem," I say.

"What?" Angel asks, holding up a sexy slip before returning it.

"That's what *you'd* do. Not me. And yet, that's *exactly* what I'm doing."

"'Cause you need to get laid."

I can't help but laugh. Leave it to Angel to state the obvious with boldness. "It has been a long time," I say, holding up a sexy bra and panty set.

"Too long, if you ask me."

"Who's asking?" I say, returning the items to the rack.

"Heard rumor they're considering making you a nun."

"That'll be the day. How about this one?" I ask, holding up a matching leopard print bra and thong.

"Nah, not you anymore."

"What? Too wild?"

"Maybe. I picture you more in satin."

"Are you telling me my wild days are gone?"

"Girl, with the dreams you have, your wild days won't ever end."

Angel selects an intricate shelf bra with matching sheer lace panties. Holding them up, she says, "This is more your style, now. Still just as sexy but with a bit more class."

"Hmmm," I say, taking the items from her. "They are nice. Wanna try on a few things?"

"Duh."

We each select the maximum allowed items and head toward the dressing room, where the saleswoman places us in side-by-side rooms. As I try on each outfit, I admire my reflection in the mirror. None really strike my fancy. I hold up the last one, the one Angel had selected, and cock my head. Perhaps.... I slip on the black sheer panties, accented with a dainty deep purple ruffle around the edges. Next, I adjust the black straps to the bra and clasp it. Standing back, I view my reflection in the mirror and can't help but laugh.

"What's so funny," Angel asks from next door.

"Nothing. Just thinking what a far cry this is from my sensible fluffy robe."

"Sally, girl, there's sensible and then there's sexy. People don't come here to be sensible. Which outfit are you trying on?"

"The one you picked."

"Like it?"

I don't answer right away, turning from side to side and looking over my shoulder to view the back. "I do. But there's nothing practical about it."

"Practical?! This isn't the place for practical."

I toy with the rhinestone-covered ball at the end of the black-corded tassel that hangs alluringly between my breasts. "But when would I wear it?"

"Whenever."

"Really? Did you take a good look at the bra?" I observe in the mirror how the satiny deep purple fabric—lightly padded, split in the middle and closely resembling two flower petals—perfectly cups the underside of each breast, not covering them, but rather, shaping them into perfect mounds with the entire breast and nipples clearly visible. "It doesn't cover *anything*."

"Not supposed to."

"Again, when would I wear it?"

Angel chuckles softly. "When you want to feel sexy."

We leave a short time later, each with a bag. Mine contains the shelf bra set and a pair of black stockings with a three-inch decorative embroidered band around the top and visible seam running up the rear. Hell, if I'm going to feel sexy, I might as well go all out.

Exiting the mall, bags in hand, I notice it's dark outside. When did that happen? Wow, we really can fall into a time warp while shopping. Wonder what it'd be like to shop forever?

Angel pulls me from my thoughts. Although I have no idea what she just said, I respond, "Uh huh." Probably not the best course of action, especially with Angel. Who knows? I could have just agreed to give her my soul.

I attempt to focus on what she's saying. But can't. What is that? That uncomfortable feeling I have. Just a minute ago I was lost in a delicious never-ending shopping fantasy and now I'm...I'm...what? Uncomfortable. No, it's more than that. All my senses are on heightened alert—again.

I glance around and see nothing. No threat. Just parked cars waiting for their owners to return. My mind's working overtime. Probably from being disoriented when I came out and found it nighttime. You know, that whole paranoid girl-walking-in-the-dark thing. Shake it off! Everything's fine. Is it? No, it's not. I can *feel* it. There is something.... Watching.... Waiting.... Like the other times. But for what? For who? Me? Angel? The both of us?

I hook arms with Angel and quicken my pace. Need to get to the car. Can't explain it. But I know I'll be safe there.

Angel protests. "Hey, what's your hurry? This isn't a race."

Oh, but it is, I think. Fragments of my premonition dream come to mind. Can't put my finger on it. But I know. This *is* a race. One of the most important ones I'll ever run. The raised hair on the back of my neck assures me of this. And the sudden gooseflesh covering my body confirms it. I shoot a quick sideways glance at Angel without lessening my pace. "Don't you feel that?"

"What? You dragging me through the parking lot like you're

running some kind of marathon?"

"No. Pay attention! Stop talking for a minute and listen. *Feel* what's out there."

"And what exactly am I trying to feel?"

"We're not alone."

A car trolls past looking for a parking spot.

"Of course we're not," Angel responds, exasperation evident in her voice. "We're in the middle of a mall parking lot. There're bound to be others around."

"But *they* all have a purpose. Going to or leaving their cars. What I'm feeling is different. Ominous. Can't shake the feeling that we're in danger."

Angel looks at me. "This isn't like you, getting spooked."

We reach our car. Get in. Lock the doors. I don't talk again until I'm heading for the exit. Shooting rapid glances at either side of the car, I scan the darkness, straining my eyes in the process. "There *was* something out there."

"Sure it's not 'cause it's dark?" Angel asks.

"That's what I thought, at first. But then I felt it. Watching me— us. Wasn't right." When the signal turns green, I'm grateful to leave. The mall. The parking lot. And whatever evil is lurking in its shadows.

# CHAPTER TWELVE

## Bitch, You Have *Nooooo* Idea!

He enjoys his stalking game immensely. He watches as the bitches exit the mall. Gets out of his car. Hidden by the darkness that envelops him, he zigzags his way through the parking lot in their direction.

*Look at 'em. Happy. Goods in hand. Wait till she sees what I've got in store for her. Won't be smiling then.*

The closer he gets, the more he senses Sally's unease. Smells her fear. He grins as she grabs Angel's arm and begins walking faster.

*That's right, cunt! Hurry up! Won't do you any good, though. When I wanna get you, ain't nothing gonna stand in my way!*

He watches Sally shiver.

*This's too rich!*

He delights in how she pulls her friend along, who's protesting all the way. He's close enough to hear Sally shush her. Try to warn her.

*Might wanna listen up to what she's trying to tell you, cunt. Never know when I might come after you.*

He nearly bubbles over with enthusiasm when he hears the panic in Sally's voice as she tells Angel that she senses danger.

*Bitch, you have nooooo idea!*

He gets as close as he dares without making actual contact, drinking in her panic like a rich perfume. His enthusiasm dims a little when he watches the cunts get in their car and drive off. But he's quick to recover.

*Next time, bitch! I'll make it more…personal.*

# Chapter Thirteen

## Princess

I go to bed early. My sleep's plagued with restless dreams. Finally, I fall into a deep sleep, so deep that nothing will wake me. Or so one would think.

Jerking awake a few hours later, I'm drenched in sweat, panting and unable to stop shaking. Another of my premonition dreams. Why won't they let me be? I try to shake the sleepy fog from my head so I can reconstruct its shadowy fragments.

A feeling of dread. Abandonment. Sticky dirt. A corner. Twisted branches. Stairs encased in concrete. The sunlight glinting off of something on the ground. What do they mean? Why can't I have normal dreams like other people? I'm sick of this! Am I going crazy? My temples pound with the onset of a tremendous headache. Always get one after my dreams. Exhausted and knowing that it's useless to try to force the pieces of my nonsensical dream together, I lie down and close my eyes, hoping that sleep will spare me the torment of more visions.

In the morning, I find myself frantic, rushing to get ready for work. Must have turned off the alarm. Shit! Can't believe I slept in again. Well, yeah, I can. That's what I do. Sleep in. I swear. If I didn't have anyplace to be, I'd sleep all the time. This whole business of having to get up early in the morning....

As I unscrew the lid on my liquid foundation, my hands fumble, and the container—lid now off—goes flying. It skitters across the counter, leaving a spidery trail of flesh-colored liquid in its wake. Just as it falls toward the floor, I wedge my hip against the cabinet. Ha!

Caught it. Reaching down, I grab hold of the bottle, triumphant in my victorious save. Then it occurs to me....

I look down and see it. The giant foundation smear down the front of my pants.

Ugh! Of course the bottle landed upside-down. *Why* would it land any other way?

If I wasn't so rushed, I might be able to see the humor in this situation. Well, that might be a stretch, but I'm sure I'll get a chuckle out of it—eventually. In the meantime, I have one leg out of my yoga pants and am hopping toward the closet. Realizing how difficult I'm making this, I stop and slip the pants off before grabbing another pair.

I nearly trip over Princess when returning to the bathroom. She looks at me like I'm a crazed uncoordinated idiot. And she's right. I am. I've really gotta slow down. Gonna break something. And quite frankly, I don't have time for that...least not right now. Perhaps I can find time to pencil in a broken leg later. What am I saying? Stop that!

Somehow, I manage to fumble my way through putting on my makeup. I have to tilt the foundation bottle severely to use what little makeup remains in it. I make a quick trip to the freestanding mirror to critique my handiwork. Striking a profile pose, I nod my approval. I then face forward and lean in close. I run my middle finger across my right eyebrow, smoothing a few wayward hairs back into place. Not bad. Okay, gotta go.

Downstairs, I scoop kibble into Princess' dog dish and place it just outside the door. "Out you go, girl." Princess doesn't move. Just looks at me. I feel a tug at my heart. She always has this effect on me. Can make me forget everything. Time. My troubles.

I kneel down beside her and take her face in my hands. Leaning my forehead against the top of her muzzle, I say, "I'm sorry, girl. Not the most relaxed morning. I promise I'll make it up to you tonight. We'll go for an extra long walk after dinner." When I mention the "w" word, her ears perk up.

Those adorable floppy yellow Lab ears are so expressive. I can tell just by looking at them how her day's gone. Next, her tail *thump thump thumps* against the cabinet, and her entire back end wiggles spasmodically. Her enthusiasm makes my heart swell, and I smile.

"Tonight, girl," I say, giving her a hug. I put her out, fill a travel mug with coffee and head for the car.

Don't have a long drive, just across town. The traffic signals are in my favor—almost all green. I have to fight the urge to press harder on the accelerator. Things are going better now. Looks like I'll get there in time. No need to speed.

I arrive at the Community Center, glance at my watch and realize I'm a few minutes ahead of schedule. Don't know how that happened. Don't care. Just glad to be here early rather than late. I gather my bag and CD player, and head in.

A few are already waiting outside the door—the eager beaver morning people. It's not normal. Think about it. If humans were meant to rise and shine at the crack of dawn, we wouldn't need alarm clocks to rip us from our peaceful slumber. Or coffee shops strategically placed just far enough apart that right about the time you finish one oversized cup of delicious brewed delight, *presto*, there's another barista waiting to take your order. No, no, no! Roosters get up voluntarily at dawn. People were meant to rise much, much later in the day.

I smile at the women as I unlock the door and click on the lights. The rest of my Hip Hop class arrives. I slip in a CD, and we progress through a series of combined moves that have all of us sweating and panting by the end. It's a good two-hour class with a nice blend of students, all adults. Some are mothers looking for an activity to call their own. Others, allergic to traditional forms of exercise, use it as a means to stay in shape. And some come to improve upon their dance skills so they can impress others at clubs.

Class ends, and everyone filters out.

Driving across town, I wonder what Ma will have for lunch. Gonna spend the afternoon with her. Been a few days since I've seen her. Don't like to lose touch. Remember well the near-decade when we had no contact.

Glad we were able to work things out. Can't imagine not being able to pick up the phone or stop in unannounced to share whatever's on my mind. Ma has always been there for me, supporting... waiting...hoping...even when I didn't take advantage of it.

I pull up in front of my childhood house. Lots of memories here. Some good. Some scary. Some sad. Memories. I've learned not to run from them. Trying to is useless. They always find me. No matter where I hide. I've learned to accept them. Scrutinize them. Learn their lessons.

Passing through the living room, I call out, "Ma? You home?"

"Out back, honey," comes her reply in a voice so familiar, so comforting that it feels like a warm summer breeze embracing me.

My eyes travel across the multitude of framed photos of my younger brother, Eric, Ma and me that denote the passage of time. Ma younger, ravishing body, twinkling eyes. And then, as the photos progress, her look becomes softer, more knowing, more dignified. Her once vibrant red hair is replaced with a brilliant snowy white. The photos of my brother do not continue. In the last one, he's a carefree fourteen-year-old, forever youthful, forever frozen in time—his life cut short.

I exit the house through the rear French doors into her magical garden. Ma has such a green thumb. I envy her. My nose drinks in the heavenly scent of hundreds of robust rose blossoms bursting to life. Intermingled is the fragrance of Night-blooming Jasmine, the vines of which cover the walls of her backyard paradise.

Looking around, I don't see her at first. But then she rises like Mother Nature herself from behind an enormous rosebush—my favorite. It's a Mr. Lincoln. Been here as long as I can remember. Still have the scar on my side from when I fell in it as a kid. Seems the prettier the rose's scent, the nastier its thorns.

We give each other a hug. Then I reach over and cup one of the velvety red Mr. Lincoln flowers in my hands. Leaning over, I close my eyes, lost in its perfume.

Ma's gentle laughter washes over me. "You always were partial to that rosebush. Even after it attacked you. How have you been?"

"Great!" I say, standing up, turning away from the rosebush. "Had my first pole-dancing class yesterday."

"That's right. I want to hear all about it. You can tell me over lunch."

We sit at the kitchen table. Ah, the conversations this table's overheard. It knows all the most intimate details of our lives. Why is it that, although we adorn our houses with comfortable furniture, we always find ourselves congregated around the kitchen table? No matter how spacious or cramped the room. Or how comfortable or butt-numbing the chairs may be, that's where we gather. To share our lives. To ask for advice. To strengthen the ties that bind us together.

Over a leisurely lunch, I fill Ma in on the details of my first class, my students, their unique personalities and how I hope to heal them— in turn, strengthening myself.

"Think this is going to work?" Ma asks.

"You know me...."

"Yes," she says, laughing. "I do. Your determination alone can work miracles."

We spend the afternoon soaking up one another's company, each reluctant to part. Hour after hour passes where we talk about everything and nothing at all. Ma's like that. She has a way of making the person she's with feel as if they're the most significant being in the world. She never rushes a conversation, devoting her time and energy to making others feel welcome, loved, special. Every time I leave her, I feel as if I've spent the most perfect day at an exclusive spa—relaxed and rejuvenated, ready to endure more of life's challenges.

Although the sun's beginning to dip lower in the sky by the time I leave, the temperature has barely dropped. It's a perfect June evening, and I look forward to my evening walk with Princess.

I round the corner into my neighborhood. Once again, a feeling of foreboding envelops me, no less significant than if someone had pulled a shroud over me. A shiver begins at the crown of my head and travels the length of my body, not stopping until it reaches my toes. What's wrong with me? Get a grip!

I attempt to shake the feeling. Arriving home, I enter the house.

But the creepy feeling intensifies and, though it's not fully dark yet, I find myself flicking on every light I come across. Dropping my purse on the kitchen table, I head to the back door. Every step closer constricts my heart a little more, making it harder to breathe. Damn it! Get a hold of yourself!

Reaching for the doorknob, something inside me screams, "No!" Instinctively, my hand recoils from the handle. I stand there, feeling as if the room's closing in on me. As I look out the window, the shadows cast by the mature trees appear ominous. Stop it! Everything's fine. If it wasn't, Princess would be barking. Princess… Suddenly, all I want is her by my side.

I summon the courage to open the door and step outside. The minute I do, an evil force wraps itself around me. My chest squeezes even tighter, and I find it hard to squeak out, "Princess. Princess!" The voice I hear is not my own, but one tinged with undeniable terror.

Where's Princess? Why isn't she coming? I call again—louder. "Princess! Come on, girl. Time to eat." Nothing. No jingling of her ID tags, indicating her approach. My summons is met with silence, deafening in its totality.

Determined now, I disregard the warnings rapid-firing their way around my brain and set out to find my companion, calling her name as I go. I walk to the back of the property and find nothing. Turning, I head toward the side of the house. Nearing the corner, that's where I first see it—blood. The minute my eyes fall upon it, my knees threaten to give out. Frantic now, I call Princess' name non-stop. I follow the trail. Along the way, the diameter of the bloody puddles increases.

Crying, I run. Hoping for the best. Fearing the worst. I follow the puddles to the side of the house where there's a concrete-framed stairwell leading down to a root cellar. Twisted branches rake at my arms and legs. I don't notice.

I arrive at the top of the stairs. My heart stops. And I know. I race down them. Princess is collapsed at the bottom. "No!" I scream. Her eyes are closed. She's not moving. The thin layer of dirt sediment surrounding her is sticky with blood. I drop to my knees and cover her body with my own. Princess, no! Oh, dear God, please, no!

After several long moments, I feel the slightest flutter of her chest. Like it's convulsing.  I raise to my knees and look down at her.  Her eye, the one I can see, is now barely open and looking directly at me.  I lay my head gingerly on her side and listen.  I can hear her heart beating—faintly, but it *is* beating.  As my body shifts, the sunlight glints across her nametag, and the fragments of my dream fall into place....

# CHAPTER FOURTEEN

## Rot in Hell, Bitch!

He's patient, concealed in his hiding place. He watches. Eventually, his perseverance pays off. Sally gets in the car and pulls out.

*That's right, bitch! Go ahead. Leave. I'll take good care of her.*

He waits until long after she leaves before moving in, just to be certain.

*Don't want any interruptions to ruin my fun.*

He stands from where he's been squatting. His thigh muscles scream their protest at having been flexed for so long.

*Fuckin' cunt! Got me all cramped up.*

Not wanting to draw attention to himself, he ignores his muscles and makes his way down her long driveway. Under his arm is tucked a plastic bag. As he approaches the gate, the mutt hears him and comes running over. She lets out a couple of warning barks and he says, "Shut up, bitch!" in a sickening sing-song voice he hopes will calm her. It does.

*Yeah, you listen to me!*

Having reached the gate, he says, "Come here, doggie, doggie," nearly choking on the words, while reaching into the bag and extracting its contents. Doesn't take long. The mutt smells the raw meat almost at once and her tail begins to wag. She sits and he reaches through the gate with his offering.

In a flash, she's up and lunges at him, biting his outstretched hand. He drops the meat, retracts his wounded hand and growls, "Fuck you, bitch!" under his breath. He looks down at the damage—two puncture wounds on top of his hand, and his right index finger has a jagged tear. Blood pours freely. Visions of opening the gate and destroying the beast that dared to bite him fill his head. Thinking of his goal, he manages to keep his wits about him and wraps his hand in his shirttail to avoid leaving a trail of blood.

He looks at the mutt who's taken his offering and crossed the yard. She lies down near the top of a stairwell and proceeds to eat the tainted meat. He takes great pleasure in watching her, curling his mouth into an evil sneer.

*Eat it all, fuckin' bitch. Serves you right.*

Turning his back to the gate, he walks up the driveway, down the street, around the corner and gets into his parked car. There he waits. From his locale, he can see if Sally returns home.

Hours pass. No Sally. He gets out of his car and walks with determination back to her house. He takes long strides down the driveway. Reaching the gate, he pauses. Listens. Nothing. He calls, "Here, doggie, doggie!" Still nothing.

He looks over the gate, then carefully opens it. He glances at where the mutt had been eating. There are only a few scraps left. He grins and approaches them with caution. Looking around, he spots her at the bottom of a concrete stairwell. She tries to get up, but staggers and collapses.

"Ain't so tough now, are you, bitch?" he says.

Reaching in his rear pocket, he pulls out a small camera and, walking halfway down the steps, snaps a couple of shots.

*These should make nice trophies.*

Done with his picture-taking, he looks at his tortured prey and says, "Rot in hell, bitch!"

He turns and exits the way he came in, being sure to latch the gate behind him.

# Chapter Fifteen

## When Will This End?

The drive to the pet clinic is horrible. Angel steers the car. I sit with Princess' head in my lap. She's cold…so very cold. Shivering and bleeding—hemorrhaging. Oh, God! Can't lose her. Hang in there, baby girl. My impatience mounts, nearly choking me. "Angel, drive faster!" Angel shoots me a desperate glance. Her face is filled with as much anguish as my own must reflect.

My resolve shatters, and I fold myself over Princess' back like a protective blanket. My vision blurs as tears well in my eyes. Squeezing them shut, I feel drops spill down my cheeks but don't bother to brush them away. Princess' body, racked by a sudden shudder, convulses. I feel every muscle in her body spasm, and then her breath catches. Is she breathing? Her body finally relaxes, and still she doesn't breathe. Panic grips me. No! "Faster, Angel! We're losing her…."

Rounding the corner, we pull into the parking lot. Angel's seatbelt is off even before we pull in. The car's barely stopped when she opens her door and rushes around to my side to help get Princess out. Together, we manage to lift her limp body and proceed through the double door entry to the clinic, leaving the car with the keys still in the ignition and the doors thrown wide open.

We approach the receptionist counter. The crown of a head, bent in concentration, slowly rises. I barely recognize the face that greets me. "Sally?" Trish says, coming around the counter. "Didn't know it was you who called." She looks down at Princess. "How long since you found her?"

I open my mouth to respond, but my mind reels. Trish? From my pole-dancing class? What's she doing here? I shake off the feeling and answer. "Maybe half an hour."

"Let's get her into a room," Trish says, opening the nearest door. Angel and I carry Princess in.

"Can you get her up on the table?" Trish asks.

In response, Angel and I hoist Princess onto the cold steel exam table. She's nonresponsive. Her limp body collapses into a heap. Moments later, the vet comes in and drills me with a litany of questions, which I'm unable to answer. Seems my faithful friend has consumed poison. But what? From where? I don't have any poison lying around.

I barely hear the vet as she informs me that Princess is hemorrhaging from her consumption of the poison—probably arsenic in the form of rat poison—as it makes its way through her digestive tract. My head feels as if it's being squeezed in a vise, and I hear the unmistakable pounding of the ocean's surf in my ears—a sure sign that I'm close to passing out. I fight the urge and take several deep breaths. The pounding noise subsides, and I struggle to compute what's been told to me. Arsenic?

"Will she recover?" I hear someone ask. The voice, my own, is shaky, barely audible and unfamiliar.

"I'm not sure," the vet says. "The poison's worked its way through her digestive system."

This nightmare's getting worse by the minute.

The vet removes her stethoscope and listens for a heartbeat. Cups her hand over the tip of Princess' nose. "Why don't you take a seat in the waiting room? We need to run some tests. Someone will come and get you when we're done."

Numb, I respond, "Okay," as I allow myself to be guided from the exam room by Trish. Before the door closes behind me, I look back and catch a quick glimpse of my baby. A man has her cradled in his arms and is exiting the room with her.

I pace. Can't sit still. Wanna rush behind the closed doors and make everything okay. It'll be all right. Don't even think it. She's gonna be fine. I caught it in time. I did. Didn't I? Oh, shit! Can't take this. Too many memories. Too much time pacing back and forth. Can't handle another loss. Not Princess.

"How can those people just sit there?" I ask Angel, indicating the other patients, an eclectic gathering of stressed individuals like me. But they're…sitting. How?! Can't stand this!

Angel eyes me. "Don't know." The look on her face is knowing, cautious. She tries to mask it, but I see. She knows I'm precariously perched on a limb that is rotted and unstable from years of abuse and neglect. I can feel the once-strong limb begin to bend and give under my weight.

Five days pass. Longest days of my life. I feel anesthetized. The tests came back, confirming what the vet surmised. Princess had, in fact, consumed rat poison. What the hell happened? Things were going so well. And then…. Can't bring myself to think….

Found the evidence. Not much of it. Princess had eaten most of a tainted raw steak that had been shoved through the fence. Who would do that? Be so cruel? And why? For what purpose? She's an innocent dog. Never hurt anyone. Never bothered anyone. Just made me happy.

Can't believe I almost lost her. But I didn't. Get to pick up my baby tonight. She's coming home! Shaky. Weak. But on the mend. And she's going to be all right…or at least they hope she will. The vet explained how only time would reveal if any long-term brain damage would arise. That could appear over the course of the next six months. Might change her personality—make her mean or unpredictable. But I don't care. That's off in the distance. For now, she's coming home!

Been visiting her every day. Hoping. Praying. Watching her get stronger. First few days were awful. No one knew if she'd pull through. It was horrible watching her body torn asunder by that diabolical poison. After seeing the slow suffering she endured, I can't conceive of how anyone could wantonly expose a living being to that…that torture, that irrefutable inhumanity.

The phone rings. It's Angel, wanting to know when I get to pick up Princess. "Tonight," I tell her.

We talk for a bit, and she comments on my excess energy.

"I'm bouncing off the walls," I say. "So excited! So much energy. Gotta get rid of some of this—"

"Why don't you go for a hike? It'll relax you."

"Good idea!"

"Want me to come?"

"No. But thanks. I think the time alone will do me good. Give me time to process everything. You know?"

"Yeah. Be safe."

"I will."


The half-hour drive gives me time to think. Maybe not a good thing. Too many thoughts of losses I've suffered. In an attempt to drown out the relentless thoughts in my mind, I reach over and turn on the radio. I flip through the stations until I come to a song by The Weather Girls. Cranking the volume, I sing along as they tell of how the weather is changing, and how it will start raining men.

Mmmm! Now there's a delicious concept—raining men. Images of Carlos' muscular back fill my mind, and just like that, I'm transported away from the endless days of stress I've endured to fantasies involving him.


Seems strange. Hiking without Princess. As I make my way through the canopied entrance to my mountain paradise, I feel as though I'm betraying my four-legged friend. Like I'm "stepping out" on her. Geez. It's just a hike. She'll come with me next time. I hope....

I navigate the first crossing of the small mountain stream that winds its way through this trail. There's a "bridge" of larger rocks, placed by other hikers to allow for crossing. The stones wobble underfoot as I hop from one to another.

The trail's a challenge. With 45-degree inclines and a base— littered with crumbled slate—that tilts severely from side to side, it's most often deserted, and today's no exception. Slipping on my headphones, I tune in my music. I'm a bundle of excess energy. I get lost in the melodies. Find myself half-dancing, half-hiking my way up the mountain, unconcerned should someone witness the shameless abandon with which I'm allowing the music to move me.

A couple of miles in, I round a hairpin turn nestled deep in a lush arroyo. Below me I hear the rush of water from the mountain stream as it tumbles over rocks, worn smooth from decades of water polishing. I notice a deer off to the side.

I slow and call out softly, "Hey there, mama." The doe stops grazing and looks at me. Suddenly, she looks past me and, startled, leaps high into the air, as if assisted by springs on her hooves, and bolts away. Her reaction makes me stop, with the hair on the back of my neck raised. What was that? Removing my headphones, I turn off the music. I scan the area, certain that I heard something. Finding nothing, I fight the unsettling feeling I have and continue on.

The arroyo's remote, heavily canopied. The sunlight pierces the dense branches of the trees, leaving little pinpricks of light upon the ground. Can't tell what time it is here. Subconsciously, I quicken my pace. Feel the sudden *need* to be free of this closed-in area. Too constricting. Too isolated. The babbling brook no longer soothes me but acts as cover to sounds that might need to be heard. Warnings.

What's wrong with me? Why am I so spooked? Must be all the stress. Haven't been sleeping well. Maybe I'm just overly tired. Plus, I'm here alone.

It's then that I realize that, since the day I found her, I've never hiked without Princess. I'm so accustomed to her companionship. Without her, everything feels wrong...different. Sounds seem more pronounced. My senses are heightened. Every snapping branch poses a threat. I know I'm being irrational. It's been a hard week. My mind's just playing tricks on me. I try to reassure myself that it's just the woodland animals making their way to the water or foraging for food.

Calm down. Stop overreacting. Since when do Bambi and Thumper scare me? Glad Angel's not here. I'd never hear the end of this. I resume walking, though at a slower pace, and try to walk with more confidence.

I traverse the remainder of the arroyo. Breaking free on the other side, I feel better as the sunlight warms my skin. I continue my ascent up the steep incline. The rhythmic drop of my footfalls soothes my mind. Calmer, I replace my headphones and turn on my music, though

I lower the volume. Song after song plays. With each, the ruffled feathers of my stressed-out nerves slowly smooth back into place.

As I crest the summit, I take time to appreciate the spectacular panoramic view. The valley sprawled beneath me, punctuated by a periwinkle blue sky, accentuated with wind-swept clouds that resemble pulled cotton. Behind me, majestic mountains stretch their massive spines toward the heavens. Random radio towers rise from their summits like spikes on cacti.

A breeze picks up, and I wrap my arms around myself, suddenly chilled. Looking at my watch, I realize I need to head back. Will have just enough time to pick up Princess.

With a lighter heart and rejuvenated nerves, I begin my descent, enjoying the scenery along the way. This really is a beautiful trail.

As I reenter the arroyo, I spot the old rusty water tank at its far end. Beside it is a stack of wood, created by fire marshals who had cleared a fallen tree. The spot always calls to me—so picturesque. But not today. Something *feels* wrong. I remove my headphones again. Can't explain it. The closer I get to that tower, the more imposing its presence feels. Every step is labored. Feels like I'm walking into a trap. I stop. Look behind me. Can't get out that way. Gotta go past the water tank. I turn back and face it. Square my shoulders. Begin walking.

Despite the heavy sensation in my legs, I quicken my pace, eager to navigate my way clear of this spot. The closer I get, the harder it is to breathe. My heart feels like it's gonna break free of my chest. I get to the water tank and increase my pace to a near-run. Once past it, my breathing resumes to somewhat normal as I slow.

What was that? Something was there. Someone. Watching me. Waiting. Felt wrong…sinister…evil.

# CHAPTER SIXTEEN

## The Fun Has Only Just Begun....

He watches Sally get out of her car and waits. She stops at the restroom before beginning her hike, and he seizes the opportunity to jog ahead. He knows just the spot. The perfect place to lay in wait for her. The trail follows only one path, and he knows she'll have to pass him eventually. And waiting.... He doesn't mind. Views it as part of the game.

He makes it to the water tower long before she does and is there, concealed and watching her, when she rounds the hairpin turn, dancing. His blood boils and hands ball into fists when he sees how happy she is. He raises his hand and, through narrowed eyes, looks at the bite marks.

*Fuckin' mutt! Should've died! Can't get to her either. Not now anyhow. Maybe later, when she's home.*

He's suddenly overcome by hatred for Sally, more powerful than even he thought possible.

*Cunt! You're responsible for this....*

He shifts his gaze from his hand back to his prey.

*Let the game continue.*

Up ahead, he spots the doe eyeing Sally and moves in a bit closer, though still out of her line of vision. But the doe knows. She catches a whiff of him, looks past Sally and bolts. He marvels in how the doe's reaction spooks Sally and delights in how she removes her headphones and looks around. From his vantage point, he sees the nervous tension on her face and feeds off of it.

*That's right, bitch! Sense me. Feel me here...watching you.*

When Sally resumes walking, he has to fight from laughing aloud at the way she attempts to exude confidence.

*Ha! Don't fool me, cunt. Know you too well. That look. That walk. You're afraid. Good! Should be. The fun's only just begun.*

He watches her back recede as she continues on up the trail.

*Best if I wait here. She'll be back.*

He settles in, suspecting it'll be awhile before Sally returns. It's a nice day and he has the feeling she'll hike all the way to the summit.

Sometime later, he senses Sally's approach long before he sees her. The closer she gets, the more she emits a fear that, like wild animal, he picks up on.

*Love that scent.*

He watches Sally remove her headphones and slow her pace, reluctant to get closer to the water tower. To him. She stops and looks behind her.

*Can't get out that way, bitch.*

Sally takes a deep inhale, probably steeling her nerves, and begins walking.

*That's right. Come toward me. Let me get a <u>good</u> look at you. Drink in your fear.*

His eyes track her every movement as she nears and then passes the tower. His heart soars when he hears her breathing become ragged and she nearly breaks into a run. It's all he can do to restrain himself from jumping out and confronting her. But he doesn't. Not yet.

*I'll let you pass today, bitch. But only 'cause <u>I</u> want you to. I rule you. Your emotions. Those close to you. Always have. Always will. And soon, very soon, you'll realize that.*

# Chapter Seventeen

## Getting Back to Normal

My drive to the clinic is filled with loud music, to drown out the disturbing thoughts flooding my head. Before long, I manage to shake the feeling of foreboding, and I find myself dancing to the beat, feeling the resistance of my seatbelt as I bump, grind and bounce along to the melodies resonating from the speakers.

By the time I pull up to the clinic, I've all but forgotten my mountain ordeal. Too preoccupied with happy thoughts of my reunion with Princess. Ah, my baby. She's coming home! I can hardly contain my enthusiasm while waiting for her to be brought to me.

The door opens and there she is—Princess, wagging her tail! The minute I see her, my breath catches. My chest heaves. My eyes well up. I rush to her. Dropping to my knees, I wrap my arms around her neck, burying my tear-streaked face against her thick neck. I brace against her seventy pounds that lean into me. Trish stands, holding the leash, patiently waiting. Not saying a word. Not rushing us.

At home, I get Princess settled. So happy to have her back. Can't imagine what I would have done if…. I stop myself. Can't let my thoughts go there. I make us dinner and place her bowl on the floor next to me. We both eat slowly, methodically—lost in our own thoughts. Happy as hell to be reunited.

That night I sleep like the dead. Don't move a muscle. Can't remember the last time I slept so well. I awake with a start the next morning, positioned the same as when I'd fallen asleep. Anxiously, I lean over the edge of the bed. Good, Princess is all right. I scrutinize her. Her deep breathing borders on snoring, and the easy rhythmic rise and fall of her chest tells me she's in no discomfort. Exhaling, I flop back in bed.

Rubbing my eyes, I turn to look at the clock. It's early. Too early for my alarm to have gone off yet. Knowing it's useless to attempt to fall back asleep—too many things on my mind—I reach over and turn off the alarm and begin my morning bed stretches before the need to use the restroom overwhelms me. I'm careful to tiptoe over Princess, so grateful that she's okay.

Just about the time I'm done getting ready, Princess comes in and snakes her way around my legs like a cat, begging for attention. Smiling, I reach down and pet her. I pay special attention to her favorite spot, giving an invigorating scratch behind her ears. Her tail wags in appreciation.

Several hours later, my students arrive for their second pole-dancing class. All seem eager to see what they will learn today. I start them out with an easy warm-up before progressing into some new moves that build upon the ones I taught last week. As before, each has her own interpretation and adds her own flourish.

Throughout class the thought keeps passing through my mind—wow, everyone's getting along so well. What's up with that? Molly, usually so clipped with her speech, strings more than a few words together to form complete thoughts. Amazing! And Trish…well, she seems downright nice—civil. The others pick up on the lighter mood and seem to enjoy themselves more than the week before.

When class ends, everyone gathers their stuff and filters out. Trish lingers, fiddling with the zipper on her jacket. She then straightens her hair and applies lip-gloss while surveying her image in one of the mirrors. Not until the last woman leaves does she turn to address me. "How's Princess? Didn't want to bring it up in class."

Who *is* this Trish? Compassionate? Thoughtful? Who is she and where did she put the woman I met last week? "She's fine," I say.

"How'd she do last night?"

"Neither of us moved a muscle."

"Her appetite?"

"Back to what it was before."

There's an awkward pause. Hell, what am I saying, all of this is awkward. I don't quite know how to deal with *this* Trish.

She fusses with a loose thread on her jacket before asking, "Do you mind...I mean...would it be okay if I see her? Just to make sure she's fine."

I smile at her softness—a true fellow animal lover.

She continues, "Wouldn't normally ask, but she really got to me— all of us—during her stay at the hospital."

"Sure. No problem. She's down the hall in my room. I'll take you."

When we enter the room, Princess, curled on her bed, sees Trish and eagerly gets up to greet her. The affection the two feel for one another is evident. Trish kneels down and runs her trained hands over Princess' muscular body. Checks her gums. Doesn't miss a single detail of her condition. Satisfied, she hugs her before standing up. The relief can be heard in her voice when she says, "Looks like she's doing great."

My heart melts for this hard woman who's as dedicated to animals as I am. We talk for a bit before heading downstairs for her to leave.

# CHAPTER EIGHTEEN

## It's a Quandary

I watch Trish drive away, then look at my watch. "Ah, shit!"

Hurrying inside, I go to the phone and dial. It rings several times before being picked up. "Hi, Sally," comes the familiar voice.

"Hey, Ma. Running a bit late. Got tied up with one of my students."

"Everything okay?"

"Yeah. Tell you about it later. Wanna settle Princess before heading out. Give me half an hour? I'll meet you there."

"Take your time. Give her a pat for me. I'll browse the stacks until you get here."

"Thanks, Ma. See you soon."

Princess appears, rounding the corner from the living room into the kitchen as I set down the receiver. Seeing her, my heart swells. Always does, but now more so. I watch her cross the room. The light catches her yellow coat. Her tail wags, not the whole thing, just the end of it. It's her discreet way of showing me how happy she is to see me, as if wagging it completely might give away how devoted we are to one another. Her floppy Lab ears perk forward a bit, causing the fur at the folds on top to appear oh, so alluringly soft, like the finest velvet. The expression on her face is the same as always when she greets me—calm, serene, at peace, denoting her universe is complete with me in it. I feel the same. Her movements are slower than normal, as to be expected. But I don't care. I'll take her in any form.

Her twinkling eyes are almost hauntingly gorgeous. They draw me in with their intensity, devotion and affection. Clear portals to her soul. I can look into them, discern their crystal clarity and read her.

Her eyes don't waver from me, never do, as I kneel before her and, cupping either side of her face, look deep into those beautiful eyes before placing my forehead against hers. Her fur feels warm and comforting against my face. We stay that way for a few moments, connecting.

Almost imperceptibly, she sits, and my arms wrap around her upper body, drawing her in close. Time and space stand still. The universe belongs to us and us alone. Hugging her, I feel re-energized. I pull away and remember to rub her ears. "That's from Ma," I tell her.

She lets out a small series of joyful barks, not piercing but enthusiastic in their delivery, and then she happily trots over to where her treat jar sits on the counter, keeping her eyes on me the whole time. I marvel at how she's able to do so without bumping into the counter. Practice makes perfect, I suppose. Heaven knows, we've done this enough times. "Want a *cooooookie*?" I ask. Princess spins in rapid circles, wagging her tail, barking heartily.

I give her a few treats, let her out to go potty and then bring her back in. Can't bring myself to leave her alone and vulnerable in the yard while I'm gone. Not after what happened. Maybe someday. Not now.

Walking up and down the aisles of the bookstore, I search for Ma. I smile as I find her where I suspected I might, in the horror section. She looks comfortable, sunk into an overstuffed leather club chair, book in hand, engrossed. Doesn't see me approach and starts when I lay my hand upon her shoulder. Recognition erases the anxiety on her face.

"Scary story?" I ask.

"No."

"Really? Then why did you jump?"

Ma closes the book, laughs and confesses, "Well...maybe just a little."

I shake my head. "Why do you read those books? They always spook you."

Ma's eyes shine. "Getting a good scare reminds me that I'm

alive."

"I'll take my reminders in the form of laughter, thank you very much. Wanna get some coffee?"

"Sure," Ma says, getting up, book in hand. "Just let me put this away."

"You're not going to get it?"

"No."

"How come?"

"Not scary enough," she replies. I eye her carefully, trying to discern if she's serious or joking. Can't tell. I turn and lead the way to the in-store café.

"Everything okay with Princess?"

"A bit tired, but my same old girl."

"Tired?" Ma asks, alarmed.

"Vet said she might be for a bit."

"Oh," she says, noticeably relieved.

We arrive at the café, place our orders and sit at a high table, facing the barista. His movements catch my attention. They're methodic, lethargic and utterly calculated in their execution.

"You had your second class today, right?" Ma asks. "How'd it go?"

"Great. The women are coming along, emerging a bit from their shells. It's revealing to watch them express themselves through their dance moves."

"Yeah?"

"They have their hang-ups, but once they start dancing, I can see their underlying personalities—the ones they're afraid to disclose any other way."

"So the dancing reduces their inhibitions?"

"Exactly!"

"Think your class can help them overcome their individual hang-ups?"

I don't answer right away, too lost watching the barista. He's tall and spindly in an Abraham Lincoln sort of way. His gangly limbs are unnatural in their movements, kind of like watching a daddy long legs attempt to prepare coffee. His jet-black wavy hair offsets pale skin

79

that is nearly transparent. It's clear that he's taken great care to comb back his unruly locks. They're so laden with grease, it's impossible to discern if he's slicked them back with oil or if it's been since the last presidency that he washed them.

With rapt fascination, I watch as his actions defy logic. He's moving so slowly that it appears as if he's not moving at all. It's like watching one of those animatronics figures at a theme park, only he's stuck. As if he's suffering a glitch in the electronic signals that transmit messages from his brain to his limbs.

Pulling myself back to the conversation, I answer Ma's question. "Hope each one will come out of her shell, bit by bit, gain a heightened sense of self-confidence and learn to feel comfortable with displaying her true self."

"Seen any progress?"

"Oddly, one of the biggest transformations had nothing to do with the class."

"Who with?"

"Trish. I told you about her."

"The abrasive one?"

"Yeah. Turns out she works at the emergency clinic where I took Princess. *That's* when I saw the real Trish. The compassionate one. Like me, she's a huge animal lover, and she took an instant liking to Princess. The feeling was mutual. Anyhow, she hung around after class today, wanting to see how Princess was doing."

"That's what you meant when you said you got tied up with a student?"

I don't answer, unable to take my eyes off the bizarre behavior of the barista. He's attending to the order before ours. Has been for quite some time. All he's managed to do is remove a cup from a stack and set the machine—reminiscent of a Jules-Verne-meets-Willy-Wonka device—to the desired settings.

The contraption begins to creak, moan and groan and finally hiss steam from its top like some asthmatic fire-breathing dragon gasping out his last breath. During all of this, the barista has barely managed to retrieve a stainless steel shot glass to capture the espresso. I fear, based on his ultra-slow trajectory, he may not navigate the short four-foot distance to set the container in place before the black fluid spills, wasted, with nothing to catch it.

Forcing myself back to the conversation, I tell Ma how much Trish's concern for Princess had touched me. As I speak, I divide my attention between Ma and watching the barista. He's systematically counting out individual ice cubes into a cup as the espresso pours into the metal container, which he managed to set in place mere seconds before the scalding black liquid began to cascade from the machine.

By this point, the Jules Verne/Willy Wonka contraption is making such an audible fuss that I fear it might just explode. But the languid look on the barista's face puts my fears to rest. As least, I hope that's calm I see and not him slipping into a coma.

The slightest trace of animation flashes across his face, as he appears satisfied that just the right number of ice cubes have been placed into the cup. And not a minute too soon, for the espresso has finished draining into the metal shot glass. The barista moves with a lack of speed rivaling that of a handicapped snail as he pours the espresso atop the ice. Wait—there's milk in there too. When did he add it? How the hell did I miss that?! Not like he was moving too fast. Must've been made momentarily zombie-like by his lacka-daisical movements, unable to register what I was witnessing.

Placing the cup atop a little counter, the barista commences stirring the beverage with a bar spoon, counting each and every swirl. Finally satisfied that the beverage has been made just so, he slides it to the anxious customer, who's so jumpy waiting for his caffeine fix that his hand nudges the cup. I hold my breath, horrified to think that the cup might topple over and the whole process might have to begin anew. Thankfully, the customer recovers and grasps the cup with not a drop spilled. Thank goodness!

Next, the barista starts the grueling slow process of making our coffees. Ma leans in close and asks, "Do you think there's a reject school of coffeemakers they recruited him from? He must be the worst one on the planet. Certainly the slowest."

I can't help but laugh. "Actually, he's not the only one. *All* the employees here are that slow."

"Really?! They can't possibly *train* them to be."

"I wouldn't be so sure. They all seem to function at the exact same mind-numbing unhurried pace."

"*All* of them?!"

"All the one's I've seen."

"And you're here a lot." Ma shakes her head in sad disbelief. "Please tell me the wait's worth it, and these are going to be the best coffees ever."

"Well…don't wanna get your hopes up."

"Oh, dear."

By the time he's done, Ma and I, stressed out from having to watch the whole painstaking process, grab our coffees and take cautious swigs to steady our nerves, as one might seeking comfort from a stiff drink.

I look at Ma, who has an expression I can't quite read. "What?" I ask.

"Huh? Not sure if it *is* good or if it's because I had to wait so blessedly long, but the coffee does taste good."

We laugh, take our drinks and stroll the various sections of the bookstore. Stopping here and there along the way, one or the other of us picks up a book, intrigued by its cover. Flipping it over or opening its jacket, we read to the other what the book is about. As expected, Ma finds her way back to the horror section where her eyes keep falling upon the book she had been looking at earlier.

Finally, I go over, retrieve the book from the shelf and offer it to her, saying, "Do us both a favor and buy it."

Ma stares at but doesn't attempt to take it. "Why? I told you. Isn't scary enough."

"Yes, but you haven't stopped glancing at it since we entered this section." I say, pushing the book closer toward her. "So, you either can't wait to see what happens next, or it *was* scary enough and hooked you long before you were aware."

"Oh, Sally, really," Ma counters, with a slight toss of her head. "Don't you think I'd know if a book impressed me?"

My arm, having grown tired of holding out the book, flops to my side, still clutching the paperback. "Didn't say it impressed you, only that it hooked you. The two aren't always interchangeable. Just take the book," I say, holding it out one last time.

Ma accepts it, feigning defeat. "Well, if it'll make you happy...."

There's an awkward silence that suddenly hangs in the air between us. I busy myself, looking at titles I have no intention of reading while Ma flips over her book and reads the rear jacket. Pulling a random book from the shelf, I glance at its cover, pretending to be interested in the ghastly image that confronts me. I look up. Ma is still scrutinizing her book, only now she's seeking answers from within its pages.

"Been wondering," I say.

She looks up, acting as though she's not hanging on my every word but doing just that, in the way only mothers can. Wish she wouldn't do that. Was hoping to catch her while she was preoccupied. Should have known better. What was I thinking? *Nothing* takes the attention of a parent away from their child.

"What, honey?" she asks in that dripping-with-sweetness way mothers have as a way to drag out their kids' deepest, darkest secrets. How do they do that? Is it some gene they have implanted when in the hospital delivering, or does it grow, gaining strength, month by month, as does their unborn child, coming to maturity the day they become a parent? Whatever it is, it's unnerving.

Realizing that I've started my descent down a slippery slope from which there's no hope for return, I ask, "Remember when my premonition dreams began as a kid?"

Ma, stopped by my random question, closes her book and focuses on me. "I do. They began right before Eric died."

I nod.

"Didn't understand what they were then," I say. "Only after did they make any sense. Thought I'd have them forever. But after you checked me into Whispering Pines, I never had another, until...."

Ma looks concerned. "They're back? When? For how long?"

"For a bit. Only now they're different."

"How so?"

"Clearer than past ones."

"You can see what's going to happen—everything?"

"No, don't get me wrong. They still feel like a bunch of fragmented pieces of a puzzle, scattered before me on a table, but the images presented with these dreams have a lot fewer missing pieces."

"Do you realize it at the time?"

"Knew something was different. But it'd been so long since I'd experienced them that…I don't know…I guess I was just shocked they were back."

"But they're clearer? You're certain?"

"Yeah."

Ma's gaze is intent. She barely blinks as she attempts to process all that's been discussed. There's a long silence. Wish she'd just say something…anything. But she doesn't. At times, she looks as though she's lost deep in thought. Other moments, she looks pained, as if even thinking about all of this is too much for her. I look at her pleadingly. Nothing. "Well?" I say.

"I don't know."

This is worse than I thought. I'd hoped Ma would have words of wisdom for me. Turns out she's just as baffled as I am. Maybe more so. What the hell?

Neither of us talks further. Sipping on the last of our coffees, we make our way to the checkout.

# CHAPTER NINETEEN

## So, We Meet Again

After parting with Ma, I head to the grocery store for a few items. The warmer temperatures have given me a hankering for a nice barbecued steak and corn on the cob.

On my short drive, my mind replays the conversation I had with Ma about my premonitions. Wish she could've given me more. Explained more. Removed some of their mystique.

As a teen, we never talked about them. After Eric died, we didn't talk at all. Losing a brother or son will do that. I was barely aware that she knew I had premonitions. Back then, my visions made me feel like a freak. When I got older and began to understand their significance, I learned to dread them, often avoiding going to bed until the wee hours of the morning or sometimes not at all. Didn't want to give my brain a chance to reveal things to come. I figured out that if I waited to fall asleep until I was literally exhausted, I could minimize the intrusion of my visions. Not always, though. Some things just had a nasty way of cropping up. But depriving myself of sleep…that helped.

I think about the time I had without the burden of my dreams. It was peaceful—serene. But the intermission's over. They're back, whether I like it or not. Can't help but wonder. Why now? After all this time?

They're always the same. Pertain to something I hold dear. Try to prepare me. Put that feeling in the pit of my stomach. The one where it seems like I'm sucking in my breath with great heaves and pulling in my abs as tight as I can. Always been that way. As if doing so can prevent the dreams from actualizing. Yeah, right. Would be nice if it worked. But it doesn't. Once I've had a dream, *nothing* keeps it from becoming reality.

Pulling into the parking lot, I locate a spot right near the door.

Inside, I grab a hand basket and head to the produce section, hoping to score some corn. On the far display, I spot it. My heart soars and my pace quickens. Funny how something as simple as corn can make my day. Grabbing a couple of ears, I place them in my basket and grab a few incidentals on the way to the meat section where I pick up a steak.

I turn to head to the registers but freeze, caught off-guard by the mesmerizing image that stands before me. I have to tilt my head back slightly to take it in. The brilliant smile offset by that delicious bronze complexion. The twinkling eyes so piercing they feel as if they could penetrate my very soul. The devilish grin that plays at the upturned corners of his mouth.

Before me stands Carlos, in all his living glory. Funny how we keep meeting in the meat aisle. Time stands still as I drink him in. His proximity's almost unnerving with the spell it casts on me. But I don't back away. He, too, has a hand basket, containing a few items.

"I see we meet again," he says, his words caressing every part of me. His voice is low, seductive. Almost throaty, it's enough to make my knees buckle, and I instinctively reach out to steady myself against him. His face fills with concern. I feel his powerful hands reach out to brace me. "Are you all right?" he asks, not releasing his hold.

I dare to gaze into his hypnotic crystal blue eyes. The ones that could have me do anything, if only he'd ask. Suddenly, I find it hard to swallow. How can I forget how to swallow? Nearly choking on my own spit, I attempt to recover as gracefully as possible lest Carlos think I'm completely inept and on a day pass from some mental institution.

Feeling the lump slowly make its way down my throat, I say, "Yes, I'm fine. Thank you. Don't know what came over me."

Yeah, right. Carlos, that's what came over me. Not sure what it is about him. Don't care. Just know that whenever I'm around Carlos, my mind turns to Jell-O and my body becomes pliable putty ready to be molded to his whim. Is this what I want? Am I ready for this? I can't ever recall a man having this effect on me. It's like I want to give every part of myself to him. Exist *for* him. Anything, just so long as he'll wrap those amazing arms around me, pull me close and never let me go. I can't take it any longer and say, "Seems we keep bumping into one another. Wonder if there's something more to this than just chance. Interested in finding out?"

He doesn't answer. Taking his time, he scrutinizes me. Not in an offensive, you're-a-slab-of-meat kind of way, but in an I-can't-seem-to-get-enough-of-you way. Know the feeling. With irresistible boyish mischief in his grin, he responds, "We could grab a bite to eat. Maybe Friday night?"

"What time?"

"Seven? I can pick you up."

We exchange information, and I head home, feeling lighter…better than I have.

For the remainder of the week, I keep myself occupied, teaching my Hip Hop classes at the Community Center and stopping at the market a couple of times for miscellaneous items.

On Friday, I get ready for my date with Carlos, thinking how quickly the week passed. At seven on the dot, my doorbell rings, and there stands Carlos, looking as handsome and irresistible as ever. We hug and he escorts me to his car.

"So, where are we going?" I ask as we head west on the 134 Freeway.

"There's this great French brasserie I was reading about in the paper. Got really good reviews."

"Hmmm…French food. Wouldn't it be easier to just poke around the garden for some snails?" I ask, grinning.

Carlos shoots me a sideways glance to see if I'm serious. Seeing my grin, he winks and replies, "Wow! Hadn't thought of that. Would be a lot cheaper, too. Let's go back," he adds, merging over as if to exit the freeway.

"No! Wait! I was just kidding. A French brasserie sounds lovely."

Entering the restaurant, I'm struck by the faux-painted walls that glow a warm umber. A band of stenciled grapes runs along the top of each wall. Their deep plum and subtle red coloring complements the umber. An old-world European style bar covers the length of one wall with a backdrop of wine holders, comprised of boxes set on the diagonal to form diamonds that the bottles are laid in, their necks sticking out, begging to be uncorked.

The tables, simple three-foot squares draped with plain white linen cloths, are arranged individually against the walls and in connected lines of twos and threes in the middle of the establishment. The chairs are rickety little things that threaten to topple over or crumble beneath one should the person be too large. They're so closely spaced that the back of one practically comes in contact with the one behind it.

The waiters, all male, display two days' worth of rough razor stubble. Loose tendrils of their dark hair fall from their relaxed ponytails to frame their faces. And they have such thick French accents that I have to replay what they say, at least twice, for it to compute.

We're shown to a table where a waiter arrives and says, "Today's specials are salmon with a cream dill sauce, served over a bed of garlic mashed potatoes or roast beef served with a red wine—No. Wait. Not that. I mean, tonight we're offering seared tuna on a bed of wild rice or lamb drizzled in a—No. That's not it either."

What the hell?! Does he even work here? He leaves, probably to refamiliarize himself with the *actual* specials, and I say, "Could you make sense of what he was saying?"

"No," Carlos says. "I think we should play it safe by ordering something on the menu."

Our soup arrives, and we enjoy it. The waiter, coming to take away Carlos' dish, says, "Sir, if you had wanted more, you should have just asked for it! No need to practically lick your bowl."

The waiter spins on his heels and leaves.

My eyes wide, I look at Carlos and say, "Can you believe that guy?"

He shrugs and says, "You know the French. With their accent, they can get away with saying just about anything."

We talk for a bit about meaningless things. Each feeling the growing attraction between us, neither wanting to openly address it. Each of our entrees is impressively displayed and mouth-wateringly good.

Carlos takes a sip of wine and says, "So, tell me about yourself. How long have you been in California?"

I swallow my bite and say, "Born and raised. Left for a bit. But I like being back. You?"

"Same. Can't imagine living anywhere else. The traffic and overcrowding aren't so great, but the weather—"

"And the beaches—"

"They're the best," Carlos says, tearing off a piece of bread.

"So, what do you do? I mean, other than go to the market—a lot," I say.

We both laugh.

"Never was one for making a big list," Carlos answers. "Would rather go every couple of days when I get the hankering for something."

"Me, too."

"Back to your question. I'm a personal trainer."

"Ah, figured you worked out," I say.

Carlos finishes his bite. "Looks like you know your way around a gym, too."

"Dance studio. I'm an instructor."

"Wondered if you might be."

We finish our meal and are offered coffee, which we accept. When we're done, Carlos attempts to summon our waiter to get the bill. *That* becomes an ordeal. You'd think they'd *want* to get paid for their service. After what seems like forever and staring down the entire wait staff as they leisurely lean against the bar, looking in our direction, we manage to get our waiter to amble over.

Outside, I lean against Carlos. "Thanks for dinner and a lovely evening."

"You're welcome."

He wraps his arm around me, and I allow myself to get lost in how right the world feels in his warm embrace. We walk back to his car in silence.

# CHAPTER TWENTY

## Chilling Revelations

In the morning, I awake refreshed. Don't think I dreamed of Carlos. At least, if I did, I can't recall. Damn! That was a wasted opportunity. Oh, well. I'll have to see if I can remedy that tonight. Mmmm...the possibilities.

Eager to just relax, I call Angel, and we arrange to have a bite to eat and see a chick flick the next evening.

Over dinner, I fill her in on my date with Carlos. "He's really nice."

"Nice? What about chemistry?"

"Oh, it's there," I say, grinning.

"Him, too?"

"Pretty sure."

"So there'll be a second date?" Angel asks.

"Hope so."

"When?"

"Don't know. Exchanged information. I'm gonna let him call me."

"What if he doesn't?"

I feel an impish smile curl the corners of my mouth as I reply, "Then I'll just have to be the aggressor."

"That's my girl!" Angel says, holding up her wine glass. "Here's to a second date."

Later that night, I fold myself under the covers hoping to delve into devilish dreams involving Carlos. But my dreams aren't of him. Instead....

* * * * *

Feel like I'm being watched as I wind my way around the side of the mountain through overgrown vegetation. I'm alone. No Princess. Seems I've been here before. I have. When Princess was in the pet hospital.

Feel vulnerable. A carefully orchestrated snare. Turn. Leave. Legs won't respond. The summit. I see him—Carlos. Facing away from me. The musculature of his back. His cinched-in waist. Warm day. Gentle breeze. Carlos covered up—no exposed skin. A beanie conceals his hair.

Pace quickens. Wanna wrap my arms around his tight waist. Almost there. Want our lips to meet. I reach out to him. He turns. I freeze. A scream caught in my throat.

I'm in my third pole-dancing class. Each student performs complex moves on her individual pole. We're halfway through the six-week session. Anticipated culmination recital.

Molly creeping me out. More than once, I've caught her watching me...just staring with an intensity that's unsettling. I approach. She's having difficulty mastering a move. "Don't ignore them," she says, in a faint voice.

"What? Don't ignore what?"

She makes direct eye contact, a rarity. "You know of which I speak."

I shake my head. "No, I don't."

"You will," is her only response before she continues her moves.

A Technicolor roof. Threat of a ticket. Panic. Slashed tires. First one. Then two. Then all four.

Class progresses. Molly and I partner up and she says, "Embrace them. Learn from them."

End of class. Molly passing through the door, saying, "You have to learn *how* to decipher them. *How* to alter their outcome."

Molly, normally so quiet. Now this?

Molly says, "Your dreams. This is all about your dreams."

* * * * *

I awake, unable to catch my breath. The sheets beneath me are soaked with sweat. The images that have been presented to me in my premonition shake me to the center of my being. What does it mean? Why would I feel threatened by approaching Carlos? And why did I scream when he turned? Then there's the whole Molly thing. Creepy! How could she know about my dreams? I've never told her about them. Am I paranoid? Is this real? Am I in danger? Feels like I am. And *this* dream was so lucid, compared to the others. It began fragmented, but then…. I think the disjointed images I used to view were better—less disturbing.

I look over at the clock, my pulse still racing. It's several hours before my alarm is due to go off. Knowing it's useless to try to go back to sleep and feeling the onset of a post-premonition dream headache, I hit the off button on the alarm and get up.

After going to the bathroom, I don my robe and head downstairs, Princess on my heels. I let her out prior to attempting to make a pot of coffee. My hands are shaking so badly that I spill a good portion of the water on the counter, missing the coffeepot's reservoir. It takes several attempts, but I finally manage to set the pot to brewing, and then I go to sit at the table. Placing my elbows on it, I comb my fingers through my hair in a desperate attempt to calm myself. Don't like this. Can't be good. Never is.

The coffeepot chirps that it's done brewing. I let Princess in on my way to fetch some. Maybe it'll help to steady my nerves. Princess never takes her eyes from me. She looks worried—like me. I drink my coffee. The second mug goes down slower, and I feel myself settling down. My headache lessens to a dull throb. I reach down and rub Princess on her special spot—right between her eyes—and ask, "Wanna go for a walk?"

Not needing to be asked twice, she springs up and turns in rapid circles, emitting a series of barks. I finish the last of my coffee, leave the mug on the table and grab her leash. A moment later, we hit the streets, which we have all to ourselves. It's still too early for much activity.

The briskness in the air feels good, and I quicken my pace to stay just ahead of catching a chill. I wind my way around the neighborhood that I know so well, barely taking notice of the surroundings. Instead, I let them ground me, focus me and strengthen my resolve that I can make it through whatever's to come. By the time we return home, it's over an hour later. Princess rests, and I prepare for my third pole-dancing class. Looking at my watch, I realize with a start that my students will be arriving in just under an hour. Where did the time go?

I let Princess out back, grab another cup of coffee (this one to enjoy), and head upstairs to ready myself. I finish just as the doorbell rings.

Class runs smoothly. My students are progressing at an impressive pace, mastering the more complex moves I assign them. Watching them grow and evolve week after week fulfills me. Makes me realize that I do have something to offer—helping others.

Trish's disposition has softened considerably and melds with the personalities of the others. Carol seems to have relaxed a bit with her perfect looks, adopting a more natural appearance that's welcoming and flattering. Alicia's looking less used up. More refreshed. More vitalized. And if I'm not mistaken, conversations flow more easily with her. She doesn't seem to be in quite the same perpetual state of stunned disbelief as when she first came to class. Pam, who already shined when she entered the class, seems to outshine even herself with her bubbly enthusiasm and natural dance ability. And then there's Molly. What can I say? Still creepy.

Throughout class, I keep a watchful eye on Molly, who, in turn, cocks her head. Silently, she watches me, almost as if she's contemplating me. Think I'd prefer if she would say something. But she doesn't.

Class ends and the women file out. Molly, having gone to the restroom, is the last to leave. Although somewhat alarmed to be alone with her, I mask my discomfort with what I hope is a winning smile. I tell her it was a good class, and I look forward to seeing her next week. She pauses and looks me in the eye—something she usually avoids. Then she says, "Don't ignore them. Embrace them. Learn *how* to decipher them."

I feel the color drain from my face, and it takes every bit of energy I have to not drop to the floor. In stupefied silence, I watch as she walks out the door without uttering another word.

# CHAPTER TWENTY-ONE

## Getting a Grip

The phone rings just as I'm closing the door behind Molly. I get it partway through the fourth ring. The answering machine clicks on, and I hear my recorded voice announce that I'm not home. "Hold on a minute." Cradling the wireless handset, I head to the kitchen where the base unit is.

What is it with answering machines? Seems they always seem to start recording at the worst time. Like now, when I am clearly home, not away, as my message indicates. Speaking of my own voice, is that what I really sound like? God! How annoying. My recorded voice drips with sweetness.

"I'm sorry," I say to the mystery caller, loud enough that I hope they can hear me over the recording. "Let me get to the machine so I can turn it off." Just then, my message ends and the sound of blank airspace, ready to record my every word, fills my ears. Great! *That* couldn't have happened earlier? I shrug off my frustration. "Hello."

"Hey, girl!" comes Angel's cheerful greeting. "Catch you at a bad time?"

"No. Just finished class and was seeing Molly out. Gotta tell you, she said some stuff that scared the shit out of me in class today."

"You okay?" Angel asks, her voice heavy with concern.

"Yeah."

"Still up for lunch with your mom and me?"

"It'll be good for me to get out. Give me a chance to change. I'll swing by in twenty minutes. Can you give Ma a call and let her know that I'm on my way?"

From the front, the restaurant is unassuming, small and has a line of people snaking its way out the front door.

Ma says, "Hope you like this place. Went here a couple of weeks back with a girlfriend. The food is really good."

Angel looks around. "Wow, is it always this crowded?"

"From what I hear," Ma responds. "A lot of famous people dine here. They seem to draw a crowd."

"We might be waiting forever," Angel says. "Doesn't look very big."

Ma smiles. "You'd be surprised."

After waiting in line for a short time, Ma, Angel and I place our orders at the walk-up window, pay and then head out to find an available table. The restaurant is an older converted single-story house with every available area surrounding it, a mishmash of various connected brick-laid pathways and patios, set up with an eclectic assortment of outdoor tables. They're covered by a colorful canopy of marketplace umbrellas so plentiful that their edges touch, forming a giant Technicolor roof. Ma was right. The number of diners housed by the restaurant is impressive. Must be nearly two hundred in all.

After circling around the perimeter of the building, we spot a lone uninhabited table calling to us. We navigate through a maze of closely spaced chair backs as we worm our way to it. It's a warm day. Despite the temperature and the close proximity of people, we find ourselves comfortable under the protection of the umbrellas and can feel the coolness of the lichen-covered bricks beneath our feet.

I find myself relaxing in this easy setting. It calms me. The stress caused by my vision and then Molly's comments begins to lose its edge.

We barely get settled at our table before our food arrives. Generous portions threaten to overflow the edges of our plates. The waiter sets down our dishes. The food looks delicious, and we each begin to eat. Taking a bite of my club sandwich, I say, "That's good!"

"I'll say," Angel responds, chewing.

"Good find, Ma. Gotta remember this place."

Ma beams, pleased that her recommendation was a good one. "The best part," she says, "is that we can sit here all day if we want.

The waiters won't bug us."

Angel finishes chewing and swallows before turning to me. "I'm dying to know. What happened with Molly?"

I hesitate before answering, not sure if I wanna spoil the relaxed mood I'm in. Deciding it might make me feel better to talk about it, I put my sandwich down and take a sip of iced tea before responding. "Molly was creepy as hell today."

"What'd she do?" Ma asks.

I tell Ma and Angel of my premonition dream the night before and then how the portion with Molly had eerily played out in class. As I'm partway through, Angel stops eating and stares at me. When I pause, she asks, "She actually said that? Specifically mentioned your dreams?"

"Yeah," I say. "Creepy. Right?"

"Have you ever told her about them?" Angel asks.

"No! Never. That's what's so strange."

Ma says, "How much do you know about this woman?"

"Not much, just what she filled out on her application and what I've been able to gather from her during classes. She's not very talkative. Whatever I've learned, I discovered by watching her."

Ma says, "Could she pose a threat?"

"No. But her comments have me thinking. I mean, really, how much do I know about these perfect strangers I've allowed into my house?"

"What about an off-site studio?" Ma says. "I wouldn't mind helping you find and set one up. Had fun decorating this one. Good mother-daughter time."

"Thanks, Ma. But I'm not going to get another studio. Although Molly's behavior is unsettling, I'm done running when something rattles my cage. Wasted way too many years of my life allowing others to influence how I feel. Not anymore. I'm the one in control now."

"Honey, that's all good, and I'm proud of you, but are you sure you're making a wise decision? One that'll keep you safe?"

"Yeah," I say, sitting a bit taller in my seat. "Molly's no *real* threat. Strange, but not dangerous."

"Well, if you're sure," Ma says. "But my offer stands."

"Thanks, Ma," I say, reaching across the table to give her hand a gentle squeeze.

We eat in silence for a few minutes before I continue. "What doesn't make sense in my dream is when I approached Carlos on the mountain and screamed when he turned around." I look at Angel and Ma, hoping one of them might have a plausible answer. Nothing. Instead, they shake their heads. Gee, thanks.

What is it with my premonition dreams? Why do I have to figure them out on my own? What am I saying? I've *never* been able to figure one out. Only after the events occur do I fully understand their meaning. Once, just once, I'd like the mystery unraveled ahead of time. Viewing the blank stares on Angel's and Ma's faces, I realize this won't be that time.

Angel looks at her watch with a start and says, "What was the time limit in the space where you parked?"

Her question jerks me from my thoughts. Takes a moment to process it. Hate it when that happens. Here I am, plugging along with my own thoughts when *whammo*, out of nowhere, someone radically changes the subject, causing my brain to sputter before stalling out. I like to think of these temporary lapses as brain farts. They come with little to no warning, pass almost as fast as they arrive and can leave a bit of an unpleasant fog in their wake.

Brain fart. Yep. That's what Angel's question just did to me. Wrinkling my brow in an attempt to get my brain back online, I search my memory banks, hoping to retrieve the information she's requested. Aha! Got it! "Two hours!" I respond, much more forcefully than I'd intended, carried away with the victory of having remembered the answer to her question.

Angel looks at her watch again. "Ah, shit!"

"What?" I ask.

"We've been here over three hours."

"What?! There's no way," I cry, looking at my watch, doing the math. Ah, hell! She's right. How did we lose nearly three and a half hours? I mean, it's been nice, hanging with Angel and Ma, but I had no idea *that* much time elapsed. Jumping out of my chair, I say, "I've gotta move the car."

"Wait," Ma says. "We'll come with you."

My mind's racing on hyper-speed. I dread rounding the corner and spotting a fluttering ticket, held in place by my windshield wiper. "No, you two take your time gathering your stuff. I'm gonna head out. I'll pull the car around to the front."

"You sure?" Ma asks.

She's talking to air, as I'm already two tables away. Looking over my shoulder, I say, "I'm sure. See you out front."

I make my way, as quickly as possible, through the maze of tables and out the rear of the restaurant. It'll be quicker this way.

The moment I clear the property, I get the uncomfortable feeling that I'm being watched. I look around the alley I'm crossing. It's deserted. But it's unmistakable. The feeling of my every movement being tracked. Scrutinized. Devoured by eyes intent to catch my every move. My skin crawls with a blanket of gooseflesh.

I quicken my pace. With every footfall, an irrational feeling of helplessness, of being stalked, settles around me, threatening to suffocate me with its intensity. I can see the end of the alley and have to fight the overwhelming urge to sprint to it.

Without warning, images of last night's premonition dream fill my mind. I can see it so clearly. All of it. The feeling of being drawn to wrap my arms around Carlos' muscular back. And then the feeling of dread when he turns, when I see his face and scream.

What's wrong with me? I'm walking so fast that I'm nearly running. I scan the alley. Still nothing. I'm alone. But I don't *feel* alone—anything but.

Clearing the opening of the alley, I see my car up ahead. No ticket. Good. More than ever, I'm desperate to get away. My hands shake so violently that I fumble with the keys. I force myself to take several deep breaths and try once again to select the needed key. I watch as my keys tumble, in slow motion, from my fingers. Damn it!

Bending down to retrieve them, I notice it. My front driver's tire is slashed. It rests like a wounded animal on its rim. Looking around, I notice that the rear tire is also slashed. A chill runs down my spine.

Time and space seem to slow to a crawl. Not wanting to, but being drawn to do so, I walk around the rear of the car to the passenger side. Both those tires have also been slashed. Holy shit!

Just then, I'm overcome with the urge to look behind me. I spin around and catch sight of a figure. Can't tell if it's male or female. He or she is covered entirely in dark clothing, complete with a knit cap. All I see is the figure's broad back, as it rushes round the corner. My blood turns to icebergs that collide against themselves as they attempt to course through my veins. There's not a single doubt in my mind. The figure I've just seen is the one from my dream.

# CHAPTER TWENTY-TWO

## What the Hell?

This can't be happening. I sit on the curb with a hard thump. My rear stings from the sudden impact. Don't know how long I sit there.

From a vast distance, I hear a familiar voice call my name.

"Sally. Sally! Are you okay?"

"Wh…what?" I look up. The effort is great. Hard to pull myself back to reality. I struggle to focus on Angel who is standing over me.

She sits and wraps an arm around me. "Your mom and I waited and waited. When you didn't show up, we got worried and came looking for you." Gesturing to the car, she asks, "What happened?"

I shake my head in an attempt to clear it. I look at my car, with its tires maliciously slashed. This can't be real. Who would do something so mean? And why?

I look at Angel and say, "Don't know. Found it this way when I came out."

"See anyone?"

Images of the person I saw rounding the corner fill my mind.

"You wouldn't believe me. *I* don't even believe it."

"Try me."

"The mystery person I saw in my dream, the one wearing the beanie—"

"Yeah…."

"When I noticed the tires, I got the feeling I was being watched. Looked up. That's when I saw the person from my dream head away from me and round the corner,"

Angel stares at me, her mouth agape. Wish she'd say something…anything. This is really scaring me. What's going on?

My dreams have never been this clear or this closely spaced to actual events.

Can't help but wonder who I pissed off. And enough to make them want to send such a clear message that they wanna disable me. Least, that's what I think they're trying to say. Whatever the message, it's doing a damn good job of spooking me.

I jump as I catch movement off to my side.

Leaning down, Ma places a hand on my shoulder. "It's okay, honey. Just me."

Angel's arm wraps around me tight, and I'm grateful. Leaning against her, I ask, "Why would someone do this?"

Ma, her phone out and already dialed, listens to the handset as she says, "I'm calling the police. This needs to be reported." Someone comes on the line and, putting up a finger, Ma turns her attention to her call. Hanging up several minutes later, she says, "They're sending out a unit. Should be here shortly. Sally, do you still have Triple A?"

"What? Yeah."

Reaching out her hand, Ma says, "Give me your card. I'll call them."

I fish in my purse, pull out my wallet and sift through a stack of plastic cards. Finding the desired one, I hand it to Ma. She flips it over, finds the number, dials and gives the operator the information requested. A few minutes later, she hangs up. "They said it's real busy, but they'll have someone out in 30–45 minutes."

"Okay," I hear myself say. I take back my card and toss it in my purse, not bothering to put it back in my wallet, the effort seeming too great. I'm suddenly exhausted. All the life seems to have been drained from me. This is all just too much—the dream, Molly in class and now *this*. I'm afraid to ask, "What next?"

Just then, a squad car pulls up and double-parks alongside mine. The driver, a slight woman with fiery red hair twisted into an unrelenting French knot, gets out and is joined by her partner, a rail-thin officer reminiscent of Barney Fife, goofy looks and all. The woman heads straight for me, not stopping, while her partner veers off to walk around my car.

The stern-looking woman takes out a flip-out pad and asks, "Who called?"

"I did," Ma says, offering her hand.

The officer looks at the proffered hand before shaking it and then says, "Officer Neilson, and you are?"

"Gloria McFee, and this," she says, gesturing toward me, "is my daughter, Sally Whitmore. Her car's the one I called about."

"I see. Who discovered the vehicle in its present condition?"

"Me," I say, standing up. "We were only away from it a few hours, having lunch. When I came out to get it...." I point at the slashed tires.

"Did you see anyone lingering around the vehicle?"

Images of the dark-clothed individual from my dream once again fill my mind, but I push them aside, knowing that the officers will think I'm mad if I mention that a mystery person from my dreams materialized in real life. "No," I hear myself answer. The voice doesn't quite sound like my own. It is strained, tired and aged.

The other officer comes to stand beside his partner and asks, "Who's the owner of the vehicle?"

"I am."

"I'll need your license and registration for our report."

"Okay," I say. I walk to the passenger side door, unlock it and rummage around in the glove box for the registration. Finding it, I hand it to the officer. He takes it and copies the information in his flipbook. I also hand him my driver's license.

Officer Neilson, looking at the two-hour parking sign just in front of my car, asks, "You say you were gone a few hours?"

Angel, who has risen to stand beside me, nearly growls at the officer, "So what? Now you're gonna give her a ticket for being parked here too long?"

In ultra-slow motion, Officer Neilson turns, looks directly at Angel and says, "*Nooooo*...I think she has been through enough today. I was attempting to establish a time line, if that's all right with you?"

Angel, realizing that I'm in no danger, backs down.

"Thank you," the officer says, dismissing Angel and once again directing her attention to me. "Do you have an approximate time you think you parked your vehicle here?"

I nod and give her the information she's requesting, while glancing at Angel. Silent words of thanks, both about sticking up for me and not mentioning anything about my mystery dream person, pass from me to her. Angel's always got my back.

"About what time," the officer asks, "would you say you found the car in its present condition, Ms. Whitmore?"

I look at my watch, do the math and tell her a time.

Ma asks, "Do you think you'll be able to find who did this? They can't be stable. To do something like this...." She sweeps her hand toward my car.

Officer Neilson smiles at Ma and responds, "We'll certainly do our best, ma'am. There are several security cameras in the area that we'll get the tapes from before we leave. Hopefully, one of them will give us something to go on."

Turning her attention once again to me, she asks, "Is there anyone you can think of who might have done this to your vehicle?"

Without hesitating, I shake my head. "No. No one."

"Are you sure? This seems to have been personal—directed at you."

"Can't think of anyone," I say.

The Triple A tow truck pulls up behind the police car and the driver gets out. He looks at my car and a long whistle escapes through his teeth. "Man, you must have really pissed someone off for them to slash both tires."

"Actually," Angel says, "all four are slashed, and you can keep your opinions to yourself."

"Sorry," the driver says, shaking his head. Looking as if he's only just noticed the police officers, he adds, "They about done with their report?"

I turn to look at Officer Neilson, who nods. "We have everything we need. If we need more, is there a number where we can reach you?"

I give her one. She and her partner leave, I assume, to go talk to nearby shop owners regarding the surveillance tapes. The tow truck driver takes my card, copies down the information and then pulls in front of my car.

The man presses a lever and the flatbed tilts, its end coming in contact with the ground. He releases the chains, stretches them long and grunts as he stuffs his ample size under my car while securing them. Within minutes, my broken car sits atop the tow truck ready to be transported. "Where to?" he asks.

"Not sure," I say, looking from Ma to Angel. Each shrugs. I look back at the driver. "Is there someplace you'd recommend?"

The man doesn't hesitate. "There's a tire shop about a mile and a half down the road. Should be able to take care of you."

I smile and say, "Thanks. Guess I'll have you tow it there, then."

Ma, Angel and I squeeze in beside the oversized driver on the short drive to the repair shop.

Two hours later, a new set of tires on my car, I take them back to their houses. I drop Ma off first, and she gives me a big hug. "Call me if there's anything you need, honey."

"I will," I say.

As I pull to the curb at Angel's, she turns to look at me. "You gonna be okay, Sally girl? I could stay with you if it'd make you feel better."

I give her a hug. "Thanks. I'll be fine. Looking forward to a quiet evening at home with Princess."

"You sure? It's no trouble."

I give her an extra squeeze. "I'm sure."

# CHAPTER TWENTY-THREE

## Got My Message?

He follows from an undetectable distance as Sally drives Angel and the other woman. They pull down a side street a block away from the main boulevard. He lets them gain distance. A block ahead, he sees Sally parallel parking and is grateful for the less frequented street. Before getting to them, he turns the corner and circles the block. By the time he returns, the three women are nowhere to be seen.

*Yeah, you bitches have fun whatever you're doing. Know I will.*

He rolls past Sally's car, smiles and continues on. Finding a parking place around the corner, he leaves his car and heads toward Sally's. His stride is measured, purposeful and reeks of confidence.

*This should be rich.*

He slows his pace a bit when Sally's car comes into view and surveys the area. Coming even with her car, he realizes his luck. There's no one else in sight. He approaches her front passenger tire, glances around once more and then squats. Pulling his switchblade from his pocket, he flips it open and punctures the tire. Looking around and seeing no one, he proceeds to puncture the rear passenger tire, delighting in the sound of air rapidly escaping. He stands and takes one final look. Observing that he's still alone, he rounds the back of the car and quickly punctures the driver's rear and front tires.

He snaps a quick photo of his handiwork and then walks away, placing the now-closed blade in his pocket. He sighs, thinking of his trophy picture and how wonderful it will be to see the look on Sally's face when she discovers his "gift."

Hours pass. But he doesn't get upset. Instead, he uses the time to think of other things he'll do to Sally. How he'll get her attention. How he'll make her pay.

*Oh, yeah, you're gonna pay, bitch!*

From his spot around the corner, he's pulled from his thoughts when he finally spots her. He smiles, watching her hustle toward her car.

*That's right, bitch. Hurry. Don't quite know what you're hurrying toward though, do you?*

Leaning around the corner to get a better view, he sees her fumble with her keys.

*Can smell your fear, cunt. It's addictive. Gives me power. And I like power…especially over you.*

He delights in Sally's anxiety as she spots first the front driver's and then the rear tire—both slashed. He watches as the color drains from her face. Not thinking, he rounds the corner and takes several steps toward her as she walks around the car, discovering the slashed passenger tires. Realizing his faux pas, he turns and hurries back toward the corner. But before he's safely around it, he feels it—her eyes boring into his back.

*Fuck! Fuck! Fuck!*

He quickens his pace, rounds the corner and keeps walking, passing his own car. He doesn't slow his pace until he's rounded another corner and walked another block. Slowing down so as not to look conspicuous, he replays the event in his mind.

*It's all right. Didn't see my face. Might be able to identify me from behind. Would that be so bad? Bet I got her thinking. Freaked her out. Love fucking with her! Maybe her spotting me wasn't so bad. Wanted her to get my message that I can fuck with her—any time, anywhere. Think she got it—loud and clear.*

# CHAPTER TWENTY-FOUR

## Dark Awakenings

Princess greets me when I get home. I'm happy for the company. I fix a light dinner for myself, add some of my table scraps to her dish, and then we go for a short walk. By the time we get back, the sky's morphing from brilliant blue to twilight greys and blacks, tinged with slight hues of green. Despite it being a nice evening, I close and secure the downstairs windows and head up to soak in a bath. After, I pull on my jammies and hop into bed to read for a bit. Princess curls at my side, grunting slightly as she positions herself. I smile. I don't read for very long before exhaustion from the day's events catch up with me. I decide to turn in.

Sleep overcomes me. But my rest is plagued with nightmares, involving my ex-pimp, Ax. The years I spent held hostage by him are a grim part of my past I choose to keep securely sealed in the catacombs of my mind. But every now and again something reminds me how Angel and I fled him and went to Las Vegas where we began new lives. No longer lowly hookers owned by our pimp, we became legitimate strippers at a high-class gentleman's club. The fear that Ax would find us was ever-present in our minds, and until the day we heard he'd been killed, we lived in constant fear.

Tonight's dreams mercilessly share visions of the savagery that Ax was capable of. Not of the things he actually did to me, but horrifying examples of what he could do.

* * * * *

Suddenly, the door crashes open. There stands Ax. He launches himself at me. He's upon me by the time I cry out to Angel for help. Lifted by my throat—suspended. Angel launches onto Ax's massive back. Pummels him. He tosses her, like a rag doll, against the wall. Ax's gun pointed at my head. "I'm taking you back home where you belong…with me." He kicks me. Broken ribs. Driving in his car. We're suddenly at Ax's place. He shoves me into a chair in the center of the room. Secures my hands and feet. Gags me. Ax knocks Angel out with a powerful right hook, breaking her jaw in the process. "No!" I scream. "Have 'special' plans for you," he says, approaching. "Not gonna kill you—too easy. Gonna make your life a living hell. Make you watch those around you suffer." Clothes torn off. Ax climbs atop. Rapes me—tearing me open. Sheets beneath me, soaked with semen and blood. Ax's legendary weapon—his ax. Razor-sharp blade glints in the dim light. It falls, again and again, making a sickening sound, as it sinks repeatedly into Angel's body. She utters bloodcurdling screams. Eyes filled with desperate terror.

* * * * *

I awake, gasping for air. Bolt upright. Switch on the light. Princess nudges her muzzle under my trembling hand. My throat's sore from restrained screams. My face is streaked with tears. With unsteady hands, I reach into the nightstand drawer, pull out my journal and begin writing.

*What the hell?! What is it with these damn dreams? Why am I plagued with them? Feel like I'm losing my mind. Fighting so hard to swallow back my tears that my hands shake violently. Can barely hold my pen. My jaw's clenched so tight that it's convulsing of its own accord.*

I'm snorting back snot and wiping away tears that won't be contained.

Don't know what this darkness is telling me. Feels like the lid on my Pandora's box has been thrown wide open. I don't know how to sort through, dodge or protect myself from its contents. Makes me wanna scream-press a button and delete all that's transpired. Not prepared for this. Don't know if I'm strong enough to face what my dreams reveal. Feel like I'm rambling. Maybe if I keep writing, all this will make sense.

Darkness abounds. Sadness threatens just beneath the surface. My dreams. Memories from my horrid past bubble to the surface like crude from the earth's core. All the past. The present. All that I was. Have overcome. Have risen above. My dream seems to indicate that they're all going to converge. But how? Oh, God!

Thought I'd risen above all of that. Had left it in my past. But did I? Doesn't feel like it now. Perhaps the clue lies in identifying it for what it is. Although I've worked so hard to conceal it, even from myself, this is the eternal wound that threatens to never heal. All-consuming.

*My time spent with Ax was horrific. Like a burn victim, the scars I sustained run deep. Might be possible to lessen the darkened shadows they've cast on my soul. But they can't be eradicated. Won't be. They're stubborn. More stubborn than I am.*

*Why am I so upset? Why am I letting this get to me? Ax is dead. Gone. Can never hurt me again, despite my dreams. I hate the way my visions affect me! After I have one, feels like I'm in a holding pattern. Waiting for the actual event to play out is awful. Wish the deep chasm of my old wounds would granulate with new awakenings instead of presenting the dreadful images I've seen in my dream.*

*Need to share this with someone. Can't carry this burden alone. It's exhausting. Angel. She'd understand. Might help. My dreams make me feel vulnerable. But I can't hide them. Gonna freak her out.*

I close my journal. Replace it in the drawer. With still-trembling hands, I rub Princess' muzzle and reach for the phone. I fumble with it as I attempt to dial.

The phone rings several times on the other end before being picked up. A familiar groggy voice mumbles, "Hmmm? Wha…?"

I grimace and take a deep breath before proceeding. "Hey,

Angel," I manage in what I hope is a cheerful tone.

"Sally?" I hear rustling on the other end. "Do you have any idea what time it is?"

"Sorry. We gotta talk."

"Now?"

"Yeah."

"It's the middle of the night! Can't this wait until morning? Till I'm a little more…human?"

Angel's weak stab at humor isn't lost on me, and I chuckle. "Afraid not."

In a heartbeat, I hear the sleepiness vanish from her voice. She asks, "Are you okay?"

"Yeah…no…I mean…I don't know. We just gotta talk. Can I come over?"

"I'll start some coffee."

"See you in a few."

At Angel's, I share the details of my dream with her. She grows pale. Forgets the mug of cold coffee in her hand. Slumps heavily against the back of the sofa. "Oh, my God," she says, leaning forward to place her mug on the table. "What does it mean? Not what I think. Can it?"

"Don't know," I say, shaking my head and draining the last of my own mug.

Angel gets up to refill our mugs. "This one was… different?"

"Never used to be so clear." I follow her into the kitchen. "Or frequent." I pause before continuing, "I'm pretty sure that person I envisioned on top of the mountain—"

"Yeah?"

I take a deep breath and am careful when selecting my next words. "I fear it may be Ax."

"Ax?! But how? He's dead. Was shot point-blank in the face…."

"I know. Doesn't make any sense. But you know how my dreams are."

"Yeah," Angel says, her voice dropping to an almost reverent level. She blows on her coffee before taking a tentative sip.

"I can't just ignore them," I say.

"What are you gonna do? Not like you can go to the cops and tell them a ghost is out to get us."

"No," I say, sipping my own coffee. "Maybe I could have Doc snoop around a bit. You know, make sure Ax really is dead."

"Want me to go with when you see Doc?"

"No. Thanks."

"Did you ever tell him about your dreams?"

"A little." I wince. "Told him about the one when Eric Angel was killed by the crossfire between Ax and that other pimp."

Angel leans over and places a comforting hand on my thigh. "Ah, girl, I know how hard that was, losing your baby like that."

I don't respond. Visions of my beautiful five-year-old son, forever suspended in time, fill my mind. My jaw clenches. I struggle to keep my emotions in check.

"What was Doc's reaction when you told him?" Angel asks.

"What could he say?" I respond, finishing the last few drops of my coffee. I look at the bottom of my mug before placing it on the table. "By then he knew me well enough to take me on my word. Not like he could really understand—"

"But he believed you?"

"Think so."

"Good. Then this shouldn't be such a hard pill for him to swallow."

"Hope not." I look out the window and squint at the bright light streaming through. "I'm gonna go now. Maybe we can both get a couple of hours of sleep before we have to get up."

"Sleep? Are you serious? I'm wide awake."

"Yeah, well…," I say, getting up to leave.

Back home, I entertain and then abandon the thought of crawling back in bed. I suspect no sleep will come and fear what I might dream if it does. No. Better to stay awake. I drain an entire pot of coffee as I busy myself, cleaning the house. By the time I'm done, not a speck of dust remains. The carpets are thoroughly vacuumed. The floors are mopped to the point I can see my drawn reflection. The kitchen and bathrooms are scrubbed to near-hospital standards of cleanliness.

Sighing, I put away the cleaning supplies and run a bath. After bathing, I select a pair of yoga leggings and a top, which I carry into the bathroom. I untwist the towel from my hair and shake it loose. Then I comb and blow-dry it. I apply my makeup, get dressed and take a step back to view my image in the mirror. The hints of dark shadows that my foundation could not conceal underscore my eyes, and my face appears thinner than normal. The twinkle in my eyes is missing, replaced with a grave look.

I turn from the mirror and head downstairs. There I riffle through one of the kitchen junk drawers. It takes several minutes, but I finally locate Doc's number. I dial the station and am informed that he'll be in later that afternoon. Glancing at the clock, I realize he'll get in just about the time I finish teaching my Hip Hop classes at the Community Center. I make myself a piece of wheat toast for the road and put Princess out to go pee. I make sure to bring her in before leaving.

The day seems to drag on and on. I find myself looking at the clock often, wondering if time is actually passing or if I've entered some time/space continuum where the hands on the clock never shift position. My last class ends. I gather my belongings and head for the door.

# CHAPTER TWENTY-FIVE

## Face-to-Face

Driving to the station, I have not the slightest idea what I'll say to Doc. How does one present that they believe a ghost is out to get them? Will he believe me? Think I've finally cracked? If I can persuade him to look into Ax's death, what will he reveal to me? A flurry of similar questions continues to swirl around my head as I pull into the police station parking lot.

I wait in the reception area at the station. It's nice enough, though its appearance cries out, "public servants work here." The slim female officer to whom I announce myself has shoulder-length, straight chestnut hair drawn back into a no-nonsense ponytail. She sashays off to the catacombs of the office and returns a few minutes later. A distinguished-looking man in his early fifties rounds a corner and walks directly toward me. "Sally?"

Although I've never met the man, I know him instantly. He's just as I'd imagined. "So good to finally meet you, Doc."

"And you," he says, as we exchange a warm handshake. "Let's go back to my office."

He leads the way around a corner. We pass partitioned desk areas. Although identical, each is personalized with photos of loved ones and with trinkets. Each of the occupants is thoroughly engrossed with his or her individual tasks. Some are on the phone. Others peck away at computer keyboards. A few look up, venturing to peer over the precariously stacked folders framing their desks, as we pass. There's a certain charm to the symphony of their office space: phones ringing, animated voices (some elevated, others hushed), the clatter of heavy

116

file cabinet drawers being pulled out and clanked back into their frames and pagers incessantly buzzing. I like the organized chaos. Reminds me of when I used to work at the strip club.

Doc, not a tall man, maybe five-ten, walks at a pace easy to keep up with. Rounding another corner, we head to the end of a long hallway where a door stands ajar. The name on the placard says Investigator Jones. I can't help but chuckle inwardly. Wonder why he didn't just have them put "Doc" on it. Aside from the very first time he introduced himself to me over the phone, he's never been about formal titles. Always stressed that he wanted to be called Doc.

We enter his office. He closes the door behind him. The office isn't spacious, just what's needed. This fact isn't lost on me and matches my impression that he's not a man interested in making a good impression through appearances, but rather through the work he does.

Motioning to a plain-armed chair across from a beat-up school-teacher-like oak desk, Doc says, "Have a seat," before rounding the desk and sitting in the well-worn, high-backed chair. We both take a moment to look at one another.

Breaking the silence, I say, "This is weird."

"It is, isn't it?" Doc says, his face breaking into a sheepish grin.

"Can't believe we've never met face-to-face before," I say, noting his grey-blue eyes and thick white hair. He appears to be taking in my appearance as well.

I know what's driven this man, who maintains a legendary reputation at the Pasadena Precinct, to become an invincible solver of cold crimes. I think of the common heartache we share—the loss of our child at the hands of vicious criminals.

I can still remember when Doc told me how his eight-year-old daughter, Caroline, had been brutally raped and then strangled by a man. I wince and recall the anguish in his voice when he told how her killer had been captured and then, due to a technicality, was released. I remember being comforted by his conviction that he would never allow another cold case to go unsolved—especially one involving a child.

I smile at the man sitting across from me. The one who found the remains of my first son and saw that justice befell the one responsible for his death. Feel like I've known this man my whole life, and yet our time spent interacting with one another was rather brief. Maybe too short. What if he doesn't believe me? Thinks I'm crazy?

I stall. "How go the cold cases?" I ask.

Doc leans back in his chair, the springs squeaking in protest. A broad smile warms his face and his eyes twinkle. "Good."

"I'll bet there are a lot of happy folks out there. I know I was when you solved Eric Angel's death. You have a gift."

"Don't know about that," Doc says, leaning forward. "Can't stand the thought of a family not having answers. That's what drives me. I'm desperate to end the nightmare of questions that keep them up at night."

"I know. You do." Without hesitating, I add, "Caroline would be proud." The slightest hint of a flinch is noticeable when Doc hears his daughter's name. I remember back to when he could barely utter her name without choking up. I'm glad to see that his efforts to ease the suffering of others have also helped to heal his own wound.

"I hope so," he says, clearing his throat. "But you didn't come here to talk about how my crime-solving is going, now did you?"

"No," I admit, shifting uncomfortably.

"What's on your mind?"

I pause for a minute. My mouth goes dry. I attempt to muster some saliva with which to swallow. None's forthcoming. Instead, I clear my throat and hear myself croak out, in a hushed tone, the name I'd hoped would never cross my lips again. "Ax." My heart beats triple time. I'm sure Doc hears it as it threatens to burst from my chest.

He doesn't respond at first. Just leans forward. Placing his forearms on the desktop, he laces his fingers together and scrutinizes me with an intensity that makes me fidget. "What about him?" he asks.

I shake my head. "I…I know this is gonna sound crazy, but I'm pretty sure I saw him."

"That can't be. He's dead!"

"I know. That's what makes this so weird."

"You couldn't have seen a dead man."

I fill him in on the return of my premonition dreams. I start with the one about Princess and tell him how that played out in reality. Then I tell him of the man atop the mountain summit I'd presumed to be Carlos, and how, in my dream, I'd screamed when he turned around and I'd seen his face. And how that man slashed my tires. I end with the most recent one about Ax abducting Angel and me. Of how he told me he'd get to me through those I care about.

Throughout, Doc runs his fingers through his thick hair, in what looks like an attempt to calm himself. Several long minutes pass before he says anything. "So let me get this straight. You think Ax poisoned your dog?"

"Yes."

"And," Doc continues, "you saw who you thought was your boyfriend on the top of a mountain, but it turned out to be Ax?"

"In my premonition."

"But you think that person slashed your car tires *in real life*?"

"Okay, I know this sounds far-fetched," I say, leaning forward and resting my hands flat on Doc's desk.

"You must, since you said you didn't report seeing anyone when your tires were slashed."

I lean back in my chair, its hard frame pressing into my back. "I didn't think they'd believe me."

"So why tell me? And now?"

"Because," I say, getting up and pacing, "this most recent premonition tells me that Ax is alive. That he's gonna start hurting those close to me." I cross the room and dispense water from a five-gallon Arrowhead jug into a paper cup. I return to my chair and look at him expectantly.

"Now," Doc says, "I'm not saying Ax is alive. According to our information, he's not. But, if he were, why would he come after you now?"

"Probably still pissed that Angel and I got away from him."

"But it's been seven years," Doc says, combing his fingers through his hair.

"Time doesn't matter with Ax. Makes it a point to get even, no

119

matter how long it takes." I pause to finish my water. "I never asked back then. Probably should've. What happened with Ax that led you to believe he was dead?"

Doc locks eyes with me. Doesn't answer right away. Makes me wonder if he's trying to figure if I'm sane enough for him to tell me the truth. "Guess you have a right to know," he begins. "During our investigation, Dan—"

"Your partner?"

"Yes. He and I hit a roadblock. Couldn't find Ax. Was like he disappeared off the face of the earth. So I spread word to certain individuals that we knew were looking for him. One of them was the twin brother of the pimp Ax shot and killed during the pimp war shootout where ultimately your son was killed in the crossfire."

Hearing his words, I flinch as images of my son flash in my mind. But I say nothing.

Doc pauses before proceeding. "Anyhow, Leonard, a high-profile crime lord from the East Coast, didn't take kindly to discovering that his brother's murderer had also killed an innocent boy. He arranged to have Ax brought to a remote cabin where he and his men worked Ax over pretty thoroughly for several days before Leonard put a pistol to Ax's temple and pulled the trigger." Doc waits while the impact of what he's said sinks in.

"Did you ever actually see Ax's dead body?" I ask.

"No. Our sources assured us he was dead."

I don't say anything. A full minute passes with the two of us just looking at one another. Then I say, "Can you dig around a bit? See what you can find? Figure out if Ax really is dead or alive?"

"I can do that," Doc says.

"We need to know if Ax is alive," I say. "My guess is that he is, and he's behind all the bizarre stuff that's been happening to me. We've gotta figure this out. You need to get him before he escalates his violence. What he's been doing so far…it's way too tame for him. I know he's just toying with me, waiting for the right moment to make his point. I couldn't stand it if any harm came to anyone I care about."

Doc's eyes meet mine. "Let's take this one step at a time. You're jumping to conclusions that Ax is alive."

I look Doc straight in the eye and say, "He is," with utter conviction.

"Let's prove that one way or another."

# CHAPTER TWENTY-SIX

## Maintaining Control

A few blocks from the station it hits me. What have I done? What will Doc find? Is Ax alive? Dead? Am I prepared to know? I drive several blocks, trying to push all thoughts from my mind. But like a slow leak, they trickle in. Just a few at first. Then the dam bursts, flooding my mind.

Ax? All this time? All the bizarre events that have happened? Ax could have...probably has been the instigator? Why didn't I know? Why didn't I sense his presence? His proximity to me. Did hearing that he was dead make me feel that I'd never be at risk again? Come on! This is Ax. He's always there. Lurking.... Waiting.... Scheming to get even.

I shake my head and slap the steering wheel. Stop it! I refuse to give that man, dead or alive, this kind of power over me. I foolishly allowed him to control me when I was young and naive. I handed him my innocence. In return, he dominated my every move and thought, every fiber of my being. Not again, dammit! Get a grip!

I pull into my driveway.

Passing through the kitchen, I notice the red light flashing on the answering machine. Angel's voice rings out when I press the button. "Hey, girl! Give me a call when you get back. Dying to know how it went."

I call Angel and fill her in on what happened with Doc. She doesn't say a word throughout. There's a long pause when I'm done. Then she asks, "Did Doc give you any idea how long it would take for him to snoop around?"

"No. I'm trying not to let this get to me. He may find nothing or confirm that Ax is dead. No sense worrying until I know one way or another."

Just then, my cell phone rings. I look at the display and see Carlos' name. "Hey, Angel. Gotta go. Getting another call—from Carlos."

"Okay. Catch you later."

I take the call just before it clicks over to voicemail. "Hey, Carlos."

"Hi, beautiful!"

"Aw! What's up?"

"I was thinking of you. Want to get together this Friday? Figured if I called you early enough in the week, I might stand a chance of being penciled into your busy schedule. Thought maybe we could do dinner—not French—and a little dancing. A new club just opened. I'd love to take you."

Dancing with Carlos does sound nice. Would be a good distraction. I push away the lingering Ax situation threatening to consume my thoughts and say, "That'd be nice."

I can hear his smile through the line as we continue to talk. We chatter aimlessly about this, that and nothing of importance. I like that about Carlos. He always knows how to make me forget my troubles, at least for a time.

"How's Friday?" he asks.

I run through my schedule in my head before answering, "It's open."

"Good. I'll pick you up at...seven?"

"It's a date."

Much to my surprise, the rest of the week flies by. Don't hear anything from Doc. But then, didn't really expect to this soon. I mean, everyone has thought Ax was dead the past seven years. Will probably take more than a few days to prove otherwise.

On Friday, Carlos arrives right on time to pick me up, and we head to a new dance club. It's nice—almost medieval in its architectural interior design. The lighting's dim, tinged in reds. There are a few individual booths set back in little alcoves, offset by rugged, stacked stone archways. We're lucky and secure one of these nests. There we dine in almost-seclusion but are able to watch the other patrons engage in various forms of self-expression on the dance floor.

There is little conversation during our meal. We are transfixed by each other's presence and the mounting sexual energy between us. Can't believe how much I've needed this—to be out with someone who ignites my passions. Every act—the lifting of a fork to one's lips or sipping wine—takes on a perverse sexual connotation. I barely blink during the meal, fearful that if I do, Carlos might spontaneously vanish. That this is all a dream, a wonderful never-want-it-to-end illusion conjured up from somewhere deep within my psyche.

Carlos finishes his meal and, placing his fork on his plate, dabs at the corners of his mouth with his napkin. Not a word is spoken. Doesn't need to be. His gaze says it all. His eyebrows lower ever so imperceptibly, and his eyes bore to the center of my soul. Almost in a trance, I lower my own fork, never taking my eyes from his.

His left eyebrow rises, slightly, powerful in its suggestion. I respond with a barely noticeable nod of my head. He rises and offers his hand. Sliding toward him across the lushly upholstered booth cushion, I take his hand and am rewarded with a powerful grip that transfers a bolt of electricity from him to me. My breathing deepens.

Carlos pulls me close and, leaning down, places a warm kiss by my mouth, allowing his lips to linger for an extra beat. An explosion of emotions surges within me, electrifying, thrilling and all-encompassing. Do I wanna be so captivated by another that I'm willing to hand myself over to them?

I ignore the policing of my mind and fall into step behind Carlos. Still clasping his hand, I feel the energy flowing between us as he skillfully navigates us to the center of the dance floor.

The music has a seductive erotic beat. Soulful in its delivery, it entices Carlos to become one with it. He looks deep into my eyes and in one graceful move pulls me against him. He wraps his arm around me and presses against the small of my back, making impossible any chance of escape. Not that I would want to.

Didn't think it possible, but my breathing becomes deeper, more rapid. I feel the heat of our bodies merge. Become one. His hips pulse forward and back in time with the music. My body responds. Our movements are perfectly synchronized. When he dips his hips and scoops forward, I anticipate his move and press hard against him. Our chests attempt to fuse. Our hips sway as one in small circles, slow and deliberate. They boldly express the sexual images playing out in our minds. Our bodies couldn't be more in sync.

The fervency between us builds. In its wake, everything around us falls away. No longer in a club on a crowded dance floor, the two of us move to our own beat, driven into a frenzy by the passions that erupt from deep within. Time and space lose all meaning. I never want this to end and can tell from the way Carlos holds me, pulling me so close he threatens to crush me, neither does he.

We're barely aware of the songs that come and go. Of dancers entering and leaving the floor. Of the minutes that flow into hours. Both of us are engrossed in the powerful endorphins coursing through our veins. Our pace never slows. Our combined rhythm merges us as one. At times, gasping for breath, our breathing takes on a rhythmic, almost hypnotic quality.

Our euphoric physical display of passion continues until the club closes. When it does, I grab my purse and head toward the door with Carlos in tow. I don't dare let go of his hand. Don't think I could if I wanted to. Our fingers seem to be permanently intertwined.

Still fueled by the sexual tension burning between us, we make it as far as my parked car, which we enter. There, our subdued passion reignites. We kiss, pet and neck, eagerly running our hands over one another's bodies through our clothing. I feel Carlos' hand slip under my form-fitting knit top. Wait! Stop! What am I doing? Here? In the parking lot? At a dance club? And with a man I barely know?

I hesitate. Pull back and say, "We have to stop. This isn't right."
Carlos looks stunned. "What?! What did I do? What's wrong?"
Suddenly, I feel like a tease.

Is that what I've become? That would be cruel. But if I'm not one of those women, why did I let things go so far? Why not stop sooner? Why not go all the way? Allow myself to get lost in reckless abandon? Because that's not me. Not anymore. That's the old Sally.

The one controlled *by* her actions.

The new me—the responsible one—emerges and tells Carlos, "It's not you. You didn't do anything wrong. This is moving too fast. We barely know each other. Hell, I don't even know your last name. To do this now, here, in this mindset would cheapen the experience. Don't think either of us wants that." I look at him expectantly.

"Vortez," he says, a little breathless, "and I'd be okay with a little cheapening."

"Would you? Would you really?" I ask. My words seem to have an effect on him. And as with me, the grip of the powerful physical spell cast over him seems to have lost some of its potency, replaced by reason. Dignity. Self-control.

"Not really," he confesses in a resigned voice barely above a whisper.

As we sit, our bodies separated, our breathing resumes its normal pace, no longer the rough panting of lust-driven beings. It's then that the most amazing feeling washes over me. That of pride. I'm proud of my ability to reclaim reason and act responsibly despite the overwhelming sexual tension driving me to do otherwise. I smile on the inside. My face must reveal some of my inner thoughts, for Carlos says, "You look so...serene. Why? Instead of being frustrated like me, you seem...content."

"I am."

Carlos recoils as if struck. "Why?! Was this just a game to you? See how far you could go? How frustrated you could make me?"

His anguish pains me. I reach out and take his hand in both of mine. "No, nothing like that. In another time, another life, I would have gladly given myself to you—right here, right now. But I've learned to appreciate and nurture the things I hold dear. And you're one of those. I don't wanna tarnish what could be with an impetuous act that we both might regret."

His countenance softens. His guarded look fades. He leans in to kiss me. I let him. It's not a lust-filled kiss, but one that conveys that he agrees and is willing to wait. He pulls back. "I suppose this means we'll have to go on a third date," he says, his eyes twinkling.

# CHAPTER TWENTY-SEVEN

## The Calm Before the Storm

Princess lies on the bathroom floor. I draw a warm bath. I slip beneath the surface. A satisfied sigh escapes my lips as I think of my evening with Carlos.

A few minutes later, I open my eyes. Look over at Princess. "Enjoyed my date." Princess gets up and comes to sit beside me. I pet her. "It was nice to get out. Have fun—on a date." I pause from petting Princess and ask, "So, what do *you* think? Is he worthy of a third date?" She barks.

A short while later, I slide between my sheets with Princess curled up on the floor beside me. Sleep comes easily.

Before I know it, my alarm goes off. Resisting the urge to send it flying across the room, I reach over and tap the off button. As I do every morning now, I lean over and look at Princess who's resting peacefully. My heart swells with gratitude that the poison didn't.... I lean over and pet her.

"Come on, girl," I say gently. "Time to get up. Have some stuff around the house and yard to do." Princess somewhat opens one eye, demonstrating that she's not fully committed to rising. She closes the eye and grunts when I poke her. Throwing the sheets back, I chuckle and step over her on my way to the bathroom. "All right, I'll let you sleep a while longer." A few minutes later, wearing my robe, I pad out of the bedroom, down the hall and am almost at the head of the stairs when I feel her nudge my leg. I reach down and rub behind her ear. "So...you decided to get up after all. Good girl!"

Downstairs, I put Princess out, pour myself a cup of coffee and set about making breakfast for the two of us—kibble for her, toast and an egg over easy for me. We eat while I skim the paper. When I'm done, I fold and place it on the table. I notice Princess looking at me, sitting at attention. If I didn't know better, I'd think she was waiting for me to fill her in on the highlights of the news.

Oh, what the hell. I look at her and smile. "They caught the guy who robbed that bank. Seems that while he was hiding out, he sustained a self-inflicted gunshot wound. Not thinking, he went to the hospital to get it treated. A staff member there recognized him from his image on the news and called the police who arrived and arrested him." I pause to look at Princess, who appears to be hanging on my every word. "Criminals can be *so* stupid! Oh, and you'll love *this* story. Apparently, there was this family from Pasadena whose dog ran away while they were camping near Lake Arrowhead. Although the family searched and searched, they couldn't locate their beloved pet. A week later, they had to give up and go home without him. That was three months ago. Yesterday, the husband opened the front door to get the paper and was greeted by his missing dog who was sitting on the doormat, wagging its tail!"

Princess *thumps* her tail, as if pleased by the report. "You liked that story, huh?" I get up, clear the dishes and, with Princess shadowing me, begin tidying the house. Finishing upstairs, I decide to leave the studio for later. I go to my room and throw on a pair of denim shorts and a spaghetti-strap top. I glance at Princess and say, "Gonna be a hot one today. Can feel it already. Best get at it."

I spend the rest of the day outside with her, me deadheading roses and trimming bushes, her chasing squirrels that foolishly wander into the yard. By evening, I'm tired and coated with a layer of dusty sweat. Just as I'm heading for the house, Princess brings me her ball. Although I just wanna go in and clean up, I can't resist her enthusiasm: tail wagging, middle and rear end wiggling from side to side and the playful *woofs* that she emits. I pick up the ball and play fetch with her, a smile warming my heart. Half an hour later, we're more than ready to head inside.

The next day, we rise and continue puttering around the yard and house. Princess shadows me as always. By the end of the day, I find myself upstairs in the studio, preparing for class tomorrow. I restock the bar fridge, set up the coffeepot to brew first thing and wipe down the mirrors so that not a smudge remains. The last thing I do is polish the brass poles with a clean cloth and a little rubbing alcohol to get off any oils. Standing back, I survey my handiwork and comment, "There, that's better," to no one in particular. Princess *woofs* and trots over. I lean down and pet her. When I'm done, I ask, "So, what do you think? Is it ready for tomorrow?" Her tail beats the air in a rapid rhythm. "All right then," I say, leaving the room.

The following morning, the doorbell rings right on time. I greet Alicia, Trish and Carol, and we head up to the studio where they settle their gear and stretch while waiting for Pam and Molly.

Once everyone arrives, I say, "Hope you all had a good week and have been practicing your routines." I pause and look around. Nodding heads confirm that they have. "And you brought your shoes?" Again, heads nod. "Good. Please put them on now. We'll go through today's routines with you wearing your stilettos so I can see how each of you fares. That'll help me determine each of your roles in the culmination recital."

"I'm *so* looking forward to that," Pam says.

"Can we invite people to watch?" Alicia asks.

"Of course! Friends, family, whoever you want. This is *your* time to shine. The recital won't be open to the public, only for your chosen ones."

"Sounds great!" Pam says.

"We still have a lot of work to do," I say. "We're already at week four of our session. The recital's in two weeks."

There's an animated yet hushed rush of enthusiastic murmurings that passes amongst the women.

As class progresses, I find myself smiling. Each woman's progress and personal growth is evident in her stylization of dance. Carol, originally obsessed about being perfect, fussing over insignificant things and hyperactively flitting from one thing to the next, has managed to slow things down. I watch her get lost in dance and notice how her moves have become slower, more sensual. As she places her foot high on the pole, I note the confidence she exudes. She reaches out toward her foot and traces the sexy curves of her leg, her fingertips traveling the length of it. Then she caresses and crisscrosses her midsection, finishing by framing her breasts.

Alicia and Trish's bond is evident, and they pair up once again. Trish's graceful moves complement those of Alicia's that scream she wants to push things to their sexiest limits. I can't help but be impressed as Trish spins and high-kicks her way through track after track of music, her need to be seen evident. She's a natural. Alicia, on the other hand, likes to remain in close proximity to her pole. She's grown to specialize in her own unique dirty dancing where she almost appears to be fucking the pole.

Pam's easy nature from the start has evolved into a playful naughtiness that leaves no doubt that she likes to get the party started and keep it going. Unlike her counterparts who seem to have discovered their repressed inner sexy selves, Pam's fun side has sprung to the surface.

And then there's Molly. Always a bit of a mystery, her abbreviated stylization of life has begun to relax a bit. And a cheekier side of her is what I now see. Today especially, I can't help but observe how there's something different about her—her moves. They've taken on a more urgent teasing nature. They appear almost impudent, irreverent but in an amusing endearing manner. She shimmies and wiggles her way through the routines almost as if *this,* today's class, is *her* recital. Odd, but then, I've grown to accept Molly's eccentricities as the norm.

Observing how much my students have grown over the past four weeks, I reflect on how much they've helped me grow. How helping them discover their true selves, the ones they can be at peace with, has taught me to be calmer in my own life. Take the whole Ax thing. In the past, that would've sent me over the edge. But I'm learning to handle stress better. And I owe my students for that.

Class ends, and Molly's the last to leave. Standing at the door, she turns and looks at me with a solemnness that I find unnerving. "I won't be here for the recital," she says.

"I'm sorry. Gonna be away?"

"No…well, sort of. He'll get me before then," she says, almost matter-of-factly.

"I don't understand. Who'll get you?" I ask.

"Ax."

As if struck in the chest, I stagger backwards and am unable to respond. In stunned horror, I watch as she turns to leave. I try to talk but can't. Oh, my God! I can't let her leave! I reach out and grab her arm with a vise-like grip.

Startled, she turns, looks at me and asks, "What?"

"Ax." I stumble through the words. "How the *hell* do you know Ax?!"

Molly looks at me with exceeding patience and calmly responds, "I've seen him."

"Seen him?!" I nearly scream. "Where?! When?!"

She looks at me, as if the answer is obvious or should be and replies in an almost hypnotic tone, "In my dreams, of course. Like you."

A thick layer of goose bumps begins at my head and folds itself around every inch of me as it travels downward toward my feet. Utterly stunned, I can't believe what I'm hearing. The world reels. I feel faint. My hand falls from Molly's arm. She reaches out to steady me.

"It's okay," she says. "Everything will be okay."

"Okay?" I hear myself ask. The voice, sounding as if it has traveled a great distance, does not sound like my own. I repeat, "Okay? How's everything gonna be okay? You said he's gonna get you. Why you, not me?"

Molly inhales deeply and then releases the air through pursed lips. "Because he knows it will get to you…. The waiting. The not knowing. Your inability to stop him."

The cogs of my scrambled brain click into alignment, and I respond, "But now we know. So we can stop him. Right?"

Molly lets go of my arm. A peaceful resignation washes over her face, and she replies, "No. We can't. You know. Ax *can't* be stopped. This is my fate." With that, she turns and walks away.

"But—" I say to her back.

She continues walking. Never looking back, she says, "Good-bye, Sally."

# CHAPTER TWENTY-EIGHT

## Desperation

Immobilized by a surge of dread, I stare at Molly's back as it recedes. How can she be so...calm? I watch her get in her car. My mind screams a thousand warnings, and yet my lips remain mute. I hear her car's engine start and blindly register as she pulls away from the curb.

At the last moment, she turns and looks at me. Our eyes lock. I feel a jolt, as her thoughts fill my consciousness. Her message is as clear as if she'd spoken. I won't be at next week's class...I'll be dead by then, it says. The thought complete, she blinks, breaking the invisible cord of communication that binds us.

My mind reels, races and screams its rejection of her message. No! Oh, my God! What am I gonna do? My brain spins on hyper-speed. My skin crawls, electrified by fight or flight. I have to *do* something. Anything. I just can't sit by and wait for this horror to play out. I won't let Ax get Molly.

She said Ax wants to send me a message. Send me a message, my ass! Who does he think I am? Still that weak, easily manipulated whore he controlled. Hardly! My heart races. Pulse quickens. Focus zeros in as if my blood's been replaced by a thousand espressos.

An image of a clock, complete with seconds, minutes, hours and days, consumes my mind. I hear its deafening *tick tick tick* as it counts down from the moment Molly drove away until next Monday's class, when I know.... We both know. Molly's pole will remain empty. Her newly discovered self-confidence and enthusiasm will be absent from my studio. She'll be gone by then.

I've *got* to tell Doc so he can protect her. Shit! Move, girl! Hurry! Maybe Doc can stop him. I close the door. Race to the kitchen. Yank open the junk drawer. Papers, receipts and business cards topple to the floor as I ferret around. Where is it?! I know it's here. My search intensifies. A plume of papers takes flight and flutters to the floor. Got it!

Reading the number from the card, my fingers fumble as they jab the keys on the phone. There's a pause that seems to last a lifetime before I hear the phone ring on the other end. It rings and rings—no answer. Come on. Be there. Just as I fear I'll have to leave a message, the line is picked up.

"Investigator Jones here."

"Oh God!" I rush, without taking a breath. "He's alive. There's no denying. I'm not just imagining it. She told me. This isn't coincidence. He's gonna get her—not me. How the hell could she have been so calm, knowing he's coming for her?"

"Sally? Is that you? Are you all right? Has something happened?"

"Yes," I say. "I mean, no. I mean—oh, shit! You've got to hurry with your investigation."

"Okay. Let's have you calm down. Take a deep breath."

I force myself to take a huge inhale, and then struggle to let the air out, controlled.

"There," Doc says. "That's better. Now, how about you start at the beginning and tell me what's happened."

I close my eyes, take another calming breath and then proceed to tell what I know. Doc doesn't interrupt. Instead, he's unnervingly silent. There's a long pause when I finish. I fear the line's gone dead. Then I hear, "She said that? That she'd seen Ax in *her* dreams?"

"Yes."

"Have you ever mentioned Ax to her?"

"No."

"Ever? Even a hint?"

"No. Never."

"Hmmm…this certainly makes things more interesting."

"Interesting?! A woman's life is on the line, and you're intrigued. What the hell?! We're running out of time. You have to protect her."

"I'm afraid I can't do that," Doc says.

"Why not?"

"We don't have any proof that Molly's in danger."

"Our dreams—hers, mine."

"Although they're unsettling, I can't dispatch a surveillance team based on a couple of *dreams*. I need something hard—concrete."

"Well, what's taking so long with your investigation?" I resume pacing.

"Unfortunately, not all stations work with the same information data base," Doc explains. "I'm having to go about my search for Ax the old-fashioned way, with a paper trail faxed to me from individual stations that I suspect might have a lead on him." He sounds tired.

I sit at the kitchen table and switch my approach. "What can I do to help?"

He responds, "Nothing. Wish you could. But we're going to have to be patient. If I push too hard, the other stations will get frustrated, sloppy with their reporting, and we'll end up missing what we need to find—hard proof."

"So that's it?" I ask, my hand shaking around the receiver. "We just wait?"

"Unfortunately, yes. I'll stoke the fires a bit under the other stations. Maybe I can finesse a quicker thorough reporting from them. As soon as I hear anything, I'll let you know."

Unsatisfied, but knowing that there's nothing else he can do, I say, "Thanks, Doc," then hang up.

My finger punches another number into the phone. I wait while the connection is made. I hear the phone ring on the other end. Once. Twice. Three times. On the fourth ring, I hear Angel's cheerful recorded voice tell me that she's not in and to leave a message. Damn it! Where are you? You need to know this.

There's a long buzz, indicating that I can leave my message. It's times like these when I curse Angel for not having a cell phone. "Angel," I say. "Call me as soon as you get in!"

I hear a pawing at the back door and let Princess in. She leans against my legs and looks up at me. My hand strokes behind her ears. "Well, that's it, girl," I say. "I guess there's nothing to do but wait." I go to sit at the table again, and Princess follows. I smile at her. I lean down and wrap my arms around her. "I'm gonna keep a close eye on you until all this is resolved. Not gonna take any chances with…."

The next couple of days are miserable. The waiting…. Angel calls, and I inform her of what happened with Molly. Then I go about my normal routine, Molly never far from my thoughts. Images of her struggling against Ax's powerful hold fill my mind. I try to push them away. A futile effort. By the end of the third day, I'm so jumpy that my Hip Hop students comment on my behavior. I apologize, stating that I have a lot on my mind. That's an understatement.

When I get home from teaching on Friday, the message light on my answering machine is blinking. Not that this is uncommon, but this time a feeling of foreboding resonates, as the flashing red beacon rhythmically cries out its warning. My hand shakes. I reach out to depress the play button. I hear Doc's voice. His tone is grave. In an ultra-controlled business voice, I hear him ask me to call him back. He has…"news."

Oh, God! This is it. The moment I've been craving, yet dreading. When the world either rights itself or forever spins out of control. Princess comes to my side, sensing my unease. I look down at her as I stroke her back, and say, "Well, this is the moment of truth."

I pick up Doc's business card and the phone and walk with the handset to the kitchen table. Princess never leaves my side. Halfway there, I try to dial and fail. The phone topples from my hand and skitters across the polished floor where it comes to a rest under the table. I get on my hands and knees and reach for it. Just before my hand makes contact, the phone rings, and I recoil as if I've been electrocuted, bumping my head smartly on the underside of the table. I rub it with one hand while fetching the phone with the other. Clicking the talk button, I say, "Hello."

"Sally," Doc says. "Where have you been? I've been trying to get a hold of you."

"I just got in and was about to call you. What have you found?"

"Ax *is* alive. We have proof. He was spotted."

My skin crawls. The temperature in the room seems to have dropped twenty degrees. Goose bumps blanket my flesh. The world stands still, then whirls into oblivion. "Holy shit!" I right myself to a slumped sitting position on the floor. My spine, having gone jelly-like, is barely able to support me. Princess licks a wayward tear that leaks from my eye. Her action reminds me to breathe.

"Sally? Sally! Are you still there?" Doc's voice sounds as if it's far away. And, in fact, it is. I look down and realize my hand lays limp in my lap, the phone barely within its grasp.

I have to force my mind to tell my fingers to curl around the handset. The effort is extreme. It takes forever for me to raise it to my ear. "Ye—" I choke on my words, clear my throat and try again. "Yes, I'm still here," I manage. "When did you find out?"

"Early this afternoon. I tried calling as soon as I heard. I've dispatched a surveillance detail to keep an eye on you. And another to keep an eye on Molly."

I don't respond at first. The news is all-consuming. My brain feels as if it's liquefied and is leaking through a sieve. I struggle to recapture some of it before it all spills through. Princess sits by my side, my arm wrapped around her. Her closeness gives me strength, and I manage to form a cohesive thought. "I have a bad feeling about this," I say, not sure whether I utter the words to Doc, Princess or myself.

"Everything's gonna be all right," Doc says.

His words don't reassure me. How can they? I know Ax. How slippery he can be. "Where is he now?" I ask.

There's a long delay, and then Doc replies, "We don't know. It's like he's disappeared into thin air."

"He's good at that. *Real* good."

"Don't worry," Doc says. "He won't get past our surveillance teams. I've pulled my best officers for the job."

"Okay," I say, knowing in my heart that an entire SWAT team couldn't stop Ax. He's too elusive.

"I'll personally check in with you each day," Doc says.

"Thanks," I reply before hanging up.

# CHAPTER TWENTY-NINE

## Waiting Until....

I'm afraid to go to sleep that night. Afraid of what my subconscious mind might reveal to me in the form of more premonition dreams. I stall, reading a novel well into the night. Turn in, exhausted, just before the sun rises.

When I awake, it's afternoon, and I'm disoriented. I lean over the side of the bed and pet Princess. She raises her head, licks my hand and then flops her head back. Apparently, she's had as rough a night as I have.

I don't leave the house that day or Sunday. Looking out the front picture window, I can spot the surveillance team Doc has placed on me. I pick up the phone a thousand times to call Molly. See how she's doing. If she's aware of the surveillance team that's watching *her* every move. But I don't. What's there to say? I don't think she'd talk to me in anything other than her creepy new cryptic manner.

Besides, I feel that to openly address it with her would only speed things up. And so I resign myself to a mindset that no news is good news. Every time the phone rings, I jump. When the postman rings the doorbell for a signature on a package delivery, I almost don't answer it. Then I remember Doc's team just outside and muster the courage to go to the door.

Sunday creeps by at an unnaturally slow pace. I find myself dialing the Time operator throughout the day just to make sure my clocks are working. By late afternoon, I relax a bit as I watch shadows, cast by the lowering sun, inch their way across the walls. Princess and I eat dinner. I relax further, settling into a sense of security that Doc's team has managed to foil Ax's plans.

Finishing the dishes, I look at the wall clock. It's just about time for the evening news. I dry my hands and let Princess out one last time. I stay with her until she's done and then bring her in, triple checking that I've locked the door.

She follows me into the living room. I go to the window and am relieved when I spot the silhouette of the surveillance team's vehicle. Allowing the curtain to fall back into place, I grab the remote and turn on the TV. Princess curls by my feet as I settle myself onto the sofa. The lead story is just beginning. A grim-faced anchor solemnly looks at the camera and tells of a senseless murder. My skin pricks seconds before they flash a still photo of the victim. There, filling the entire screen, is Molly, smiling back at me. I recoil from the image.

Holy shit! Holy fucking shit! He did it. Oh, my God! Ax killed Molly! I feel my stomach retch and barely make it to the toilet.

Exiting the bathroom, I hear the phone ring and pick it up. "Have you seen the news?" Doc asks.

"I just did. What the hell happened?"

"Don't know. I've just finished debriefing the surveillance teams that were watching her."

"And…?"

"Nothing. Like you, she was at home all day. They didn't see anyone enter or leave the house."

"They obviously missed something. Ax was there. I know it! He killed her…just like she said he would. Like in her dream. What about me? Am I next? I…I can't talk about this right now," I say, hanging up.

# CHAPTER THIRTY

## Lead Story

Ax leans back in his chair and grins at the report the news anchor is covering. It's the lead story.

*Lead story. Like that.*

As the anchor goes over the details, Ax reflects on how thorough his homework had been. He'd taken his time, studying each of Sally's students. Followed them. Watched their mannerisms. Wanted to be sure to pick just the right cunt. The one whose death would have the biggest impact on Sally.

Almost from the beginning, he'd set his sights on Molly. He'd noted how she dripped of insecurity. And he knew that trait would compel Sally to care about helping her the most. He could envision Sally going to extra lengths to pull Molly out of her pathetic shell.

*Aw, how touchin'. Fuckin' bleeding heart. So predictable. That'll be your downfall. But for now, it cost that bitch her life.*

Ax sighs heavily, basking in the afterglow of Molly's murder.

*Of course, it was creepy how the cunt knew my name. Seemed to know I was coming for her.*

At first, he'd thought she might be a bore to kill. Offer no resistance. But in the end, just like all the rest, she'd livened up. Come out of that wallflower shell of hers.

*Put up a good struggle.*

Ax reaches over and picks up a snapshot from the end table. It's of Molly. Eyes open. Mouth agape, forever frozen in a tortured scream. Ax smiles, warmed by the memory.

# CHAPTER THIRTY-ONE

## So, He Really Did It

After hanging up, I sit there for a long while, Princess alongside me. I stroke her fur in an attempt to calm myself. "Damn, girl! Can't believe he killed her." What am I thinking? Of course he did. This is Ax. He can't be stopped. A shudder runs down my spine, and I can't help but wonder. Who's he gonna set his sights on next?

I look down at the phone still in my hand and dial. It takes only a couple of rings before Angel picks up. "Hello?"

"Hey."

"Sally? Just saw the news. That woman who was murdered, wasn't she one of your students?"

I fill my lungs with air in an attempt to...I don't know. Brace myself? Gain courage? I exhale and then say, "Yeah. That was Molly."

There's a long pause on the other end. "Holy shit!"

Hearing her state my own thoughts, I'm suddenly exhausted and lean forward. Rest my face in my hand. I remain that way for several moments while collecting my thoughts.

"Talked with Doc?" Angel asks.

"Just got off the phone with him."

"What are you gonna do?"

"Nothing."

"Nothing?! Give me a break. There's plenty you can do—*should* do."

"Such as?"

"Stay inside. Bolt the damn doors. Don't answer them for anyone, no matter what!"

"Angel, you can't be serious. I'm not gonna become a prisoner in my own house."

"Will if you're smart. Besides, won't be forever. Just till they catch Ax."

I take a deep breath and say, "Appreciate your concern, but I won't let fear of what might happen cripple me. If Ax is determined to get me either directly or through others, he's proven he can."

"Fine!" Angel says. "If you won't listen to reason, then at least promise you'll be careful."

"I will."

"What about Doc?" Angel asks.

"He's gonna keep working the case. Locate Ax. Bring him in. In the meantime, I'm gonna call my students and cancel tomorrow's class. Not up to it. Bet they're not either."

"Probably best. Let me know what happens. Okay?"

I hang up and go up to the studio where I retrieve my students' list of phone numbers. Calling each of them proves painful. Some have heard of Molly's death and are in a state of shock. Others I have to break the news to, and their stunned silence is…. But I manage.

Princess, normally eager to go for a walk, doesn't pester me to go for an evening walk. She knows I'm not up for it. Not tonight. When it's dark. When *he* could be out there. Waiting. Lingering. Watching.

I check to be sure the doors are locked, click off the lights and head upstairs where I draw myself a bath. Several minutes later, I slide into a protective cocoon of bubbles. The scent of lavender surrounds me, yet barely registers.

An hour later, despite it still being relatively early, I find myself in bed, reaching for my journal.

*He got her—Molly. Ah, Molly…. Why you?*
*Of all my students, you'd come so far.*
*You'd started out so…abbreviated. Everything*
*about you reeked of it. Like you felt you*

*were the biggest burden on the world. And then, with my help, you began to open up. I was just beginning to see the amazing woman within you. Why couldn't we finish what we began? What we both wanted- needed? You to be whole. You reminded me so much of myself. Wanted to fix you. Down deep, I knew that would finish my own healing process. But now.... Ax. That bastard robbed us both. What the hell am I gonna do? Acted all brave to Angel. I'm anything but. This has gotta stop. Ax has to be stopped. Can't imagine ever seeing him again. What would I do? What would I say? What would he do? Oh, fuck!*

I close my journal. Put the cap on my pen. Reach over and pet Princess goodnight before turning off the light. I lie there, hoping sleep will overcome me and wash away the tremors of trepidation within me. Instead, I find myself staring at the ceiling.

# CHAPTER THIRTY-TWO

## Oh, My God!

I awake in the morning. Sunlight, streaming through the cracks of the closed blinds, warms my face. I lean over and see Princess sleeping peacefully beside me. She looks content. Glad someone got a good night's sleep. Not me. Tossed and turned the whole night.

I lie back in bed and close my eyes. Progressing through my morning stretches, I feel the stress of the previous day's events in my aching muscles. I replay my conversation with Angel and grow angry. I won't let Ax control my life again. I can't.

Princess gets up and nudges my hand with her muzzle. An idea teases my mind. I toy with it. Should I? Is it safe? Fuck it! I'm not gonna hide. Not again. This time I'm taking control.

The thought complete, my mind's made up. I look at Princess and say, "Hey, girl. Wanna go for a hike today? Should ease my stress. You know, fresh air, exercise." Princess barks.

An hour later, I'm caffeinated, we've eaten a light breakfast and we're driving to Chantry Flats—my favorite hiking spot. On the drive, I replay the reactions of my students to Molly's death.

Pam, usually so vibrant, had sounded flat as if all emotions had been drained from her. Alicia slipped into her old self. Conversing with her was forced. Through halting dialogue, she told me she'd seen the news. I could hear her light a cigarette and take drag after long drag, rapidly exhaling smoke in between. Trish had reacted tersely, stating she'd never really gotten the chance to get to know Molly due to her being so withdrawn. Carol, the most pragmatic of the bunch, tried to assess what may have happened. Who might have been responsible. If there was anything Molly could have done to protect herself. I made it a point to cut my conversation with Carol short.

I pull into the parking lot and within minutes, Princess and I are descending the steep slope to the base of the canyon. With every step, I can feel my burden lessening. I inhale the sweet scent of pine mixed with other indigenous plants. Princess and I cross the stream and veer to the left where we come to a fork in the trail, leaving behind the wide path and hikers.

We venture up a path that leads to Mt. Wilson. I look at Princess. "Long or short hike?"

She cocks her head.

"Can't decide, huh? Me either. How about we play it by ear?"

Princess wags her tail.

Within minutes, the trail becomes steep and narrow—only about two feet wide. Some places are narrower, causing us to concentrate on our steps. The distraction is good. The sheer edge of the mountain is to our left. A thousand-foot drop falls to our right. Princess, eager to see what's ahead, takes the lead as we walk single-file. Every once in a while, I stop to appreciate the view.

We climb and climb. There's a vast canyon that spreads away from us with the tops of its majestic pines rising above the land like razor stubble. The sky's a brilliant blue. Not a cloud in sight. The sun's rays fall upon us and warm our skin.

I feel relaxed. Calm. In my element. Here I'm at peace with the world and don't allow thoughts of Molly or Ax to weigh me down. This is my time—to process all that's happened.

We twist and wind our way up the mountain. Off to our right, the crashing of water can be heard far below. We've risen above the top of one of the waterfalls. I stop to look over the edge and see a collection of people below. I see an elderly man, sitting on a large rock. Several children, their shoes and socks off, splash in the lagoon at the base of the falls. Their laughter resonates against the steep canyon walls, and I can't help but smile at their enthusiasm. I stay there for a bit, my bird's-eye vantage point offering me a clandestine view.

Princess grows restless, and we continue on our way. The trail becomes steeper. The drop-off to our right more formidable. We continue another mile or so before the needle-thin radio towers atop Mt. Wilson come into view. Just then there's a fork in the trail. If we hang to the right, we'll continue up to Mt. Wilson's summit—a good hike. I look at Princess and ask, "Wanna go?"

She wags her tail and barks.

We continue on. It feels good to put distance between us and other hikers. Up here, we have the whole mountain to ourselves. I relish the peace and solitude it provides. Makes me feel untouchable. All thoughts of Molly and Ax have long since been left behind.

Princess and I make it about halfway from the fork to the summit before hunger gets the better of me. Damn! I wanted to make it all the way to the top. Knowing it's a long hike to our car, I head back the way we came, Princess trotting in front of me. As we near the fork, her body stiffens. Her head lowers. She slows her pace. I feel it, too—the change. Something's not right.

I look over my shoulder. The trail is clear. Up ahead, there's a sharp bend. Princess's ears perk forward. Her tail, until just a minute ago wagging, is now dropped in a straight line, almost motionless. She hunches her shoulders down. A shudder begins at the base of my neck and travels the length of my body.

I stop and pull back on her leash. She turns and comes to me, placing herself in front of my body. I know this stance. She's protecting me. I squat down and wrap my arms around her. "What's wrong, girl?"

She turns and faces the trail ahead. I feel the muscles in her body tense. A slow growl emits from her. Every fiber in my being tells me to avoid turning that bend. My mind scrambles for a solution. I look behind me. What I see is daunting. A long steep trail that leads to the summit of Mt. Wilson. The chances of coming across anyone on it are near nonexistent.

To our right is the sheer side of the mountain. To our left, an unimaginable drop. Shit! We're trapped. Why'd I come here? Bad idea. I hug Princess tighter. My heart's threatening to burst from my chest. And although my blood's racing, I'm very, very cold.

Princess, who had been leaning against me, bristles and pulls away. Her whiskers push forward. A low grumble of a growl pours forth its warning. Her lips blow little puffs of air in between. And then it happens.

She lunges forward, barking and snarling. I'm dragged with her, refusing to let go of her leash. She manages to pull me along a good eight feet. I'm so preoccupied with struggling against her leash that I don't notice what's captured her attention.

"Princess, no!" I plea. "Stop!"

That's when I hear it—the voice I'd hoped to never hear again. My blood turns to ice at the sound of it.

"Princess," it says. "So that's the bitch's name. Should've fuckin' killed her."

Slowly, I raise my eyes, terrified at what I know stands before me. Of whom. Ax.

Oh, my God! I gasp for air. My knees threaten to give out. Princess, in a frenzy, tries to get to Ax, a black version of a Paul Bunyan complete with a cinched-in waist and muscle-clad body. He creates a formidable barrier. I pull on her leash, but she's too strong and breaks free. In horror, I watch as she rushes Ax, who calmly approaches her. She launches herself to attack and manages to sink her teeth into his leg.

"You fuckin' bitch!" he snarls, reaching out to grab her leash. Gives it a quick jerk. Suspends her above the ground as blood begins to soak through his pants. She releases her bite and struggles and kicks against the noose of her choke chain as it shuts off her ability to gasp for air.

My eyes fall upon Ax's face, one I hoped to never see again. The gunshot wound that was supposed to kill him horribly disfigured it. The hairs on the back of my neck stand at attention when I notice the dark clouds in his eyes. I watch his face grow stormy. I know that look.

He swings Princess to his side, hovering her over the thousand-foot drop.

I lunge forward, desperate to save her. "No!" I scream.

Ax smiles. Princess kicks and flails. "That's the last time the bitch'll bite me," he says. His eyes lock with mine, his menacing, mine pleading. He pauses. Smiles. And then he releases his hold on Princess' leash. She disappears from sight.

"*Noooo!*" I cry. I rush to the edge and drop to my knees, praying to see her. I do, on a ledge far below. Her body lies motionless. I strain my eyes to catch a glimpse of any signs of life. Oh, my God! Did her rear leg just twitch?

My heart swells. Though my legs feel unstable, I get to my feet, square my shoulders, whirl around and take a step toward Ax. Don't want him to see my fear. Not that he can't smell it. He's uncanny. Knows when he's triggered fear. Delights in it.

Ax grabs a handful of my hair and yanks me up to his scarred face. "You fucking bastard!" I yell while pummeling his chest with my fists.

Ax lets go of my hair, pins my hands at my sides and leans down, his face even with mine. "Do I have your full attention?"

"Yes," I growl through clenched teeth.

"Good! Time we have a little chat. You know, catch up."

# CHAPTER THIRTY-THREE

## You Bastard!

Ax gives me a shove. I stumble backwards, lose my footing and rake my back against the jagged mountainside.

"Lot's happened since you left me," he says. "Suppose you heard about me and Leonard."

"Who?"

"The twin brother of the pimp I killed when your motha fucka brat got in the way."

I narrow my eyes. "He didn't get in the way."

"Fuckin' brat was always underfoot."

"If that's so, why'd you hold him hostage every day? Why not just let him be with me?"

"Come on, bitch. You're smarter than that. Holding onto him made you work your debt off to me."

"Debt?"

"Yeah, you fuckin' cost me a fortune not working those six weeks."

Pulling myself away from the rock wall behind me, I approach Ax. "Well, pardon me! I was busy having a kid, my body ripped apart and trying to recover so you could pimp me out some more."

"That's why the little bastard had to pay."

I begin pacing. My blood boils. Tears fill my eyes. I fight to contain them. "That *bastard*," I choke on the word, "was my son. He had a name, Eric Angel. He was an innocent little boy who didn't deserve to be your prisoner, treated like something expendable."

"Ha! He *was* expendable," Ax says, laughing, the corners of his mouth curling into a cruel sneer. "Proved that, didn't I?"

I lose my battle of withholding my tears. Their moisture burns my cheeks. I stop pacing but don't respond. Visions of my beautiful son fill my mind. His brilliant eyes—so full of life. His contagious laugh—that of my brother's. His enthusiasm for life. How he made me try harder. Want to be a better person. A better role model.

A memory of how he loved to watch squirrels flashes through my mind. Marveling at their tightrope act on the telephone wires, he'd say, "Mama, look. I wanna do that."

I'd ask, "Do what, baby?"

Always the same, it was then that my son would turn his attention from the squirrels he loved and look me in the eye. His were hypnotic. Clear. Wise. In them was knowledge that no little boy should possess. His eyes would bore into the center of my soul, and he would say, "Be free. I wanna be free like they are."

My heart would shatter with his words.

Then he'd ask, "Mama, do you ever think we'll ever be free?"

I choke back my pain and glare at Ax.

"That's what I thought," Ax says. "Now where were we before that brat of yours came into the conversation? Oh, yeah, my run-in with Leonard. For three days, he and his muscle tortured me. Then they shot me in the face. Left me to die."

"Too bad you didn't," I hiss.

In an instant, I feel the back of Ax's hand across my face. My head snaps to the side from the impact. His words slice through me. "Fuckin' cunt! Remember your place."

I resist the urge to rub my face where I can feel the welling up of Ax's hand impression. I cross my arms over my chest in an act of defiance and glare at the man before me. "Place? I don't have a place. Not with you. Not now. Not ever!"

Ax throws his head back and laughs. "Really? Is that what you think?"

"That's what I know!"

"Thought you could just walk out? That there wouldn't be any consequences?"

"There weren't."

Ax takes a step closer, and despite my resolve to not, I recoil.

"Guess again. With me, there are *always* consequences. Leonard and his muscle found that out the hard way. *Really* enjoyed 'taking care' of them. By the time I was done, each was begging for his life. Yeah, *enjoyed* ignoring that request. And with you, there have been consequences. Think about it."

The harsh realities of Ax's words sink in, as visions of finding Princess poisoned at the foot of the stairs and hearing of Molly's death fill my mind. I stare at the man before me. He has no soul. Never did. He cares not about the wake of misery he leaves behind him, only that it serves his purpose.

I dare to look him in the eye and say, "That was pretty fucked up, poisoning Princess and killing Molly."

Ax's face erupts into an evil grin, one that makes me shudder. "Now *those* were fun. But only the most recent in a long stream of contact I've had with you. Come on, bitch. Think. You can come up with the others."

I flinch, narrow my eyes and take a step back. "What are you talking about? I haven't had any contact with you since the day Angel and I fled."

"But *I've* had contact with those close to you."

I don't respond. My mind whirls on hyper-speed, trying to make sense of what he's telling me.

"Let's start with your husband."

"James?"

"Was that his name?"

I remain silent. A storm of warning flags rain down in my mind, as I fear what Ax will reveal.

"How'd you like the little *souvenir* I gave him?"

I tilt my head, confused.

"You know, that scar down the side of his face."

"That was you? *You're* the one who attacked him?"

I remember getting called by the hospital that James had been mugged. Me sitting alongside his hospital bed, waiting, hoping and praying that he'd wake up. Trying to calm my stomach when it threatened to retch when I saw the angry patchwork of green, black, purple and yellow bruises that covered his face. Trying not to flinch when I saw the jagged scar that extended the length of the side of his face, despite the best effort of a top facial plastic surgeon.

How many times did I caress that scar, grateful that I still had my husband? Wondering who could have been so cruel. Never imagined Ax. Shit! And now, standing before me, I see the man responsible. "You bastard! Why? Why would you hurt James?"

"To serve as a reminder."

"Of what?"

"That I'm always here. Watching you. Waiting. Scrutinizing your every move."

"But I didn't know that was you."

"Do now. And the look on your face—priceless. How fuckin' dare you think you could just walk away? That I wouldn't track you down. I own you, bitch!"

My head reels from the reality that Ax is the one who mugged and then carved James' face. Oh, my God! He was watching me? All that time? All the while I thought I'd been rid of him. That I was safe. And James had to pay for my leaving Ax?

I'm pulled from my thoughts when I hear Ax's voice. "What about the care package you got on the three-year anniversary of your brat's death? Like it? Have a nice binge? Should've been enough there."

I flash back to finding the unmarked brown package containing a three-day crack supply and pipe on my front porch.

"That was you?" I ask. "Always wondered who could have been so heartless. Should've known."

I recall how I'd taken the package and its contents and gone to meet with my sponsor, Claire, and how good I'd felt when we tossed it in the nearest dumpster.

"No, I didn't binge." I spit the words at Ax and stand a little taller. "I'm stronger than that."

"Really? Didn't seem so strong when your baby died a few days after you gave birth to him."

My mind fills with images of an intricate webbing of lifesaving tubes pumping fluids in and out of my second son. Of how he, James Charles, Jr., having been born three months premature, had struggled to cling to life.

I close the gap between Ax and myself in a few decisive steps. "Don't you dare speak of my son! You had nothing to do with him."

Ax looks down at me while crossing his arms over his chest, a bemused smile adorning his face. "Sure about that?"

I recall how James Charles, Jr. had been gaining strength each day. Of how I'd been in the room with his father at the time that the monitors had inexplicably shrieked their alarms. Wait. My son *had* been getting stronger. All the hospital staff said so. And then.... No. Can't be. Ax couldn't have had anything to do with *that*. It was just a terrible tragedy. But what if he had? What if my son could still be alive?

Ax uncrosses his arms and begins circling me, like a lion its prey. "Let me jog your memory. Remember that new orderly, the one who checked on your son earlier in the day?"

I recall the images of that day, forever seared into my psyche. The one that initiated cataclysmic events that forever altered my life. I picture the orderly's face and how the regular nurse, Anne, had questioned his presence. I turn and look at Ax who's now behind me.

The scarred remains of his face contort into a satisfied smirk. "Ah, you do remember. Yeah...he was a friend of mine. Owed me a little *favor*. Did a good job of repaying his debt. Wouldn't you say?"

The reality of what Ax has just revealed makes me stumble backwards. Feeling as if I've been kicked in the gut, I double over and gasp for air. Oh...my...God! My baby. My beautiful son. Another beautiful son. Ax killed him? He killed *both* my sons. What the fuck!

I rush at Ax and pound his chest again as I scream, "You bastard!"

Ax grabs each of my wrists and holds them with a vise grip. "Yeah, thought you'd like that," he says. "Just another way to help you remember. Making my point?" he says, forcing my hands down to my sides.

I raise my eyes and look at him but make no response.

My mind flails against the truths he's revealed. Every tragedy.... My most significant heartaches.... My first son shot and killed. I can barely bring myself to think of how Ax disposed of his body in a shallow grave in the mountains. And my adoring husband. Attacked and forever scarred by Ax's cruel hands. James *hated* that scar. Made him self-conscious of the ones he bore on his chest and thighs from the car fire that had claimed both his parents' lives—him being the only survivor.

The pounding of a headache begins between my temples, and I grimace when I think of my second son. So vulnerable. Struggling for life. Fighting to be with his daddy and me. I feel my stomach flip and then retch. I clamp my mouth shut, unwilling to give Ax the satisfaction of seeing how he's affecting me.

Yeah, Ax, he's the epitome of evil from the core of his being. There's no good in him. No hope. Ax is just...*Ax*.

The intricate pieces of the puzzle Ax's been carefully constructing over the past seven years fall into place. I see it all. How he had been watching me. How I'd been lulled into a false sense of security, believing that he'd been killed. How I went on to live my life. How I'd unwittingly placed others in his crosshairs. How I'd wondered a thousand times how one person, me, could be the recipient of so much seemingly unconnected tragedy. But there was nothing random about any of it. The monster standing before me orchestrated it all.

My hands ball into fists at my sides, and I grind my jaw at the overwhelming totality of this awareness. Every muscle in my body tenses, wanting to destroy Ax. The final piece of the puzzle slips into place, and I say, "It was you who slashed my tires that day."

Pleased, Ax smiles. "Not as satisfying as sinking that same blade into your husband's face and ripping it open—but close. And the look on your face when you came out.... Kept getting better—you walking around your car, realizing *all* the tires had been slashed."

"That *was* you I saw in the knit beanie, rounding the corner."

Ax exhales. "Yeah, hadn't planned on you spotting me. Did get you thinking, though, didn't it?"

I scrutinize the man before me and choose my next words carefully, uncertain of the response I'll get. "So, what's next in this little game of yours?"

Ax smiles. "Thought you'd have figured that out by now, bitch."

"Why don't you tell me?" I say, keeping my voice steady.

"One loved one at a time, cunt. That's how I'm gonna get to you.

One loved one at a time," he says, shoving me again. I lose my footing and fall to the ground. He grins. "And that cunt, Angel, and your mother…. I'll save them till last. Make you sweat that out." He kicks me hard in the side and then turns and walks away without another word.

The wind having been knocked out of me, I clutch my side and gasp for air. My eyes fall upon his receding back. I pull myself into a sitting position and attempt to steady my breathing. In. Out. One breath at a time. My breathing returns to normal. There. Better. Much better.

My mind struggles to digest all that I've just learned—what Ax's responsible for. Of all that's happened. It's then I remember. Oh, my God! Princess! I clamor to my feet, clutching and grabbing at fistfuls of dirt in the process. I run to the edge where Ax had released his hold on her leash and peer over. There below is the ledge. Or is it?

I look from side to side, trying to get my bearings. That's the spot, but Princess is nowhere to be seen. With a mixed cocktail of elation and dread, I scan the area, desperate to find my dog. Where is she?

# CHAPTER THIRTY-FOUR

## What's Next?

I continue to scan the area where I last saw Princess. I see a path that leads down away from the ledge where she fell. It's the only way off the ledge and is partially concealed by treetops. But it looks as if it leads to the houses below where the trail forks. I take a final look and then take off running down the trail. My side, where Ax kicked it, burns and makes running difficult. I end up lurching along at an awkward lope. I navigate my way across narrow passes, desperate to find Princess.

She's got to be okay. Right? I mean, she was on the ledge. And then she wasn't. Thank God for that ledge! Had to have moved on her own accord. No one was down there. I know Princess. She'd do anything to get back to me. To save me. To get at Ax. Even if it meant having to go the long way back.

She's gotta be heading to the bottom. If I could just go faster. But what if she's too injured? Oh, God! What if the effort to get back to me is too much and she collapses? Will I find her? Shit! Should've taken more time to map out the trail. Don't know if I'll be able to find the right one when I get to the cabins.

I pick up my pace, clutching my side to stem off the pain. Every breath feels like a knife stabbing into my side. At one narrow passage, I slip on loose gravel and almost pitch over the side. Slow down. Won't do Princess any good if I fall over the ledge.

Seems like forever before I see the fork up ahead. I glimpse a gathering of hikers. They appear to be circled around something. It's then that I know. Gasping for air and with my side on fire, I double my speed and bolt toward them, calling, "Princess! Princess!"

Some of the people turn to look at me—the mad woman descending upon them. A man looks from me to the form on the ground and then back at me again. Our eyes lock. Unspoken words pass between us. He clears an opening just as I arrive at their circle.

I see her, Princess, lying on the ground. I drop to my knees beside her, desperate for a sign that she's okay. That she *will be* okay. A thousand images of her pass through my mind. Angel and me finding her, as a young pup, abandoned in the box at our condo in Vegas. Luigi, Mama Pearl and the rest of the gang at the strip club rallying around her and making her the club's mascot. Discovering the softer side of Luigi as he spoiled her rotten with custom food dishes, plush dog beds and bejeweled dog collars. Of the many hikes I'd been on with her. Of how she'd been there for me—always. And now it's my turn.

I lay my hand on her side. The only words I can muster are, "Princess. Come on, girl."

With those simple words, all my hopes and fears and ambitions spring to life. This is my baby. My heart and soul. The one constant that's been there with me through thick and thin. I've told her all my secrets. And she's listened, patiently. She's heard me rant and rave when the world gets me down. She's allowed me to bury my face against her strong neck when I've cried endless tears. She's made me laugh when all I thought I could do was cry. She's shored me up and given me time and space when I needed them. In my darkest hours, she's given me a reason to get up each day. To keep trying. To forge ahead in hopes of achieving something better. I can't imagine an existence without her. Don't want to.

Beneath my hand, I feel her side raise and then lower—a labored movement, hitching and halting. She raises her head and looks at me.

She's alive! My heart soars. I wanna drape myself across her and hug her tight but resist the urge, fearful that it might complicate her injuries. Instead, as I've done a thousand times before, I scratch behind her ear. She lets out a contented sigh and lowers her head, looking exhausted. I drop mine to where our faces meet. I stroke her face and muzzle. Within me rages a storm of disconnected and conflicting thoughts. Thank God, she's alive! That bastard, Ax. How fucking dare he! At the thought of Ax, I hear someone say a ranger's on the way. Moments later, one arrives, a woman in her early forties. What am I gonna tell her? How will I explain?

The ranger introduces herself and asks if I'm the owner. I tell her I am. She asks, "What happened?"

My mind spins and reels on hyper speed, attempting to come up with a plausible explanation that'll keep Ax's involvement out of it. I can't mention him. For all I know, he could still be watching me. No, I've gotta keep silent about him, at least for now.

"We were hiking the trail to Mt. Wilson," I say. "Princess slipped and went over the edge. Tried to hold onto her leash, but she was too heavy. She landed on a ledge below where I couldn't get to her." I pause to stroke Princess' face. "Didn't know what to do. Got up and paced. A few minutes later, looked over the edge, and she was gone. Took off running and found her here."

My heart racing, I'm sure the ranger will see through my deception. I force myself to steady my breathing and make a silent prayer. To my relief, the ranger accepts my fabrication and offers to drive Princess and me back to our truck so I can get her to a vet. I take her up on her offer. Once at my truck, we load Princess. I thank the ranger and head out.

I wind and drive my way down the mountain road, mindful of Princess who is lying on the seat beside me. Once we hit a straight stretch, I call Angel. When she picks up, I rush to tell her what's happened—the truth. She's stunned. Tell her I'm on my way to the vet with Princess. She agrees to meet me there. When I pull into the parking lot, I see her car.

As I get out of the truck, she rushes to me and gives me a hug. "Sally girl, I'm so glad you're okay. When you told me about Ax—"

"Let's get her inside."

"I let them know you were on your way. They're waiting."

Angel helps me carry Princess into the pet hospital where we're met by an orderly who shows us into a room. We lay Princess on an exam table. Her breathing is ragged. Her eyes closed. And her nose, always a shiny black, has taken on a dull, dry appearance.

A few minutes later, a vet enters the room. I tell her what happened—well, the version I told the ranger. She examines Princess, who barely moves, and tells me she'd like to take some x-rays. I agree. Angel and I wait while they take Princess to prep her.

No sooner does the door close behind them than Angel turns and says, "Holy crap, Sally. Tell me everything. You...*saw*...Ax? *He's* the one who did this?"

"Yeah. Said he's been watching me ever since we left him."

"But Doc said he was *dead*."

"Apparently not. Still alive and as big a bastard as ever. Princess tried to protect me. That's when he dropped her over the ledge. What he told me next was terrifying."

"Can't imagine what's worse."

"How about finding out that he's been responsible for *every* tragedy that's taken place in my life since the day I left him."

"How?"

I look at Angel, not wanting to worry her, but knowing I have to tell—everything. When I'm done, she sits there, a stunned look of disbelief and horror upon her face. Long minutes pass before she says, "Holy shit! We've gotta *do* something. Stop him."

"Yeah, I know. But first, I'm gonna concentrate on Princess. Then I'll go to Doc and tell him what's happened."

"Sally, I'm scared. What you've told me...it's creepy, even for Ax. I knew he was dangerous, but this proves he's—crazy."

Just then, the vet reenters the room, several x-ray films in her hand. She crosses to a backlit box on the wall, turns it on and slides the first film in. She points to a spot on it—Princess' right front leg. "Do you see it? There's a break." Not waiting for a response, the vet replaces that film with another, of Princess' chest. "And there," she says, pointing, "she's broken a couple of ribs." The vet turns to look at me. "One of which punctured her lung."

"Oh, God!" I say.

"She needs surgery to repair the damage to her lung." She slides that film out and puts up the one of the broken leg again. "And with this," she says, pointing at the film, "I'm going to have to use a plate and pins."

My chest heaves, and I force myself to ask, "Will she be all right?"

The vet clicks off the display and looks at me with compassion. "There's no reason to believe that she won't be able to fully recover. But it's going to be a slow road back, and the surgeries won't be cheap."

"Cost doesn't matter. Whatever it takes to make her better."

"All right then, but she'll need extra care after."

"Again, whatever it takes. Just *please* make her better. She's all I've got. I couldn't bear to lose her."

The vet smiles. "She'll be fine."

With those words, images of others stating the same about my dead brother, dead husband and dead son fill my mind. A shiver overtakes me.

Angel, reading my thoughts, wraps her arm around my shoulder and gives it a squeeze. "This time's gonna be different, Sally girl. You'll see. Princess is gonna be fine."

I look at the vet. "Can I see her?"

"Of course. I'll have one of my technicians take you back."

Angel remains in the exam room. I follow the tech, winding and turning through the hallways until we see her. Princess lies on an x-ray table, asleep. The tech explains how they had to anesthetize her to get clear shots.

I go to Princess and stroke her side. I lean into her ear and whisper, "Come on, girl. Fight. For you. For me. For us. And to defeat that bastard, Ax!"

I give her a final hug and am led back to the room where Angel is. After having signed the necessary forms, I leave Princess at the pet hospital.

In the parking lot, I look at Angel and say, "I need to call Ma and let her know what's happened."

"Might be better in person."

"Hmmm…probably right."

"Want me to come with?"

I look up at my friend, my rock. "Would you?"

"Sure. I'll follow you there."

"Hey, Ma," I say into the phone on the drive to her house. "Okay if Angel and I stop by?"

"Sure. Everything okay? You don't quite sound like yourself."

"Princess got hurt. I just left her at the vet's. They're gonna have to do surgery."

"What happened?" Ma asks.

I resist the urge to blurt everything out. "I'll explain when we get there."

"O…kay. Drive safe, honey."

Ma's words are like an embrace. I smile. "I will. See you in a few."

Arriving at Ma's house, I let Angel and myself in. "Hey, Ma, we're here," I call out.

"In the kitchen," she says. "Just put on a fresh pot of coffee. Come on in."

Over two pots of coffee, I tell her everything that's happened. In between stunned silences where the color drains from her face, Ma manages to regain her composure enough to ask questions. I answer them as best I can. But the ones she poses about what we should do…. All I can do is respond, "Need to tell Doc what's happened. All that Ax confessed to."

"Doc's got to offer you better protection, then," Ma says.

I look first at Angel and then to her. "It's not me who needs protection."

There's an uncomfortable silence. No one knows what to say, aware that the words I've spoken ring true. A short time later, Angel leaves, the three of us having decided to meet at the police station in the morning.

Ma and I talk for a bit, and then I ask, "Would it be okay if I stayed here tonight?"

She looks at me, full of compassion. "Sure, honey. Your room's made up. Stay as long as you want."

"Thanks. Can't bring myself to go home to an empty house. Not tonight at least."

# CHAPTER THIRTY-FIVE

## Things are Looking Up

I sit in the reception area of the police station, waiting with Ma and Angel for Doc to come out. The station's abuzz with energy. Officers come and go. Some carry files. Others escort individuals to their offices. What I see before me is an expanse of navy blue.

After what seems like forever, I look up, deciding if I should remind the receptionist that we're still here. Just then, an officer heads our way. "Sally?"

"Yes?"

"I'm Inspector Kowalski, Doc's partner."

He offers his hand. I shake it and say, "This is my mom, Gloria, and my friend, Angel."

Dan nods at them. "Nice to meet both of you. Doc said for me to bring you back."

We follow him round a corner and Dan raps his knuckles on Doc's open door, saying, "Okay if we come in, pardner?"

Doc sees us and gets up. "Come in, please." He motions to chairs that Angel, Ma and I settle ourselves into. Dan leans against the doorjamb.

Doc looks at me and says, "If you don't mind, would you please recap what you told me on the phone? That way we'll all be on the same page."

I take my time outlining all that I learned from Ax in Chantry Flats. Of how he'd been stalking me and been responsible for all the tragedies I'd endured over the past seven years. Of how Ax delighted in crucifying me with each new revelation.

I tell how I don't think they'll be able to catch him. How he *always* manages to stay ahead of the law. Don't know how he does it. Wish I could figure it out so I could bring him down. But he's unstoppable. Seems that whatever Ax wants, he gets. And what he wants most now is to hurt me. Strip me of everything I hold dear.

As the thought enters my mind, I have to fight hard to push the images of two dead sons, a mutilated husband, Molly murdered, Princess poisoned and then being dropped off that cliff out of my mind, lest I dissolve into a puddle of tears. That won't get us anywhere. Right now what we need is to put our heads together to come up with a way to trap Ax. A way to best him at his own game.

"With Ax, you're gonna need your best officers," I say. "He'll run circles around any inferior ones. Even your finest will have their work cut out for them."

"If what you say is true, then it would appear Ax is good at what he does," Doc says. "Especially managing to stay off the radar for the past seven years."

"Clever man," Dan says. "But not infallible. Every crook gets sloppy sooner or later."

"Not Ax," Angel says. "He's made an art out of fucking with people and not getting caught."

"That may have been true in the past, but we found some evidence that he might have been in Molly's house," Doc says.

"Really?" I ask. "What?"

"A knit beanie, matching the description of the one you saw the person wearing as they rounded the corner, after you discovered your car tires had been slashed. Our lab's running tests on it now."

"Detective Jones," Ma begins.

"Doc, please."

"Doc, when Sally came to you after Molly approached her, you offered both women protection. That didn't help Molly. And now Ax has threatened all those close to my daughter."

Angel says, "Scary as hell how he's known everything about Sally, those close to her, and how you knew nothing about it."

"Exactly," Ma says. "So what are your current plans for protection?"

Doc says, "Things are different now. Until the incident with

163

Molly, we weren't aware that Ax was even alive, having thought he'd been killed. And even after the Molly incident, we weren't certain that Ax was behind everything. But now, with the discovery of the beanie and Ax having approached Sally, things are different."

"Don't worry," Dan says. "We'll get him."

I let out a heavy sigh. "I'm not sure Ax is getable."

"Trust me," Dan says. "Even the elusive Ax can be caught."

We talk a bit longer. Dan and Doc ask questions and attempt to answer the ones Ma, Angel and I pose to them. By the time we leave, I'm feeling a bit better. And although I know it's probably foolish, I sense the slightest glimmer of hope that maybe this time Ax will screw up, and we'll be able to get him.

Ma, Angel and I stop at a café on the way home. There, over a light lunch, we discuss our visit at the station, our concerns and how, overall, we feel somewhat better.

Later, Ma drops Angel at her house and then heads to mine. "Honey, sure you're fine with going home?" she asks. "You're more than welcome to stay with me."

"Thanks, Ma. Appreciate the offer. I'll be okay."

She pulls up to the curb. "All right, but if you change your mind, just come on over."

"I will," I say, leaning over to give her a hug.

My phone begins to ring when I'm closing the front door. I hurry to the kitchen. Pick it up and say, "Hello?"

A pleasant-sounding woman greets me and tells me that she's calling from the animal hospital where Princess is.

My breath catches, and I ask, "Is everything all right?"

"Yes. I was calling to let you know that Princess' surgery went well. She's in recovery now. The doctor wanted me to call to inform you that she'd like to keep Princess here for a few days of observation."

"But I thought you said everything was okay."

The woman's voice takes on a soothing tone. "It is. The doctor would like to keep a close eye on her. You can pick her up Friday."

Relaxing, I say, "Okay. The doctor indicated that extra care would be required. What's that entail?"

The woman tells me the particulars, and we agree that I'll get Princess on Friday. Wow! Feels like a massive weight's been lifted from my shoulders. Princess is coming home! She's gonna be okay! That bastard, Ax, didn't get her—close, though.

My mind flashes to Ax, dangling her over the cliff. I push the memory aside, refusing to allow thoughts of Ax to dampen my happy mood. I reach for the phone and call Angel and then Ma to share the good news. Both are thrilled. It's decided that they'll come over Friday night to celebrate.

I hang up and set about readying the house for my baby's return. The woman from the pet hospital had mentioned that it might be challenging for her to navigate stairs, at least for a bit. As I prepare for Princess' arrival, my soul soars more with each task completed.

I move Princess' bed downstairs. As I grasp it, her scent is released. I smile at its familiarity. I place blankets and a pillow for me in the entry closet. Know Princess. She won't stand to be separated from me. I'll sleep downstairs with her until she's healed enough to go up and down the stairs. I set my travel toiletries in the downstairs bathroom, knowing that it will comfort Princess to be able to lie outside the door while I get ready. Next, I bring down a few outfits and hang them in the office closet. That should do it. Now the only time I'll have to go upstairs will be to teach my class on Monday. I'll watch Princess over the weekend. See how she does. Then I'll make a decision as to how to leave her downstairs while I go up to teach my class.

A few hours later, my phone rings, and I hear Carlos' voice on the other end. "How have you been?" he says.

"Okay."

"Just okay?"

"It's been kind of hectic."

"I wondered if that was the case. Left a couple of messages but hadn't heard back."

"I'm sorry," I say. "There's been some…stuff going on."

He waits, not pressuring me. Like that, his patience. Calms me. Gives me courage to proceed. And I do. I tell him all that's been happening.

When I'm done, there's a long pause. I fear he may be deciding the best way to get off the line. Instead, I hear him say, "I'm so sorry for what you're going through. I'd wondered why you hadn't made contact or returned my calls since our date last week. Now I know why. At least, I hope that's the reason."

I smile. "It is. Everything just got so…. What with the appearance of Ax and then Molly…. God, it's all such a mess. I can't believe I brought this on everyone."

"Stop that!!! *You* didn't do anything. Ax is at fault."

Hearing Carlos' reassurance, I smile. His words bathe over me like a gentle caress, enfolding me in their safety.

"Appears you could use a break," he says. "Let me take you out tonight. Away from your worries. To a place where the only things that matter are the two of us."

My brows knit together, and I have to swallow back the lump that forms in my throat. "Even after knowing everything, you still wanna take me out?"

"Of course."

"I would have thought you'd flee in the other direction. You know, too much to deal with."

Carlos' next words make me melt. "I like you," he says. "The fact that Ax has hurt someone I care about…that doesn't make me want to flee. Instead, makes me want to wrap you in my arms and protect you. No. I'm not going anywhere, unless you tell me to."

I'm unable to speak. How did I get so lucky? How do I express my gratitude? Where did this compassionate man come from? How can I share just how much his words affect me? I can't. I know these aren't the best circumstances under which to pursue a relationship, but I'm drawn to Carlos. To his strength. His compassion. To the amazing calm he casts over me. I don't know how he manages, but in his presence, I feel my universe slip into alignment, even now. I like the sensation. Makes me feel—complete. Whole. Something I haven't felt since the day James died.

"All right," I say.

"I have the perfect place to take you.  One where you'll forget your troubles and get lost with me." Carlos' smile jumps through the line.

"Sounds perfect."

# CHAPTER THIRTY-SIX

## The Ebb and Flow of the Waves

A short time later, my doorbell rings. I rush to the door, bag in hand, to find Carlos with a broad smile. "Hello, gorgeous," he says.

He reaches over and places a delicate kiss on my lips. His touch is gentle, as if it's not even there. The minute our lips meet, I feel an electric surge of passion pass through me. I lean against him and wrap my arms around him, responding to his kiss with a more insistent one of my own. We remain lip-locked for what seems like forever. Time and space cease to exist. And with each ticking second and beat of my quickening pulse, my worries of Ax fade into oblivion.

Carlos pulls back and looks at me. He doesn't say anything at first. No need to. The expression on both our faces speaks volumes.

"Ready to begin our adventure?" he asks.

"I am."

"Got everything?"

I hold up the bag.

He grins, and his eyes sparkle with a boy's charm. "Good. Let's go, then."

We navigate the highway with the top of his convertible down. I lean my head back, close my eyes and smile. A second later, I'm drawn from my bliss when I hear Carlos ask, "What are you thinking?"

I open my eyes and turn to look at him. I let out a contented sigh and say, "Appreciating how wonderful tonight is."

"It is perfect."

Carlos exits Pacific Coast Highway, turning into a private drive. He pulls up to a guard kiosk where a man says, "Hello, Mr. Vortez.

Good to see you again."

"And you, Mark."

"I'll buzz you right in."

"Thank you. Have a good night."

"You, too, Mr. Vortez."

I look around. Carlos navigates the car through charming streets, lined with immaculate quaint houses. "This is nice. Live here?"

"I wish. My family's vacation house is here. They come down on the weekends."

"Ah, so we have it all to ourselves," I say, laughing. "Am I to presume, Mr. Vortez, that you have illusions of taking advantage of me?"

"No, unless, of course, you want me to. My intent was to take you somewhere private, away from the rest of the world, where we could get lost in the roar of the ocean and be lulled by her waves."

"Sounds perfect."

"I'd hoped you'd think so. You seemed like the type who would appreciate a night stroll along the beach and a moonlit picnic dinner alongside a bonfire."

"You're quite the romantic."

As we turn into a driveway, a charming single-story house stands before us. Its siding is painted light grey with white trim that accentuates its wood-paned windows. Reminds me of pictures I've seen of homes in Cape Cod. We get out of the car. Carlos leads the way into the house, holding the door open for me. We pass through an expansive living room and are drawn to a rear balcony with an impressive view.

Carlos opens a sliding door, and a salty breeze greets us. I precede him out to the balcony where I rest my arms on the railing. I take a deep inhale and allow my gaze to wander the length of the beach below. A few individuals are still bodysurfing. And others dot the sand, lying on bright-colored beach towels. My vision passes beyond the breakers. "Oh, look," I say, clapping. "Dolphins! See them?" I point in their direction.

"I do," he says, smiling at my girlish enthusiasm.

"I adore dolphins! Have for as long as I can remember. Eric, Ma and I used to make a game out of seeing how many we could spot while at the beach." Although I'm still looking at the dolphins, I can feel Carlos' eyes on me, taking in my every gesture and fascination. I turn to him. "Can we go down?"

"Do you need to change first?"

"Already got my suit on," I say, revealing my bikini top strap.

We descend a staircase that spans the side of a steep cliff and make our way down to the sand. Halfway there, Carlos turns to look at me. "Back at the house, you mentioned that your mother, Eric and you used to watch dolphins. Who's Eric? Haven't heard you mention him before."

A thousand images of lazy days spent at the beach with my baby brother flood my mind. They don't make me sad or cringe as they once did. Now I gain comfort in being able to recall the time we shared. Of the many waves we rode together. Of the endless tide pools we explored. Of the shell collecting we did, comparing our bounty at the end of the day. Of the sandcastles we'd spend hours making, patiently sprinkling sand spires upon our masterpieces, only to beg our mother to be able to stay long enough to watch the surf wash away our efforts.

To Carlos, I respond, "Eric was my little brother."

"Was?" he says, stopping and taking my hand. "I'm sorry."

"It's okay. Happened a long time ago."

"You don't have to tell me if you don't want to."

"No, it's okay. We were teens, celebrating my having just gotten my driver's license. I drove us to the beach that day. Had fun, catching one good set after another, until the last wave. It was bigger than either of us expected. Caught us off-guard. We over-paddled and pitched over the top—headfirst. I got out. Eric wasn't so lucky. Broke his neck when his head hit bottom. Couldn't move. Took in too much water. The official cause of death was drowning."

"That's terrible. How awful for you to have to go through that alone."

"Yeah. Messed me up for a *long* time. But finally came to terms with it."

Carlos puts down the basket he's holding and wraps me in an embrace. The spicy scent of his cologne comforts me, and I press against him. My head rests against his chest. I hear his heart *thump thump thumping*. I like that. It soothes me. He hugs me for a bit before pulling away. He picks up the basket, and we walk side-by-side, my hand clasped in his.

I like how neither of us feels the need to fill every moment with endless chatter. There are times, like now, when the solitude of silence is a welcomed friend. Wish more people knew how to enjoy quiet moments. So much needless talk ensues between people.

We make our way down to the beach where he lays out a blanket near a fire ring. He sets the picnic basket atop and turns to look at me. "Want to go for a walk?"

I tilt my head and penetrate his soul with my eyes. They communicate my appreciation. "I'd like that."

We remove our shoes, roll up the legs of our jeans and head off in the direction of a large rock formation farther down the beach. Moist sand squishes between my toes, and I wiggle them in delight. Occasionally, the water rushes at us too fast and splashes our pant legs as it runs over our feet, ankles and calves. We don't attempt to get away, though. Just allow the water to go where it will.

Carlos wraps his arm around my waist. We fall in step with one another, and I lean against him. We talk about this and that. Then I say, "I have something to confess," not looking at him or slowing my pace.

"You do?"

"After that first time when I saw you in the parking lot of the market—"

"When I rescued your runaway onion?"

"Yes. Well, I saw you another time."

"When we decided to go on a date?"

"No. There was another time." This I say hoping he won't stop and look at me.

"Why didn't you say hi?"

"I was gonna, but then…. Well, there was this little boy. He ran up to you with a bunch of bananas and called you Daddy."

"Ah, you must have seen Anthony, well, Tony. He's my son."

"You didn't mention you have a son." I stop and turn to look at him. "I feel awkward asking, but where's his mother?"

Carlos stops and lets out a sigh. "No need to feel awkward. It's a natural question. Anne—that's his mother—didn't seem to take to motherhood or being a wife, for that matter."

"What happened?"

"Just before Tony's first birthday, she left us. She filed for divorce and gave up her parental rights."

I clasp Carlos' hands in mine and say, "That's awful! I've never understood how anyone could walk away from their own child."

"Me either. But that's what she did. Anyway, Tony's a great kid—my best bud. He doesn't remember her. Someday I'll have to explain everything to him. But he's too young now."

"Is he about four?"

Carlos smiles, the proud smile of a father devoted to his child. "Yeah, just had his fourth birthday last month. How about you? Any kids?"

We turn and head back toward our blanket. On the way, I share about Eric Angel and James Charles, Jr. and the events that surrounded their deaths. By the time we arrive at the blanket, neither of us has much to say. A silence befalls us as we sit, lost in our own thoughts, watching the ebb and flow of the waves.

Nothing calms my mind as quickly and as thoroughly as the ocean. Within minutes of gazing over its expansive surface, I'm lulled into a deeply relaxed, almost hypnotic state. With each crashing of the waves on the shore, truckloads of stress and negative energy melt away, leaving me feeling calm, tranquil and at peace.

The ocean lures me. Lulls me with its melodic harmony of swells rising to waves and then crashing against the shore. Gazing out over its expanse, I instantly know my place, my insignificance in the universe, and I submit to its power and grace.

Everything that surrounds its glory and splendor is never the same. No two waves, no pod of dolphins, cluster of seals or reverent gathering of surfers is identical. Each has its unique footprint. I never tire of drinking them in. I revel in filling my mind with all of them, as the static of my brain is turned off, replaced with the symphony of the ocean.

As the sun begins to dip in the sky, I turn and look at Carlos. "Let's go for a swim."

A devilish grin warms his face. "Before we eat?"

"Sure. Why not?"

"Aren't you supposed to wait thirty minutes between the two?"

I laugh. "That's an old wives' tale. Besides, that's only for swimming *after* you eat."

"In that case, sure."

We strip down to our suits and head for the waves. Carlos runs full-force at them and dives under one. I take my time getting wet, luxuriating in the way the water feels as it wraps around my body. Carlos comes up behind and scoops me up in his arms.

"Hey!" I protest.

"Time for you to get wet," he says, grinning and heading toward the waves.

"*Noooo!*" I cry, just as he plunges both of us under the water.

He has a secure hold on me and pops us up on the other side. "Now, that wasn't so bad, was it?" he asks, placing me back on my feet.

I splash water at him in a playful gesture. He reciprocates. Before long, we're engrossed in an all-out water fight and helpless to stop laughing. After, we ride a few waves. By the time the sun appears to extinguish itself where the horizon meets the water, Carlos and I head back to our blanket. He sets about starting a fire to warm us and asks me to lay out our meal.

The fire springs to life, and Carlos joins me. We dine on lobster pate that we spread on butterfly-shaped crackers, havarti cheese with dill, fresh berries (which we feed to one another), and a delicious cabernet sauvignon. The wine makes our cheeks glow in the flames. We cuddle, me sitting between his legs, my back to his chest. His arms encase me and make me feel protected.

"What are you thinking?" he asks.

"What made you want to become a personal trainer?"

"Actually," he says, "that's how I met Anne. She was one of my clients. And I'm thrilled I got Tony out of the deal. I've always liked working out, and being a trainer works out well with having to play Mr. Mom. I can make my own hours, for the most part, and when I need assistance, my parents live close by and help out." He looks at me. "How about you? How long have you been dancing?"

"As far back as I can remember," I say, as visions of my brother and then Angel and Eric Angel and I silly dancing fill my mind. "When I moved back here from Vegas, I saw an ad in the paper for a Hip Hop dance instructor at the Community Center. I applied and got the job."

"Do you like it?"

My face lights up. "I love expanding people's boundaries through dance. It's so rewarding to see their truest selves emerge through the expression of dance. And then, a few months back, I got the crazy idea to help women boost their self-esteem through a pole-dancing class."

"Why pole dancing?"

"Well, I used to be one."

"A stripper?!" Carlos asks, unable to conceal his surprise.

"Yeah. Saw a lot of women overcome their shyness and self-confidence issues through becoming pole dancers."

"Really?" Carlos says. He looks at me for several long moments before saying, "So, ever do anything about your class idea?"

"Started a six-week class with five students. Well, I *had* five students, until Molly.... Have our final class this coming Monday."

Carlos smiles a broad grin, similar to an overly enthused Cheshire cat. "Now *that* would be something I wouldn't mind seeing."

"I'll bet. Sorry, you can't. They're private lessons."

"Darn. How's it working out? Accomplishing what you wanted?"

I beam like a proud mother. "Yeah! Each of them has come *so* far. I'm proud of their efforts and enjoy seeing who they're evolving into."

"*Evolving* into?"

"Who they were meant to be before life, circumstances and garbage got in their way."

Carlos and I talk long into the night. Wrapped in a blanket and warmed by the fire, we stay cozy. We talk about everything and nothing. About our hopes and dreams. About life's disappointments and immeasurable joys. We talk about our relationships with our families and what true friendship means.

By the time the last ember of the fire flickers out, I feel as though I've known Carlos my entire life. He shares that he feels the same. We're amazed by how paralleled our lifestyles, lives, philosophies and passions are and can't help but wonder where the other's been hiding. Why our paths haven't crossed before now.

We gather our stuff and head back up the stairs. At the top, I wrap my arms around his waist and say, "I'm so glad we didn't allow our hormones to get the better of us at the dance club. Wouldn't have been right. Would've cheapened the experience. But now...."

Carlos pulls back and grins, "Are you implying what I think you are?"

I don't answer. Instead, I engage him in a passionate kiss. When we pull apart, there's urgency to his step as we return to the house. We barely make it to the door before we begin heavily stroking and kissing one another. He fumbles with the keys. I fumble with his belt. He manages to get the door open just as I undo his pants. They fall to the floor. He steps out of them and frantically slides his hands under my top and pulls it over my head with one hand while cupping a breast with the other. The whole while, we're standing in the doorway— door still open. We step inside. He kicks the door closed. Our breathing is ragged. We struggle to grope, kiss and disrobe one another as we head to the bedroom. A trail of shed clothing marks our path.

# CHAPTER THIRTY-SEVEN

## Far From Over

I awake Friday morning, happy as can be. Today I get to bring Princess home from the vet's. I've missed her so much. Not having her as my constant shadow felt...wrong, like I've been out of sync. Funny how we can grow so accustomed to someone being such an integral part of our lives that we don't notice the daily impact they have on us—until they're not there.

Each morning I awake and lean over the bed to say, "Good morning," to Princess. It's only when I see her empty bed that I remember my companion won't be there to flank my side. That I won't be able to share my thoughts with her. That I won't be able to rub behind her ears. But all that changes today. She's coming home!

Although it's only been a week, I know the pet hospital must be getting tired of my calls. I've checked in with them every day to follow her progress. Most days, I'm connected to Trish who's willing to take the time to fill me in on how my baby's doing, the little things she knows I'll appreciate, the ones the other staff members don't think important enough to share. I still can't get over that Trish is such an animal lover. That she has a soft side. Each time I talk with her, I'm left wondering who's more excited about Princess' recovery—her or me?

I hustle through my cat-like stretches and then get up, eager for the day to progress. I look at the clock on the nightstand. It reads 8:00 AM. They told me I could pick Princess up at four. I can wait that long. It's only eight hours. I go to the bathroom, wash my face, brush my teeth and apply makeup. I use these rote tasks to help slow me down. To curb the frustration I'm feeling with having to wait so long to get Princess.

I pad my way to the closet and pick out an outfit to wear to teach my Hip Hop class. I can already feel that it's gonna be a warm day, so I select a pair of three-quarter length leggings and a sleeveless top. I pull my hair back in a ponytail and take a moment to admire my reflection in the full-length mirror.

The smile I feel in my heart about being reunited with Princess is evident on my face. It's erased the worry lines—caused by everything with Ax—that have etched my forehead. My eyes look brighter today—more full of hope.

Still can't get over how I never used to be able to look myself in the mirror—too unhappy with who I saw reflected back. Glad that's all behind me. I eye myself and approve of what I see. I make my way downstairs where I grab a mug of coffee and a yogurt before heading out the door.

At the Community Center, I enter my classroom where an assortment of middle-aged women has begun to gather. Most are mothers who have dropped their kids at school, grateful for the break. I'm surprised to see Carol from my pole-dancing class.

"Hey, Carol," I say. "What brings you here?"

"Thought I'd fit in some extra 'me' time. You mentioned this class," she says, lowering her voice and looking around, "and I thought it might enhance my pole dancing. It's okay that I join, right?"

"Absolutely! Glad to see a familiar face. You'll find this class to be a lot easier. But one will help the other."

Carol smiles and takes her place with the other women. I watch her during class and can't help but be impressed by the new woman she's become—the confident playful one my pole-dancing class released from within her. This Carol stands in sharp contrast to the one who walked through my door five weeks ago. I think about how closely correlated my own growth is to that of my pole-dancing students. How, as they evolve, so do I, bolstered by the good I'm doing. When class ends, I approach her. "So, what do you think?"

"You were right. It was easier. Enjoyed the fast beat and pace of the dancing. Different from the one at your studio. I think I'm going to enjoy this class."

Gathering up my things, I smile. "See you Monday?"

"I'll be there."

I run several errands, grab a bite to eat and stop at the market before heading home. Once there, I tidy the upstairs and clean the living room. As I walk past an end table, I lean down to inhale the aroma of a spring bouquet that Carlos sent to me after our evening together at the beach. Visions of that night, of our getting to know one another and of our passionate lovemaking fill my mind.

He'd been the kind of lover I'd thought he'd be. Gentle, yet commanding. Loving and attentive, yet insistent. Passionate. Satisfying.

I think of how we never made it to the bed. Our needs overrode our patience, and we ended up collapsing onto the floor of the master bedroom where we entangled as one, revealing the secret treasures of the other. Our first time making love had been near animalistic in our frenzy to fuse with one another. After, we lay together, my back nestled against his front, his arms encasing me.

I close my eyes and can almost still feel the warmth of his body against mine.

We'd rested and then opened a bottle of wine that we shared as we talked about our lives. It warmed my heart that he hadn't been put off by my having been a stripper. Instead, as we lay there spooning, he'd asked me questions, which I answered. I didn't feel ashamed telling him about my time spent on the stage. And when he asked what it had felt like to strip while dancing, I was inspired to show him.

The master bedroom had a four-posted bed with tall vertical posts that I twirled and wrapped myself around as I danced to the music that played in my head. All the while, I seduced Carlos with my eyes, conveying my deepest desires. I didn't feel shy about sharing that part of myself with him and, to his credit, he didn't look at me like a slab of meat but as a valued human, willing to express herself to him through the art of dance.

When I finished, he stood and came to me where I knelt on the bed. He swept me up in his arms and climbed atop the bed himself. In a fluid motion, he laid me on the mattress and stretched out beside me where he traced his fingers across my body as if the sensations they felt were forever fusing me into his mind. I, too, took my time exploring his body, feeling its every curve and the tone of his muscles. The second time we made love, we lingered. Carlos was slow to build the momentum and whenever near the point of climax, his or mine, he'd back off, adding to our ecstasy, before building the heat again.

I think of how we made love throughout the night until the sun rose, never tiring of the other. Always awakening some new discovery—some hidden treasure of delight that needed to be explored. After our last lovemaking, we'd cuddled as one and fell into a deep sleep—one of sheer exhaustion and satisfaction.

The next morning, I'd awoken to the enticing aroma of the breakfast Carlos had cooked for me, one fit for a queen. When we finished eating, we took a stroll along the beach before he drove me home. Later that day, the flowers had arrived.

I stand from smelling the flowers and head to the kitchen where I clean the coffeemaker and set up a fresh pot to brew the next morning. The phone rings.

"Hello?"

"Hi, Sally, Doc here."

"Oh, hey, Doc. What's up?"

"I wanted to share the good news. He got sloppy—Ax."

I find myself holding my breath.

Doc continues, "I just got off the phone with our lab. They confirmed that the DNA on the knit beanie found at Molly's is Ax's."

Can it really be? The all-elusive Ax may have missed a beat? No way. Ax is *way* too smart for that. This has gotta be a setup. Part of some elaborate plan.

"When are you gonna pick him up?"

"We're not—yet."

"Not yet? When do you plan on getting him? What more does he have to do? You just said you have proof he was at Molly's."

"For now, we'll ask him to come in for questioning."

"You actually think Ax is gonna volunteer to come in and have a nice little chat with you? Do you have any idea who you're dealing with? Fuck *asking* him to come in! Wouldn't it just be better to go and arrest him?"

"We're gonna play this cool. Have him come to us. In the past, Ax was mighty sure of himself. Relished any opportunity to rub our faces in that we had nothing on him."

"Yeah, like with my son."

I think of how crafty Ax is. Would be just like him to flaunt things in the faces of the authorities. He's clever. Way more than anyone gives him credit for. But what if he *has* slipped up this time and given the police a way to catch him? To put him away. To get him the hell out of my life—once and for all. It wouldn't make right all that he's done, but....

I'm drawn from my thoughts by Doc saying, "We'll let Ax think he's in control until he's here and then...."

"So, you've got him?"

"I wouldn't wanna hedge any bets, but, yeah, we're fairly confident...at least for Molly's murder."

Thoughts of Ax's evasiveness crowd out my hope. "But how can you be sure? Ax is slippery. Look at all he's done to me, either directly or indirectly. And yet, you still have nothing on him for those. Probably never will. He's *that* good. And if you're not convinced, just look at how he managed to avoid being killed after being shot point-blank in the face. Point-blank in the face! Who does that? Gets up and walks away? I'm telling you, the man's unstoppable. His getting sloppy and leaving behind his beanie worries me. He's not that stupid. The fact that you found it and have been able to link it to him leads me to believe that he wanted you to. That it's all part of some elaborate plan he's got."

"You don't think that perhaps you're giving him too much credit?"

"Ax is *everywhere*! He knows my every move and those of people I care about—always has. Always will. He's proven that by what he told me up in Chantry Flats."

An image of Ax yanking Eric Angel from my arms as he still suckled my breast fills my mind. Eric Angel had protested being deprived of his feeding with loud cries. I'd begged to be allowed more time with my baby. And Ax...the look on his face...it had been of sheer delight at our anguish.

"Ax is a demon," I say, "who thrives off the pain, suffering and destruction of others. He's not human. Has no compassion. There's not a sincere bone in his body. And yet, you think he's gonna just come waltzing into the station because you *ask* him to?"

"As I said, he's done it before."

My blood boils, stomach churns and heart aches as old wounds, long-since scabbed over, are ripped apart. "And that got you, what? Not only were you unable to hold Ax accountable for my first son's death, but he stalked me, unmonitored, for all those years. And now you want me to believe that you'll be able to beat Ax at his own game. That's all this is to him, you know—a game. One where the pawns are real people."

I take a deep breath and exhale slowly. "I can't believe...no, I won't believe that you've beaten Ax until I see him behind bars. And even then...."

Doc and I talk for a few more minutes until an awkward silence fills the line, and I tell him I have somewhere I have to be. We hang up, neither of us satisfied with the way the call has gone. Doc meant it to be good news, but every fiber of my being is screaming that things are far from over with Ax.

# CHAPTER THIRTY-EIGHT

## Good to Have You Home, Girl!

I hang up with Doc and place calls to Angel and Ma, who are just as skeptical of the news about Ax as I am. We keep our conversations brief, agreeing that we'll talk more when we're together. It's decided they'll arrive at five, enough time for me to return from picking up Princess.

I look at the clock on the oven and realize it's time for me to get her. I'm so excited! I grab my purse, keys and run out the door. A minute later, I'm back to get my shoes. Can't believe I forgot them.

On the drive to the pet hospital, my mind replays my conversation with Doc. Memories of Ax, his savagery and ruthlessness, fill my mind. I try to block them, but they threaten to flood my consciousness like a burst dam. In a desperate attempt to drown out my thoughts, I turn on the radio.

Music always calms me. Takes me away from whatever troubling event I'm enduring and transports me to a place where I can let my guard down—a bit—to take a few cleansing breaths. I flip through the stations before landing on one that's playing a song I like. One with a base beat heavy enough to drown out the oppressive memories of Ax.

Pulling into the parking lot of the pet hospital, I feel better as I've managed to stuff the foreboding memories of Ax back in my mind's file cabinets and have closed and locked their drawers.

I remove the keys from the ignition and take a deep inhale. I'm slow to let the air out. With it passes the last remnants of my stress. Thoughts of being reunited with Princess make me smile, and I head inside.

Trish's face brightens when she sees me. "I know someone who's gonna be *real* happy to see you."

"How's she doing?"

"Moving a bit slower than normal, but she should be fine. Might wanna keep her off stairs for a few days, though."

"Have everything set up so the two of us can stay downstairs."

"I'll go get her," Trish says, taking Princess' leash from me.

What seems like an eternity passes, and then I hear it, the *click click clicking* of Princess' nails on the linoleum flooring. She rounds the corner and nearly pulls the leash from Trish's hand when she sees me. I rush to her. Eager to wrap my arms around her, I kneel but stop short. There's something that looks like a soft straw sutured into the lower part of her chest. I look up at Trish.

She sees my worried expression and says, "That's just a drain tube from when we had to repair her punctured lung. We'll have you return in a few days to have it removed."

"Is she sore? Can I touch her?"

"She's fine."

As we've been talking, Princess has been snaking her way around my legs like an overenthusiastic cat. I kneel down and wrap my arms around her neck. The minute I do, she leans her whole weight against me. Surprised, I topple backwards onto my rear. Princess seizes the opportunity to place her right casted front leg in my lap, and she licks my face. I don't fight it. Laughing, I rub behind her ears.

Feels wonderful to be able to do that—touch her. Look at her. Enjoy her. I'll never take that for granted, not after all this. The file drawer in my mind cracks open a bit, and the image of Ax dropping her over the cliff tries to make its way to the surface. I don't let it. I won't allow that bastard, his image and beastly ways to taint my reunion with Princess. He has no right being in our lives and certainly not any of our happy moments. I'll deal with him later. But for now, this time is about my baby and me being reunited.

Greetings over, Princess steps off me but not before her tongue places a delicate lick on the tip of my nose. She stands back a bit and barks as if to say, "What are you sitting on your rear for? Get up! We have places to go!"

Trish and I both laugh. I get to my feet and am handed Princess' leash. She drags me toward the door. I try to pull back, to rein her in, but she's infused by a surge of adrenaline. Halfway through the door I say over my shoulder, "Can I call you once we get home to make that appointment?"

"We'll be here," Trish says, chuckling.

I help Princess into the truck. She settles on the seat beside me, head in my lap. I like that, the weight of her head pressed into me. Makes me happy. Evokes a new protectiveness in me. One that won't allow anything else to happen to her—no matter what. I pause to look down at her before starting the engine and think, my baby's back. My shadow's back! Tears well up in my eyes. I have to blink them away to see the road as I drive us home.

We arrive at the house, and I get Princess situated. She explores the downstairs and seems surprised to find her bed there. She looks at me.

I cross the room and stroke her fur. "Thought we could bunk down here for a few days. Kinda like a girls' sleepover."

Princess tilts her head.

"It'll be okay. I'll be right beside you on the sofa."

Hearing this, Princess lies on her bed. I position myself at the corner of the sofa, just above her, my feet tucked under me, as I read a book.

At five, Ma and Angel arrive and let themselves in. Princess gets up to greet them. They wince when they see her.

"Poor baby," Ma says, bending down to pet her.

Angel rubs behind Princess' ear with one hand and offers me a bottle of wine with the other. "To celebrate her homecoming," she says.

I take the bottle and look at the label. "Mmmm…. My favorite."

We head to the kitchen where I open the wine and pour each of us a glass, which we take (along with the bottle) to the backyard, followed by Princess. I start the bar-b-cue, and we sit at the patio table while Princess makes her way around the yard, refamiliarizing herself with it.

Angel takes a sip of her wine and says, "So, they think they've got

184

him—Ax?"

"That's what I'm told," I say.

"I don't believe Ax slipped up," Angel says. "He wants them to catch him."

"Why would he want *that*?" Ma asks.

I look over at Princess, who has just finished sniffing a daisy and is passing by the stairwell to the root cellar. She pauses and looks down the stairs as if remembering. Then she continues exploring.

Ma follows my gaze and says, "She's moving slower than normal. But I'm amazed at how well she's getting around."

I look at Ma. "Doc said they're gonna play it cool with Ax. Make him think they just wanna bring him in for questioning. That way he won't know something's up and try to disappear."

"Ax is good at that," Angel says.

Princess walks over to my gardening table. Under it, I have terracotta pots that are nested together. Something catches her attention in one of them, and she jams her nose down in it, toppling over the stack in the process. Several crack. A lizard emerges and makes a mad dash to escape her probing nose. Ma, Angel and I laugh as Princess hobbles after her prey like a peg-legged pirate. The lizard makes short work of outdistancing her and climbs the stone wall where it disappears into the neighbor's yard, the ones who don't have a dog.

A little while later, Ma, Angel and I make dinner in silence, each of us lost in her own thoughts. We resume talking as we dine alfresco. Ma takes a bite of her burger and chews. I can see it—her worry. It's always presented itself the same way. Deep worry lines crease her forehead and the corners of her eyes. She tries to relax them. Her effort is futile. I know her too well. She looks at me, sees that I've read her, swallows and says, "Do you think Doc can keep you... us...safe?"

I glance at Angel before answering. Our eyes lock momentarily, and pages of unspoken dialogue pass between us. I take a sip of wine and refill each of our glasses before saying, "No one's safe from Ax."

Ma scrutinizes me. "Then how come you look so calm?"

"Calm? I'm not calm, Ma. I'm scared to death." I scan the yard.

It's getting dark. I call Princess. Can't stand the thought of not being able to see her every minute. Of not being able to protect her. Of not knowing what lurks in the darkness. Princess comes and sits by my side where I stroke her fur, lost in thought. A few moments later, I look up at Ma and say, "I'm terrified that Ax will jump out from the dark corners and attack me."

Angel says, "But that's not his style—going after you. You know how he works." She looks at Ma and then back at me. "Tell her. Be honest."

I take a sip of wine and let out a heavy sigh as it warms a path down to my stomach. "Angel's right," I say. "Ax is cruel. He won't hurt me directly, at least not yet."

Ma tilts her head. "But I thought you—"

"He'll destroy each and every living being I hold dear. And when he's robbed me of everything, *then* he'll kill me."

There's a horrified look on Ma's face as the totality of my words sinks in.

"It won't be quick," I continue. "Or merciful. Not with Ax. He'll take his time. Enjoy torturing me. Reminding me of everything he's taken from me, and how much he enjoyed doing so. Then, when he's broken me, he'll kill me."

The color drains from Ma's face. I hate upsetting her, but Angel's right. She has a right to know. Just wish I could spare her somehow. No one says anything for a bit. Our meals are forgotten, our appetites lost. Princess lies by my side. The only sound that can be heard is the *thump thump thumping* of her tail. Like a metronome, it ticks away the awkward silence that's befallen us.

We finish the wine, and then Ma and Angel help me clean up. After, we head inside, closing and locking the door behind us. Ma and Angel stay a bit longer. We make idle conversation, each wary of broaching the subject of Ax again, lest any more harsh realities be revealed.

A short time later, Ma and Angel head home. I get in my pajamas and lie on the sofa, while Princess settles herself on her bed beside me. I replay in my head what I'd told Ma, wishing that there could have been a better way to tell her, to prepare her. But there wasn't. Not when Ax is involved. When he's thrown into the mix, nothing's easy. Things get messy. People get hurt. I hope Doc's able to get Ax before he strikes again.

I lean over before clicking off the light, cradle my head in my hand, and pet Princess. I take my time running my fingers over her soft coat. I caress behind one of her ears and then the other. Finally, I run my fingers down her muzzle and transfer a kiss from my fingertip to her shiny black nose. Her tail *thumps* the ground, and she starts to get up. "No, no, it's okay, girl. Lie still. Missed you." Princess looks up and then lays her head in between her front paws, indicating that she's ready to sleep. I take another moment to admire her before turning off the light.

# CHAPTER THIRTY-NINE

## Why So Many Poles?

Princess nearly drags me up the front porch steps, anxious to be home. Our walk this morning was good. Needed that. To get out. Connect with nature. Slow things down a bit. Spend some quality time with Princess. Though hindered by her injuries, she was eager as ever to try to chase squirrels up towering trees.

There's no chill to the air. Love days like this. Wish it could always be summer. There's nothing better than crawling out of bed and not shivering my way to the bathroom. And when it comes time for me to choose what to wear, I don't feel like I'm racing the clock to keep hypothermia from setting in.

I do love my house, but older homes can be drafty. Mine is one of those. Doesn't matter how much I turn up the thermostat in the winter, I still feel cold. Can't help but wonder how folks managed a hundred years ago. Weren't they affected by cold?

Princess, impatient, paws the front door.

"Hold on, girl," I say, struggling to get the door open.

Princess looks up and barks as if to encourage me to go faster.

"All right! All right, already," I say, directing my full attention to the door.

I manipulate the key in the lock, another quirk of older houses. The locks never seem to work smoothly. James used to say that our front door reminded him of his trying to get in his bachelor apartment. He'd say, "A little muscle, a little finesse and presto, in we go."

I feel the tumblers click into place. I look down at Princess and say, "Abracadabra," while swinging the door open and unclicking her leash.

She rushes inside, her casted leg making an awkward *thump* each time it connects with the hardwood flooring. She heads straight to her water dish in the kitchen where she settles in for a long drink. I'm right behind her and notice the light flashing on the answering machine. I depress the play button and am greeted by Carlos' voice. "Hey, beautiful! Hope your day is off to a great start. Want to make it even better? Give me a call."

Hearing his warm voice makes me smile. Princess, upon hearing Carlos, stops drinking and barks once. I look at her and ask, "So, girl, think I should call him now or make him wait a bit?"

Princess, hearing the playfulness in my voice, circles several times while barking loud enough to make the kitchen echo.

I dial the phone. "Let's find out what he's got up his sleeve."

Carlos picks up on the first ring. "Hey, Carlos. Expecting my call?"

"Hey, gorgeous!"

"*Oooo*, I'm moving up in the world. Have gone from beautiful to gorgeous. If I hang up and call back, will I get elevated to a whole new title?"

"You're in a good mood."

"Princess and I just got back from a walk."

"Sounds like it did you good. Interested in keeping that good vibration going?"

"Ah, you silver-tongued fox."

"Let's get together tonight. I want to see you."

"You do?" I say, the coyness in my voice not the least bit hidden. "We could get together. But it would have to be here. Don't want to leave Princess alone. Not just yet, anyway."

"How about I make things simple and bring us dinner."

"Mmmm...sounds great! How about five?"

"See you then."

"Hey there, girl," Carlos says, kneeling down to pet Princess, who wags her tail and manages to lick the side of his face. Carlos smiles and says, "I'm not sure I know you well enough to have you take advantage of me. Besides, my girlfriend here might get jealous."

Looking up at me, he says, "Wow, Ax really did a number on her."

We head into the kitchen, followed by Princess, where I help Carlos set the bags on the counter. "Smells wonderful," I say, taking a deep inhale.

"Hope you like it."

"Are you hungry now, or do you want me to give you a tour first?"

"Hmmm…." Carlos says, looking toward the living room and then at the bags on the counter. "Good food? Tour? Good food? Tour? I vote for a tour."

"You got it." I interlace my fingers into his, while heading out to the living room. I explain how Princess and I are bunking downstairs until she feels well enough to navigate the stairs.

"So, you teach your classes from here?" he asks.

"From the upstairs studio. Wanna see it?"

"Thought you'd never ask."

Still holding his hand, I head to the stairs with him walking behind me. I pause and look back at him after climbing a few steps. "You've been thinking about my shiny brass poles ever since my bedroom demonstration at the beach house, haven't you?"

Carlos doesn't answer, at least not with words. He raises his chin slightly, looks me in the eye, and it's then that I see all his truths revealed.

I raise my eyebrow, turn and continue heading up. We enter the studio. I let his hand go as I turn on lights and cross the room to watch his expression.

Here, in my studio, I'm in my element. I feel free. Calm. Myself. Able to express myself. Watching Carlos take it all in for the first time is a bonus.

He looks at the mirrored walls, raised center stage and toward the six shiny brass poles, glistening in the studio lighting. A sly smile begins to curl the edges of his mouth and by the time he takes in the poles, he's grinning widely. "Why so many poles?" he asks.

I reach out and caress the pole I'm beside. I lock eyes with him and run my fingers up and down it. I'm not nervous or shy. I convey the confidence I'm feeling as I cross to the second pole and place my free hand on my hip, caressing my cinched-in waist and curvy hips.

Wrapping my fingers around the pole with the other, I tilt my head in toward the pole, arch my back and circle it. Out of the corner of my eye, I catch a glimpse of the light reflecting off my auburn hair as it sways. I let go and sashay my way to the third pole. The whole while, I don't take my eyes off of Carlos, who I believe may have stopped breathing.

I reach the third pole and grab it with my right hand above my head. My left arm brushes against one of my breasts as I grab hold of the pole at chest height. Next, I raise my left knee and stroke the pole with the inside of that leg. I hike my leg up high on the pole and tilt my head back, letting my hair cascade down my back where it brushes seductively against the curve of my lower back.

Releasing that pole, I head to the fourth pole and spin around it. Then I make it a point to cross by Carlos and pause momentarily in front of him as I cup the side of his jaw with my hand. It's then I realize that he's still breathing or has just resumed. He takes a deep inhale and kisses the inside of my wrist.

I leave him and head to the fifth pole where I press the front of my body against it while grasping it with both hands overhead. I peek from behind the pole so I can see him and wiggle my hips ever so slowly to the music I hear in my head. I create an illusion of snaking my way down the pole by bending first one and then the other knee, still swaying my hips from side to side.

I depart that pole and head to my own, located at the center of the stage. I reach high over my head and grab it with first my right and then my left hand. Giving a little hop, I allow the tops of my feet to wrap around the pole. I shimmy my way, inchworm style, up the pole almost to the ceiling. Unable to help himself, Carlos approaches me like an insect drawn to the blue light of a bug zapper. I smile and wait for him to make his way to me.

He stands just below me. I surprise him by releasing my hands from the pole, legs wrapped around it, and gracefully arch my back as I bend down, my head approaching his. I summon him to me with a slow curl of my finger. He raises up on his toes—excited, expectant. I cradle either side of his face in my hands and kiss him long and hard.

When Carlos' breathing becomes ragged and his need insistent, I pull away. He's panting—hard. So am I. I smile and ask, "Now do you understand why there are so many poles?" in a husky voice.

I let myself off the pole. Carlos takes a step toward me. I playfully dodge him.

The look on his face is that of a sad puppy as he asks, "Why? Why would you do *that* and then step away?"

"But you brought that delicious-smelling meal downstairs," I say. "It would be such a shame to let it go to waste."

"I have no intention of letting that happen," he says, tracing a loving finger across the mask of freckles that splash across my nose and cheeks. "We'll eat after...."

"After?" I say, pouting out my lower lip. "I'm not sure I have enough energy after my show. How about we eat first and then maybe...."

"Maybe?! After a performance like that. Maybe? You're killing me!"

I smile at him and caress the side of his face. "Shhh...it'll be okay."

"I don't think you understand," Carlos says, wrapping an arm around my waist and pulling me close. "I'm in serious pain here."

I rise up on my tiptoes, place a chaste kiss on his lips and twirl away from him while saying, "Then I guess we'd better eat so we'll have energy for later...."

# CHAPTER FORTY

## Ax and Wayne

The phone rings several times. With each unanswered ring, Ax's fury grows. Four rings. Five rings. Ax snaps the pencil he's holding.

*Where is that motha fucka?! He knew I was gonna call. Where the fuck is he?!*

The phone's answered on the sixth ring.

"What the hell took you so long?!" Ax roars.

"I couldn't get to the phone right away."

"Why the hell not?" Ax growls through clenched teeth.

"Well," the man coughs on the other end, "if you really must know, I was in… the bathroom."

"Don't give a shit what you were doing!" Ax yells. "When I call, you…pick…up the god-damned phone."

"But—"

"No buts! Fuck! I've wasted enough time with you already. You have the stuff or not?"

"I…well…." the man squeaks. "Not yet, but I will," he says, his voice withering from Ax's verbal assault.

Ax paces back and forth in an effort to calm himself.

*I need this motha fucka. Least till I have the stuff, and then….*

A smile plays at the corners of his mouth.

"I…I'll have it for you by the end of today," the man says.

"I'll call you at eight. Don't disappoint!" Ax slams down the phone and paces like a caged animal.

*Everything rests on this fucker coming through. How the hell did it come to this? I don't depend on others. How could I've been stupid enough to leave my beanie at that cunt's? What the hell's wrong with me? Now I've got that motha fucka cop breathing down my neck.*

His ears still ringing from Ax yelling at him, Wayne stands dumbfounded for a minute before hanging up. He snaps out of his daze and looks at the clock.

*Don't have much time.*

On the drive to the station, Wayne grumbles half to himself, half to no one, "Can't believe I'm doing this. But I can't let it get out—not that I'm gay. Would be the end of my career at the station. How the heck did Ax find out?" Beads of sweat dot his forehead, and he wipes them away with the back of his hand.

*Get a grip, man. Can't go in there nervous. They'll know something's up.*

Wayne makes a conscious effort to breathe in until his lungs can no longer expand and then exhales, slow and steady. He almost grows light-headed from the effort but manages to regulate his breathing. His sweating slows.

A half a mile later, he sees the police station and pulls in the rear drive. He parks his car. Takes a few more calming breaths. Views himself in the visor mirror to ensure he looks calm. He grabs his ID badge and heads to the door, where he punches in the access code.

As he makes his way to his destination, he notes there aren't many people around.

*Good! Sundays are usually lighter days. Fewer people the better.*

A man walking toward him says, "Hi, Wayne."

As they pass, Wayne says, "Hey, Doug," in what he hopes sounds like a level voice not reflective of the battle raging within him, the one that has him wanting to puke or empty his intestines.

Doug slows his pace, scrutinizes Wayne and says, "You okay, man?"

Wayne averts his eyes, feigns a cough and says, "Coming down with something." He feels sweat trickle down his armpits and his back.

"Take it easy," Doug says, continuing on his way.

On the drive back to his place, Wayne keeps looking in the rear-view mirror to make certain no one's following him. Several miles from the station, convinced that no one's behind him, he relaxes.

*I can't believe I did it. Got everything. Ax will be pleased. Hope this is the end of it. Don't trust him. I want him out of my life!*

Wayne enters his apartment with fifteen minutes to spare. Setting the items on the counter, he goes to the kitchen where he pulls a bottle of whiskey from an overhead cupboard. He pours himself a finger's worth and tosses it back, shuddering as the bitter liquid burns its way down his throat and warms his stomach. He pours himself another two fingers' worth and goes to sit on the sofa. He eyes the items on the counter from across the room.

"Good lord!" he says, taking a sip. He places the glass on the coffee table, kicks his feet up and leans his head back, closing his eyes.

*Ax should be calling any time.*

As if on cue, the phone rings. Wayne answers on the first ring and hears Ax's baritone voice on the other end say, "Well?"

"I got it."

"Everything?"

"All of it."

"Meet me at nine," Ax says.

Wayne can hear the pleasure in Ax's voice and takes another sip of his drink. Ax gives him directions that he scribbles on a pad next to the phone. He hangs up and finishes his drink in celebration of having succeeded in his task.

*Just got to give the stuff to Ax. In less than an hour, all this will be over.*

Ax makes his way to the location, well acquainted with it, and arrives first. Stepping out of his car, he feels a sense of power wash over him. He inhales and admires the city lights far below. Then he lets out his breath.

Not long after, he hears the unmistakable sound of approaching car tires moments before headlights round the corner and come into view.

He puts his hand up to shield his eyes as Wayne pulls his car up alongside him. He watches Wayne get out. He narrows his eyes in bemusement, watching the manner in which Wayne reaches into the car to grab the items.

*What an idiot. If he'd just kept to fucking girls, none of this would be happening. But he didn't. Couldn't. Sex. Gives me leverage—every time.*

Wayne approaches and hands him a folder and the beanie. A hopeful smile pulls at his mouth. He says, "I also erased the computer file with the DNA results. So, this makes us even. Right?"

Ax doesn't answer. Instead, he snatches the items and views them by the light of the full moon. He takes his time to flip through each page of the hard copy file that contains the definitive match of his DNA to the knit beanie, which he crumples in his other hand. Satisfied, he places both items on the hood of his car and takes a step toward Wayne, who stiffens but holds his ground. "Not quite," he says.

In a flash, Ax produces his trademark hand-held hatchet from behind his back and, in one fluid motion, swings it low. It slices deep into Wayne's right calf muscle, and he smiles as he feels the blade graze bone.

Wayne's face contorts to one of agony. He collapses to the ground. Clutching his leg, he emits an animalistic howl. "What the—"

"Shut the fuck up, asshole!"

Wayne's eyes widen. His body rocks back and forth as he struggles to stifle his cries.

Ax says, "Wanna know how I feel about you?"

Wayne doesn't answer, too lost in the pain that threatens to override his mind.

"I asked you a question, motha fucka," Ax says. He kicks Wayne hard in the back of his calf, sending a spray of blood arcing through the air.

Wayne bellows his agony and scrambles backwards like a wounded animal, dragging his injured leg in the process.

Ax smiles and says, "Gotta tell you, motha fucka, your

screams…music to my ears."

"Wh…why?" Wayne manages.

Ax closes the distance between Wayne and him in two strides and leans down. "Didn't think you was gonna walk away, did you?"

"But…we had a deal," Wayne says, flinching from Ax's close proximity.

Ax throws his head back and roars with laughter. "We had a deal," he mocks. "You are the stupidest motha fucka I've ever met," he says. "And I've met quite a few."

Still clutching his leg, Wayne scoots farther back, smearing the ground with a trail of blood.

Ax kneels beside him. "Seems like you got a nasty cut. Here, let me take a look."

Wayne's efforts grow frantic. His good leg kicks up dust. His hands claw at the dirt. He tries to scootch farther away. Ax grabs his wounded leg with a vise-like grip. "Where you going?" He pulls out his switchblade, flips it open and leans in. Wayne eyes grow wide with terror. Ax takes a moment to enjoy Wayne's gaping wound. The muscle, sliced through, resembles that of a raw chicken breast cut in half. He jabs the knife into the exposed meat of Wayne's muscle, twists the blade and calmly asks, "Does that hurt?"

Wayne flails and screams. He tries to pull away from Ax and his probing knife. But Ax kneels on Wayne's leg with his knee. Ax cups a hand over Wayne's mouth and says, "Shut up, motha fucka!" He pauses for a minute. An evil grin spreads across his face. He produces a bandanna from his rear pocket and gags Wayne. When he's done, he shoves his knife deeper into Wayne's exposed muscle and carves out a chunk. "How about this? Does *that* hurt?"

Desperate, crazed, Wayne reaches toward Ax and claws at any part of his tormentor he can connect with. His nails rake a jagged path down the good side of Ax's face.

Ax stops his torture. His hand flies to his wounded cheek where he feels blood—his own—seep between his fingers. He narrows his eyes and bores them into Wayne with an intensity meant to make the man drop dead. "You motha fucka! Nobody hurts me and lives!" he roars.

Wayne's eyes widen like those of a cornered animal. With every ounce of strength he has, he struggles against the hulk of a man pinning him to the ground.

Ax reaches beside him and fetches his hatchet. Wayne's efforts of resistance rise to unbridled passion and his gag comes off as he struggles to free himself. Ax throws his head back and laughs. The sound is not human but one born of pure, malicious, evil intent.

He leans in so close that his face is directly in front of Wayne's and says, "Come on, motha fucka. Struggle some more. I like it when you fight. Gives me a *good* workout."

He raises his hatchet high overhead. Its blade glints in the moonlight and then stands frozen mid-air for a moment before coming down and slicing through Wayne's right bicep. Wayne shrieks. Ax smiles and raises his blade again and allows it to bite into Wayne's right shoulder and then thigh. Over and over the blade finds its mark, accompanied by Wayne's desperate clawing, shrill screams and pleas. With each new strike, fresh blood soaks the ground and splashes across Ax, driving him into more of a killing frenzy.

Long after Wayne's limp body has collapsed backward against the ground, Ax continues to sink his hatchet into the corpse, delighting in the sound it makes when its blade strikes bone. Sometimes he feels the bone splinter, and groans of satisfaction emit from deep within him. Finally, he grows bored. He gets off of Wayne and stands beside his shredded remains. From his rear pocket, he pulls a small camera and snaps a picture. Then, disgusted with how quickly his fun ended, Ax kicks his broken toy.

He steps over Wayne's body and heads to his car. From the trunk, he fetches a shovel and begins digging. Thirty minutes into his task, Ax pauses to look at a spot about fifteen feet away. He sets the blade of the shovel on the ground and rests his chin against the top of its handle, smiling.

Visions of the many times he'd been here fill his mind....

His gaze shifts to the next hill over. A dark cloud passes over his eyes. He recalls how the police had swarmed that spot when they found the remains of Sally's bastard son. He shrugs off his disgust.

*How ironic.  Thought they could catch me.  <u>That</u> didn't work out so good for 'em.  And if they find this body...they won't get me.  I'm Ax.  No one catches me!*

He laughs aloud.

*Don't know who they're dealing with.  What I'm capable of.  How many motha fuckas I've killed and scattered through these hills.*

Filled with a sense of triumph, Ax resumes digging.

# CHAPTER FORTY-ONE

## Not Again!

I awake in a pool of sweat. Heart racing. Breathing ragged. Body trembling. Beams of predawn light stream through the cracks between the curtains. I turn my head and view Carlos, still asleep beside me on the living room floor. Lying on his stomach, his arm's draped across my midsection. I slide from beneath it, careful not to wake him. Despite it being warm, my body is wracked with a shiver, and my head begins to pound with a headache.

Princess follows me as I make my way into the kitchen. It's there that the enormity of my dream hits me.

Oh, God! Not again. How?! How the hell does he always manage to do it? I lean heavily against the wall where I slide to a sitting position. I wrap my arms around my bare legs. Princess sits at attention by my side. I rest my head on my knees and attempt to recall the elements of my dream. Unlike those in the past or even more recent ones, this one seemed so much clearer—in a way.

There had been dirt. Tires crunching loose gravel. City lights below. And Ax. Oh, God—Ax!

My mind flails against the image of him. I hug my legs tighter. My fury rises to the surface over my hatred of the man who so completely turned my world on end. Robbed me of my youth. Terrorized me. Murdered my first son. My second. Attacked my husband. Tried to kill my dog—not once, but twice. My mouth twists into an unconscious snarl.

In my dream, Ax was smiling. Happy. Held hidden knowledge. The image terrifies me. Nothing but the total annihilation of another makes Ax that happy. There was another man. Though his face was partially obscured, I swear I've met him before but can't place where. Doesn't matter...I hope. Ax is the one who concerns me. Why's he smiling? What's he know?

Hill in the distance. A shovel. Goddamn! Why isn't it clearer? Fuck! I feel the fogbank of blurred memories begin to squeeze out other recollections of my dream. But I fight it. I squint my eyes closed and hug my legs even tighter, my nails digging into their flesh. Concentrate! I've got to see it all. This time, I *must* know. My head feels like it's in a vise with someone tightening the screw. I ignore the pain, too consumed with salvaging the memory of my dream before my mind swallows it forever. Phone calls—lots of them. Blackmail. A meeting. But why? How could that meeting make Ax so happy? Moonlight glinting off a blade. Oh, shit! The pieces of the dream fall into place. Ax has killed again. Eric Angel. What does he have to do with this? Shallow grave. At the meeting, Ax killed someone—that man. Who was he?

My mind races. My head feels like it might implode from the effort of remembering. I see Ax. He's walking away, not from me but from someone else. Who? As the person comes into focus, my mind rejects the image. No! It can't be. Not again. God fucking damn it! Not again. Ax is walking away from Doc, smiling in triumph.

I feel a hand on my shoulder. I jump and scream, simultaneously. Princess is up in a heartbeat. My eyes fly open. I look up. Carlos is standing beside me, a worried look on his face.

"I woke up and you weren't there," he says.

It's then that the tears begin. Not a little. Not one at a time. But a deluge. Carlos drops to his knees and pulls me against him. "Shhh, it's okay, baby. I'm here."

I melt against him, wrapping my arms around him in the process. Princess settles down beside me. I grip Carlos as if my very life depends on it as wave after wave of frustrated tears cascade, splashing against my legs. Though I try, I can't shake the image of Ax walking away from Doc in triumph.

He knows something. They're not gonna get him. That bastard! He'll slip through their fingers once again. Always does.

Carlos rests his head against the top of mine. "Baby, what's wrong? Please let me help."

"It's Ax," I say, my voice muffled from pressing my face into his chest.

"What about him?"

I pull back and look up. "I had a dream. He's killed again."

Carlos looks down at me. "How can you be certain?"

"I don't know how, but he's gonna walk away from Molly's death. Doc won't be able to get him." I look into Carlos' eyes. They're filled with compassion, concern and a deep sense of protectiveness. "My dreams are never wrong."

"Call Doc."

Carlos helps me up, and I head to the bathroom, Princess on my heels. I splash water on my face and catch a glimpse of myself in the mirror. What's reflected back is an image of an exhausted me. One who's tired of losing to Ax. Always feeling like I have to look over my shoulder. Once, just once I wanna get that bastard. Every fiber of my being craves victory over him! I reach for the hand towel and pat my face dry. I brush my teeth and go to locate Carlos.

He's in the kitchen and has a pot of coffee brewing. The sun's risen. Although it promises to be a hot day, coffee sounds good. I let Princess out back, and then I come up behind Carlos and wrap my arms around his waist. "Thank you."

He places a hand over mine and says, "For what?"

"For being here—with me."

Carlos turns in my arms and looks down at me. "I told you, the fact that Ax has hurt you makes me protective of you. And remember, I'm not going anywhere unless you tell me to."

I smile at Carlos and lean my head against his chest. "Thank you for being you."

"You're welcome. Now, don't you have a call to make?"

I let Princess in. Her tail wags, and her cast makes soft *thuds* on the kitchen floor with each step. I lean down and rub behind her ear. "Good girl."

She follows me to the junk drawer where I sift through the top layer of papers before finding Doc's number. I dial it and sit at the kitchen table while waiting. Behind me, the coffeemaker's beeper indicates it's done brewing. Carlos pours each of us a mug, adding creamer and sugar to mine. He takes a tentative sip of his and then sits in the chair across from me.

Doc picks up, and I fill him in on the elements of my dream, ending with, "Ax knows something you don't. He's gonna walk."

"Not a chance," Doc says. "His beanie was found at the scene. And we have a positive DNA match on it. No disputing that."

"I understand what you're saying, Doc." I look over at Carlos, who nods. "But my dreams are never wrong."

There's a pause on the other end.

"Doc?"

"Still here, just thinking. Perhaps your history with Ax and his reappearance is what's making you uneasy to the point that now you're having dreams about him."

"Don't patronize me."

"I'm not. It's just that you and Ax have had a lot of history together. And his recent reentry into your life...it's gotta be unsettling. Wouldn't you agree?"

"Well...."

"You don't think there's the slightest chance that what you saw in your dream might've been influenced by all of that? Perhaps you're reading something into the dream that wasn't there?"

I take a sip of my coffee and cradle the phone with the side of my cheek. Carlos reaches across and clasps my free hand, giving it a gentle squeeze.

Doc adds, "I'm not saying Ax hasn't killed again. We both know he's capable. But for him to walk away from Molly's murder...no way. The case we've got against him is airtight." Doc clears his throat. "Maybe what you saw in your dream wasn't Ax walking away from *Molly's* murder but from the murder of the other man in your dream?"

"Hmmm...." I take another sip of coffee. "Hadn't thought of that. There *were* a lot of jumbled images. Maybe...."

"Tell me more about the other man."

Doc and I talk a bit longer. By the time we hang up, I'm feeling better. Though I still have a slight nagging feeling that prickles the back of my mind—always is where Ax is concerned—Doc has managed to convince me that the evidence they have against him is concrete. That there's no way Ax will be able to circumvent it. Before we hang up, Doc promises to call me after Ax comes in for questioning tomorrow.

Carlos pours more coffee, and I make toast. We nibble and sip while I fill him in on what Doc shared. I look at the clock. "Have time to go for a walk with Princess and me before you have to head to work?"

Carlos looks at his watch. "Maybe…. Still have to get home and cleaned up. But my first client doesn't arrive for an hour and a half. Sure, if it's a short one."

I grab Princess' leash, and we head out.

# CHAPTER FORTY-TWO

## It Worked!  It Really Worked!

As I wash, I remember how nice it had felt to walk hand-in-hand with Carlos, Princess alongside us, as we made our way through the maze of my neighborhood's streets.  I like the calming effect Carlos has on me.  How being with him makes everything seem manageable.  In the past, all this garbage with Ax would've had me spiraling out of control.  But now, I don't allow my imagination to get the better of me.

I close my eyes.  A sense of calm washes over me.  Doc's right. There's no way Ax can wiggle his way out of the proof they have. Take the beanie.  Dan was right.  Every criminal gets sloppy sooner or later…even the elusive Ax.  Just had to give it time.

With that thought, I view the clock on the counter.  With a heavy sigh, I realize Ma will soon arrive.   I wrap myself in a towel and, looking through the partially open door, I see Princess, lying on her bed.  She's facing me.  I think she's grateful I've been staying downstairs with her.  I know if I'd tried to go upstairs to sleep without her, she would've struggled to shadow me, to navigate the stairs despite her cast, healing ribs and punctured lung.

As if sensing that I'm thinking of her, Princess gets up and comes to the bathroom.  She nudges the door the rest of the way open and enters.  She snakes around my legs, tail wagging.  All of this I watch, not saying a word.  Don't have to.  Silent words of communication convey how much I love her.  How grateful I am she's still with me. That she'll heal.

She stops circling me and sits by my side.  I kneel down.  I hug her and hear the *thump thump thumping* of her tail on the floor keeping rhythm with the beating of her heart. I lean in close to her ear and whisper, "Can I keep you…forever?"

Princess turns her head and places a delicate lick on the tip of my nose that makes me laugh.

"Good girl," I say.

She heads back to the living room where she lies down on her bed. Still facing me, her head rests between her two front paws. I eye her cast. Thoughts of Ax fill my mind. Only this time, those images are of him behind bars. Of Doc's satisfied grin as he personally locks the cell behind Ax. I sigh. I'm comfortable with this image.

There's a knock at the door. I look at the clock. Must have been daydreaming longer than I thought. That'll be Ma. A moment later, I hear her key in the lock. The door opens and she calls, "Sally? I'm here."

I emerge from the bathroom, towel still wrapped around me. "Hey, Ma," I say, giving her a hug. "Thanks for coming to keep an eye on Princess during my class."

Ma heads into the kitchen. "Coffee?"

"There's a fresh pot."

Princess gets up and follows her. Ma reaches down and pets her. "Good girl."

Ma pours herself a mug of coffee and returns to the living room. "So, what time does your class start?"

"The women should arrive in a half hour," I say from the bathroom where I'm halfway dressed.

Ma pokes her head in and asks, "Want some more coffee?"

I check mine. It's almost empty. "Yeah, if you wouldn't mind," I say, offering the mug.

Ma takes it and heads off, Princess still following her. A few minutes later, she returns and hands me a steaming mug. I've finished getting dressed and am putting on my makeup. Ma leans against the doorjamb and watches me.

I see her in the mirror and turn. "What?"

There's a look of contentment on her face when she says, "Nothing. Just enjoy watching you get ready."

I resume applying my foundation and eye makeup and take a

moment to look at my reflection. I turn to face Ma. "Mind if I go upstairs and get the studio ready?"

"Go ahead," Ma says. "I'll let the women in when they arrive—give you a few more minutes to tidy up."

"Thanks, Ma," I say, passing and placing a kiss on her cheek.

Upstairs, I barely have a chance to turn on the lights, set a pot of coffee brewing and wipe down the poles before I hear the doorbell ring, announcing the arrival of my students. Within the next few minutes, we begin class.

The women talk animatedly about their culmination recital tonight. Some are nervous that one of our classes was eliminated, wondering if they'll be ready to perform. I assure them they'll be fine. I ask each to give me a list of how many spectators they've invited so I'll have enough chairs set up. I can't help but smile as they tell me, with pride, the number. Six weeks ago, not a single one of these women would have believed that they would *want* to have others come and watch their transformation. I'm happy for them.

When class ends, Trish lingers. "How's Princess doing?" she asks.

"Really well! Wanna see her?"

Trish's face lights up. "Can I? I miss her. She's a special girl."

We head downstairs to the kitchen where Princess eagerly greets her. Trish runs her hands over her. Checks her drain tube. "When are you bringing her in to have this removed?"

"Later today," I say.

She stands back and watches Princess walk. "She's doing great. Should be able to tackle the stairs in the next few days."

I thank Trish for having taken such a special interest in Princess while she was at the hospital and for following up on her. I'm glad I've gotten to see this softer side of Trish. I suppose good things can come from tragedies.

I make Ma and me sandwiches. We take them to the back patio. Princess explores each and every bush, no doubt hoping to flush out a squirrel or some hapless critter to chase. We watch her as we eat. I fill Ma in on my dream and subsequent call to Doc.

"Think they've really got him?" Ma asks.

"Even Ax can't find a way around the DNA on the beanie," I say.

"And your dream?"

"Think Doc's right. I must have misread its jumbled images."

Ma looks concerned. "But you think Ax has murdered again?"

"That much I'm sure of."

"Think they'll question him about it?"

"Can't do anything until they have some proof, especially with someone as slippery as Ax. But the good thing is, they'll probably arrest him for Molly's murder after questioning." Ma relaxes a bit, and I continue, "Then they can sort out the other murder…whoever he was."

Ma asks, "You recognized him?"

"Couldn't begin to say from where, though."

Ma and I fall silent while we finish lunch and then do the dishes. I accept her offer to come by later, during the recital, to watch Princess. She helps me set up chairs for the expected viewers and then heads out.

Several hours later, Ma arrives just prior to my students and their guests. She sees to answering the door and keeping an eye on Princess. I head up to the studio. The spectators take seats around the room while I talk with my students off to the side. Ever-present on my mind is that one of them—Molly—is missing. I've no doubt my students feel her absence as well. But I'm proud of the way they're handling themselves.

Couldn't help but notice how they were smiling and chattering with confidence when they entered the studio. They're walking in their five-inch come-fuck-me acrylic heels as if they've been wearing them for years. And although it's only been six weeks since class began, their already shapely legs have toned significantly. The stilettos accentuate this fact, which isn't lost on the guests.

It's not just my students' physical appearance that's changed. Everything about their demeanor has shifted—in a good way. I smile inwardly as I recall the misfit group of lost women who, not quite sure what to expect, entered my studio a month and a half ago. Of how some had challenged me. Others had meekly asked how this might work.

I'm so excited about tonight. Feel like it's taken forever to get here. Can't believe it's really happening—the recital. All my hopes and dreams for these women…tonight will be their night to shine. The time when they get to show how much they've grown. Where I get to sit back with pride and appreciate all their hard effort and revel in their personal growth as I realize the fulfillment of my own dream.

I discuss final pointers with them and then dim the lights and start the music. Each woman goes to her pole. Pam and Trish have the middle ones with Carol and Alicia flanking them.

Although Trish has more experience, everyone decided to have Pam take the lead. Even she, who at the onset of the class was terrified of being center stage in large gatherings, was excited by the idea. As an orchestral number comes on, she introduces each of her classmates, ending with herself. She gives an impromptu speech about how she hopes the audience is ready to have a good time and experience the rebirth of each of the women at the poles. Pam's speech is sexy, alluring and captures the attention of every person present. Her voice never wavers, showing how she's completely at ease. I can't help but be impressed with her.

The first song of the recital begins and Trish, standing alongside her pole, reaches her right hand high overhead and seductively wraps her fingers, beginning with her pinky and ending with her thumb, around the pole. The other women follow her lead. Carol, originally nervous and hyperactive to a fault, tilts her head slightly and locks eyes with various audience members. Her moves are slow, calm, purposeful and sexy as hell. Her newfound confidence is revealed in how she lets herself go with the music.

She places her left hand on her hip, arches her back and juts out her chest and rear. With slow deliberate steps, she slinks and sways her way around the pole, her legs taking her weight as she lowers down a little every now and again. She returns to her full height and rotates her hips in a circular motion, gently gyrating.

As the tempo of the song builds, Alicia, who used to hide behind a mask of heavy black eye shadow, heavier black eyeliner and dark glossy lipstick, leans her back against the pole. She reaches overhead and grasps it. Pushing her chest out, she bends and straightens her knees, giving a little wiggle in between.

From there, she progresses by seductively arching her back, pulling away from the pole slightly and swaying her hips from side to side as she moves up and down. No longer looking like the used-up ex-hooker I learned she is, she displays dignity and grace as she allows herself to sink deeper and deeper into the music. She gently rolls her head from side to side in beat to the music. As the song comes to its crescendo, she alternates between moving her head in sexy circles and performing little figure eights with it. Her pageboy straight-cropped hair swings freely in the process.

When the next song comes on, Trish bedazzles the crowd when she steps away from the pole, right hand still held high, and twirls under her own arm as if being spun around by another dance partner. Her spin complete, she tilts her head back as far as it will go, the ends of her flaming red hair seductively brushing against her rear.

Hers is not a move born from anger as it might have been in the beginning. What I see now is softer Trish. One who has learned she can maintain a greater sense of strength by allowing others to view her compassionate side.

Leaning into the pole, she raises her left leg and slides it up and down. Pulling back a bit, she swirls her hips in slow circles while lowering herself onto her knees. Once there, the pole pressed up against the middle of her chest, her right hand strokes it while she shakes her rear in beat to the music.

Pam raises her left knee to a bent position and shifts her body so that her pole's along her right side. From there, she arches her back and leans back as far as she can. In perfect harmony, each of the women synchronizes her moves.

As that song comes to a conclusion, my students resume standing in front of their poles, backs to them, hands grasping them from overhead. The women transfer all their weight to their right legs and hike their left high in the air, pulling their raised knees in close to their chests. With an unexpected grand finale flurry, each kicks out her left leg and then slowly sinks to the floor.

The audience gives a standing ovation. My students beam. My heart swells with pride, and my eyes moisten with tears. They've each come so far. I couldn't be more proud of them. It worked! It really worked—my concept of a pole-dancing class rebuilding the broken spirits of women who have been beaten down by life. I blink away tears, as I comprehend the performance I've just seen is the realization of my dream and the evolution of each of my students.

# CHAPTER FORTY-THREE

## Walking Out

Tuesday morning dawns bright and hot. Ax exudes an air of confidence as he struts up the steps of the police station. His stride is easy. His demeanor calm. His anticipation of the upcoming interview with Doc, palpable.

*Gonna enjoy fucking with 'em cops!*

Ax makes direct eye contact with the receptionist when he announces himself. She questions his need to talk with Investigator Jones and, in response, he says, "That's between me and him." His voice lowers an octave, a menacing warning hidden just beneath the surface when he adds, "Just get him." Without waiting for a reply, he turns his back to the woman and crosses the room to view the alerts on a bulletin board hanging on the wall.

*Damn cunt! Who the fuck she think she is, questioning me?*

There's a momentary pause while the receptionist tries to figure out how to handle the situation. The corners of Ax's mouth draw up to an evil sneer when he hears her pick up the phone and call Doc's office to announce his arrival.

*Yeah, that's right, bitch. You do what I say!*

An officer comes to the desk and calls, "Ax?"

Ax takes his time turning around, a placid expression on his face, and says, "Yeah?"

"This way," the officer says.

Ax follows the man into the recesses of the station. They stop before a room where Interrogation Room A is written on the plaque beside the door. The officer motions for Ax to enter. He pauses in the doorway, observing the interior, before entering.

There's a long table. Doc is seated on one side. His partner, Dan, indicates a chair on the other. "Have a seat."

Ax says nothing, walks to the chair, pulls it out and sits. It creaks when he leans against it. Once Ax is seated, Dan sits at the head of the table.

Doc looks Ax in the eye. "You understand why you're here?"

"Something about some bitch gettin' killed. Don't know what that's got to do with me, though."

"Allow me to enlighten you." Doc pauses, gets up and begins pacing. "Our investigators found a knit beanie at the scene of the crime."

Ax doesn't say anything. Instead he bores into Doc with an intense stare. Doc doesn't back down from the look and says, "That beanie had *your* DNA on it."

Ax kicks his feet up on the table, crosses his arms over his chest and says, "Is that a fact?"

*Think you're so fucking smart. Think you have me—me, Ax. Ha! No one gets me.*

Dan reaches over and says, "Feet off the table," sweeping Ax's feet from the surface.

There's a *thud* when Ax's feet hit the floor, and he has to reel in a flash of anger.

*Motha fucka! How dare he touch me!*

Doc gets up and circles the table, coming to stand beside Ax. "Cut the crap," he says, leaning in close—close enough for Ax to smell lox and cream cheese on his breath.

Ax waves his hand in front of his nose. "Man, your breath stinks!"

Doc straightens and walks to the other side of the table. Ax notes the confidence with which he takes his time.

Doc sits in his chair. The left side of his mouth pulls up into what appears to be a barely concealed smile before saying, "We've got you this time."

Ax's face erupts into a knowing grin. He looks from Dan to Doc, laughs and says, "Seem pretty sure of yourself."

*Idiots!*

"No way you're going to be able to beat the evidence," Dan says.

Ax doesn't respond.

*Arrogant pricks! Look at 'em. So triumphant. Naive bastards.*

A full minute passes. As the silence continues, Ax sees what he'd hoped for—dawning realization that presents itself as doubt on Doc's face. Ax grins and views Dan, who looks at his partner. Silent words pass between them.

Ax waits long enough for Doc to shift uncomfortably in his seat.

*Yeah, squirm, motha fucka.*

Ax says, "Wanna see this proof you say you have."

Doc nods to Dan, who gets up and leaves the room. "Certainly."

Doc and Ax eye each other from across the table while Dan is gone. Minutes pass—the only sound is the ticking of the second hand on the industrial wall clock. Ax takes immense satisfaction in each passing minute without Dan returning. Five minutes elapse. Six. Seven. Ten minutes after he left the room, Dan returns. He stands in the doorway. The color seems to have drained from his face. Deep worry lines crease his forehead when he says, "Pardner, can I talk with you?"

Ax notes the grave expression on Doc's face when he sees Dan's expression.

*Excellent!*

Doc gets up. He and Dan leave the room, closing the door behind them.

Ax watches them through the observation window. Dan says something to Doc, whose face goes pale. Despite the door being closed, Ax hears Doc roar, "What?!" before turning to look at him through the glass. Doc turns back to Dan. An animated conversation takes place between the two. Doc slams his fist against the wall. Ax smiles. Dan places a hand on Doc's shoulder. Doc pulls away and paces back and forth, combing his fingers through his thick white hair. Every now and again, he looks at Ax. He turns and says something to Dan, who gestures as if to say, I don't know.

Ax delights in the defeated look both men bear when they re-enter the room. The icy recesses of Ax's heart warm when he notes how Doc seems to have aged since stepping out. Lacing his fingers behind his head, Ax leans back in his chair and says, "Where's your proof?"

There's contempt in Doc's voice when he says, "I don't know how you did it."

*And you never will.*

Ax says, "Nothing on me?  Guess I'm free to leave."

Doc makes a sweeping gesture with his hand and says, "Just go," in a voice barely above a whisper.

Lowering his arms, Ax leans forward and says, "What's that? Didn't quite hear you."

Ax notes the fury smoldering behind Doc's eyes when he glares at him and says through clenched teeth, "You're…free…to…go."

*And now for the final blow.*

When he's at the door, Ax turns and looks at Doc.  "So tell me. Does watching me walk out of here make you feel the same as when the detectives screwed up the investigation of your little girl's case, and you had to watch her murderer walk away scot-free?"

Doc kicks the chair nearest him, sending it crashing into the table. He lunges toward Ax with alarming speed.  His fist draws back.  In a heartbeat, Dan's beside him, holding Doc's arm back.  "Calm down, pardner."

Doc struggles against Dan.  He looks at Ax and growls, "You leave her out of this, you bastard!"  Bits of spittle spray Ax's face.

Ax throws his head back and laughs.  "Might want to get that temper under control," he sneers, before walking out.

# CHAPTER FORTY-FOUR

## It All Comes Down to This

Princess and I enjoy our morning walk. The sun's shining bright. Its rays feel good against my skin. Princess sniffs bushes we pass, hoping to flush out a squirrel. Despite her finding none, she trots with a happy gait. She's getting good at walking with her cast—almost like it's not there. Had the drain tube removed. And she's not favoring her side any longer. Can't believe how quick she's healing.

I reach down and scratch behind her ear. Her tail wags in response, and she looks back at me. Our eyes lock momentarily. I swear she smiles at me. "Good girl."

She turns her head and quickens her pace, pulling me along. My heart swells with love. Can't help but smile. We continue on our way. A few blocks from home, I think back to last night. The success of my pole-dancing class' recital. How excited the women had been. Of how proud I was of their accomplishment. Not one messed up on her moves. Their routines were fluid and resonated with their newfound self-confidence.

After class ended, I was thrilled to see how appreciative their loved ones had been of all the hard work they'd put into their performances. Still can't get over how my idea worked. *My* idea. An ex-hooker. Ex-stripper. Ex-crack addict. By taking a group of women, detached from themselves, and introducing them to stronger, whole, self-confident beings who could appreciate their own worth, I managed to further my own healing. Watching them grow has taught me a lot, and I'll never forget the looks of contentment on their faces when they hugged me good-bye.

As I smile at the memory, Princess nearly drags me up our front porch steps. Inside I hear the phone ringing. At first, I decide to let the machine get it, but then think it might be Carlos and hurry in.

I pick it up just after the answering machine does and say, "Hold on. Let me turn this off."

I press the stop button. "Hello," I say, unclipping Princess' leash. She trots off to get a drink.

On the other end I hear, "Hi, Sally. Doc here."

I note a strain in his voice—one that snaps me out of my carefree mood and puts me on guard. "What's wrong?" I ask.

"Ax came in for questioning this morning."

"And…?"

"He was his normal self—cocky, arrogant."

"How'd he react to his DNA being found on the beanie?"

"I'm sorry, Sally," Doc says, sounding exhausted…no, not exhausted, defeated.

"What are you trying to tell me?"

Visions from my dream try to surface. I push them away. No! I won't let them. Everything's fine. Doc assured me that they have Ax this time.

"I don't know how he did it," Doc says.

"Did what?" I ask, needing but not wanting to hear the answer.

"We no longer have the beanie with Ax's DNA on it."

The room begins to spin. I find it difficult to concentrate as I walk to a kitchen chair to sit down. "What the fuck?!" I hear myself say. My voice sounds strained—not my own. In it is harbored an unbridled fury. My blood boils. A thousand images of Ax screwing me over, of his abuse, of his fucking with my life spring to mind, and my head pounds with the onset of a mighty headache.

"That's not all," Doc continues.

I don't respond, knowing that he'll proceed whether or not I want to hear his words.

Doc lets out a heavy sigh and says, "Somehow the computer results of the DNA and the hard copy file have vanished as well."

"Of course they have," I say. "I tried to warn you."

"In short, we have nothing on him," Doc says. "I wish I had better news for you. But without any evidence, we've had to drop the case against Ax for Molly's murder."

I don't say anything. Nothing to say. Should've known. My dream tried to warn me. Never should've allowed Doc to fool me into thinking that the police would get Ax. He's too clever for that. Always has been.

"Sally?" Doc says. "Are you still there?"

"Yeah," I say in a clipped tone. "Just thinking. Guess that's it then. Thank you for trying."

"Don't be like that, Sally."

"Like what?"

"Calm. Appreciative."

"Calm? I'm not calm. Just realize that there's nothing you or the department can do to stop Ax. Now it's time for me to accept things and move forward."

"What does that mean?"

"Nothing. Just babbling. Thoughts are scattered. Thanks again for all your help. Gotta go."

"We'll keep an eye on Ax," Doc says.

I hang up and head upstairs to my bedroom. From the nightstand table, I retrieve my journal and a pen. I stack the pillows against the headboard and sit on the bed, filled with a new resolve. I open my journal and begin writing.

*This time's gonna be different. Ax won't win. Been going about this all wrong. Hoping the police would be able to get him. Beat him at his own game. He's too smart for that. Should've known. Ax always manages to slip through their fingers. Functions outside the norms of civilized society. Adheres to his own laws of recklessness and disorder. Only thing he seems to understand is lawlessness.*

*Chaos. Pain. Suffering.*

*Fine! So be it. Now I know what I have to do. It's up to me. Can't believe this didn't dawn on me before now. Time for me to go back in my past. Tap into my resources there.*

*Just like my students, I've learned something about myself. I'm stronger, more self-confident. And I recognize my own self-worth. I won't lie down for this. Won't let Ax get away with Molly's murder or continue wreaking havoc in my life. I'm not without power where Ax is concerned.*

*This isn't over—not by a long shot. Ax is going down. I know who I have to contact. Who can stop him. Who can put an end to the menacing reign of Ax—once and for all. My old stripping boss, Luigi.*

I recall how Luigi, an ex-mob member, became Angel's and my surrogate father, exacting an unparalleled protectiveness over us. Ours was a tearful farewell when we left the club and our life of stripping. Luigi made it a point to tell us that he considered us family. That if there was ever *anything* we needed, all we had to do was ask. That he took care of family....

I close my journal, cap my pen and lean my head back. My headache is subsiding. Not gonna let Ax get to me anymore. I feel invigorated. Empowered. In control. My resolve is set. My mission determined. If it's the last thing I do, I *will* get Ax. There's nothing that can stop me now.  And with Luigi's help….  Oh, yeah, this time, Ax is gonna meet his match…and lose!

I reach over and retrieve the phone from the nightstand.  I dial. The phone rings several times on the other end and is then picked up.

"Hello."

The sound of his familiar voice washes over me and fills me with a warm glow, causing all my worries and concerns of Ax to vanish.

"Hey, Luigi," I say.  "It's me, Sally."